LION

THE WILL SLATER SERIES BOOK TWO

MATT ROGERS

Join the Reader's Group and get a free 200-page book by Matt Rogers!

Sign up for a free copy of '**HARD IMPACT**'.
Meet Jason King — another member of Black Force, the shadowy organisation that Slater dedicated his career to.

Experience King's most dangerous mission — action-packed insanity in the heart of the Amazon Rainforest.

No spam guaranteed.

Just click here.

BOOKS BY MATT ROGERS

THE JASON KING SERIES

Isolated (Book 1)

Imprisoned (Book 2)

Reloaded (Book 3)

Betrayed (Book 4)

Corrupted (Book 5)

Hunted (Book 6)

THE JASON KING FILES

Cartel (Book 1)

Warrior (Book 2)

THE WILL SLATER SERIES

Wolf (Book 1)

Lion (Book 2)

"Bad company corrupts good character."

— MENANDER

P eter Forrest gazed out over his empire, all forged from nothing, and wondered just how the hell he'd managed to slip so far down the rabbit hole.

Corruption never begins with a raging fire. It trickles into your life with an insipid flicker, so small you barely notice, and the effect of its power compounds until you're swimming in shit so thick it becomes impossible to crawl out. Forrest started on that path long ago, and its hold hadn't properly seized him until weeks previously.

By then, it was far too late.

He stood on a wide steel walkway, staring out over an emporium the size of five plane hangars laid end to end, walled off at the distant edges but sporting a glass-domed ceiling worth tens of millions. The rectangular expanse rested atop two of the largest skyscrapers in Macau, connecting the two structures together to form an upside-down U.

The entire complex had come with a construction cost of more than five billion USD, a fortune that Forrest had spent his entire life amassing in mostly legitimate ways. Of course, no businessman is truly noble in the sense that at some point ethics have to be thrown out the window in favour of cost-effectiveness, but until his venture into Macau he'd considered himself a good man.

Funny how debt repayments can waste away any shred of morality, he thought.

Mountain Lion Casino & Resorts had culminated with a final bill — including construction, labour, government taxes, and a million unexpected costs that came along with a project of this size — of close to six billion dollars. Everything was calculated in USD, which added a further blow to his Australian fortune. Converted to his native currency, he was looking at eight billion.

The project had been a dream since his early childhood, and he'd been relentless over the last thirty years amassing his fortune.

Mining ventures in Western Australia had paid off and he'd funnelled the obscene profits into real estate, capitalising on the booming Australian market. It had left him with enough wiggle room to green-light the construction of what would amount to his magnum opus.

But nothing ever unfolds the way it's supposed to.

A cluster of movement from the edge of the walkway tore Forrest from his thoughts. He flicked his gaze away from the magnificent view and turned to observe the grim procession heading straight for him.

Three triad thugs, each of them in their late twenties with a decade of experience causing unimaginable pain under their belts, hauling a baccarat dealer from one of Forrest's VIP rooms in their wake. The young kid's lip was bloody and his right cheek had already begun to swell. Forrest briefly considered grimacing but squashed it down.

The injuries were nothing in comparison to what might come next.

From underneath the walkway, a throaty growl resonated up through the cavernous space.

He shivered in anticipation.

The trio of triad goons deposited the dealer in a pathetic heap at Forrest's feet. The kid spat a mouthful of blood onto the steel walkway and slumped over, shoulders hunched. Forrest knew exactly what this side of the business called for. He wouldn't allow a shred of remorse to infiltrate his demeanour.

He crouched by the young guy's panting frame and slid a thin smartphone out of his pocket. He navigated wordlessly to a cropped portion of surveillance footage and thumbed the play button, allowing a bird's-eye-view of a red-carpeted VIP room to play on the screen. It focused on a young Filipino man — the same man lying dejectedly before Forrest — making random bouts of eye contact with a pair of high roller gamblers on either side of a luxurious baccarat table. Forrest sped up the footage, allowing the guy to see the extent of his deception.

Over and over again, the twin parties placed the same bet on opposite sides of the game, ensuring that their total combined bankroll remained even. The dealer did his best to shield the proceedings from the security cameras dotted around the room, but nothing got past Forrest.

'You see what you're doing?' Forrest said — the first words he'd uttered in hours. Despite having lived in Macau for years now, he still sported a thick Australian accent. 'I see what you're doing.'

The Filipino guy spoke rudimentary English. It was a requirement for the job. 'I don't know what this is...'

'Of course you do, buddy. We run this same system in ninety percent of our VIP rooms. And you fucking know that. It's basic goddamn money laundering 101. Bet the opposite sides of the table so it looks like you've had a crack, then make off with millions in supposed "gambling winnings". You want to know how many times I've seen it? Hundreds, mate. Maybe thousands. But the dealers declare when the members of their VIP room wish to partake in this little racket. They take commission for allowing these wealthy men and women to launder their dirty money on our premises, which gets passed up the food chain. You know this. But you tried to act like it wasn't happening in your room, and you kept the profits for yourself. Admit it and I might take it easy on you.'

'Yes,' the man said, staring at the floor.

'Well, that didn't take much persuasion. Why'd you do it?'

'I thought I could get away with it. Money for family.'

'You thought you deserved it more than me?'

The Filipino guy shrugged, refusing to make eye contact. 'You have a lot of money, sir.'

'I owe a lot of money,' Forrest said. 'You have no idea what my financial situation's like. Look around you, for fuck's sake. Any idea how much a place like this costs?'

'A lot, sir.'

'Spot on. You know what happens if money launderers get the idea that they can get away with leaving me out of the cut? One of my cash flow systems gets cut off. I can't make repayments. This whole empire goes tits-up. You want that to happen?'

'No.'

'It looks like you do.'

'I'm sorry. I didn't think.'

'No you didn't. Because you didn't consider the consequences if I found out. What kind of precedent do you expect me to set?'

'What?'

The Filipino could only manage single syllables now, his face paling and his hands shaking. He was scared shitless. As he should be. Forrest didn't look forward to what he had to do next, but he was left with no other choice.

'This is business,' he said. 'I have to look at the big picture. If I give you a slap on the wrist and let you get back to your job, do you think that'll scare these gambling sharks into obeying me? Power's everything out here, champ. You should have thought that through before you messed with a system as new as mine.'

'New?' the kid said. 'W-what does that have to do with it?'

'I need to establish myself in this market. I'm the new kid on the block. Sure, my casino's the biggest, and my profits are obscene, but if I show myself as a pushover I'll get run out of here as fast as possible. Got it?'

'Why are you telling me all this?'

'Because I want you to know this isn't personal.'

Even though he was approaching fifty, Peter Forrest had the strength of a man twenty years younger. He sported little muscle or fat on his frame, but there was uncanny power in his wiry physique. He had grown up on a farm in the Australian outback, and that strength had remained in his bones. He clamped a hand down on the back of the young dealer's neck and hauled him over to the side of the railing.

The guy began to struggle. He squirmed restlessly under Forrest's grip, and a battle of willpower seeped across the walkway with toxic intensity. The atmosphere tightened, as if every ounce of nicety had been sucked from the air all at once. Perhaps the man knew what was coming.

Forrest doubted it. He kept this section of Mountain Lion off-limits for good reason. Only the triad knew about it. They'd been the first to suggest using it as a form of punishment. Eventually, Forrest had conceded.

'You know how this place got its name?' he muttered in the dealer's ear, keeping his voice low for no good reason other than to appear menacing.

'You have lions, don't you?'

Forrest flashed a glance at the triad thugs waiting patiently behind them in a tight semi-circle. 'Rumours must spread.'

'They up here?'

'Down there,' Forrest said, jerking a thumb at the strange open-topped enclosure below the walkway.

The lush jungle had grown thick across the cylindrical space, providing a sanctuary of sorts for its two occupants. Below the enclosure, the rest of the complex's upper level spread out in an amalgamation of amusement parks, restaurants, atriums, walkways, and shops all open during daytime hours to the general public. This section of the resort had been elevated and cordoned off in such a way to provide Forrest a sweeping view of his work while obscuring the sensitive details from the general public.

Of course, at this hour of the night the cavernous space was a ghost town, devoid of any living creatures except the two beasts underneath them.

'They're Tsavo lions,' Forrest explained, leaning over the railing to catch a glimpse of the darkened artificial jungle below. He knew the Filipino dealer couldn't care less — and was likely trying not to faint or shit his pants — but he didn't often get the opportunity to tell the story. 'I've had a fascination with lions ever since I was young. I dreamed of owning a place like this, looking out over my empire.

And then slimy fucks like you try to strip me of my fortune.'

'Man, I was just—'

'You know why I got Tsavo lions?'

The dealer didn't respond. Beads of sweat had broken out across his forehead, and his cheeks had reddened as he strained against Forrest's vice-like grip on the back of his neck. He clutched the railing with white knuckles, terrified of the possibilities.

'They're a rare breed. From Kenya. They've got no mane. Only a couple of thousand of them in existence. Goddamn expensive. But I wanted the most vicious lions I could get my hands on, and after I heard the story of the Tsavo Man-Eaters I couldn't pass up the opportunity to throw a couple million in the direction of whoever was willing to sell me one. You heard that story, champ?'

Silence. Lips pursed.

Forrest squirmed, frustrated, and continued.

'Back in the 1800s. A pair of the devils set to work mauling workers along a railway line in Kenya. Killed one hundred and thirty-five of the poor bastards before they were finally shot. What a *story*, hey? Vicious motherfuckers. No-one knows why they're so aggressive, but I had to have them. It's kinda symbolic, you know? I had to be aggressive with my businesses to get where I am. I just had to have them. No matter the cost.'

He realised he was ranting, sharing information he would never ordinarily disclose due to the knowledge that the poor dealer in his grasp wouldn't be around to hear it for much longer.

He composed himself and settled into a steely mood.

'Anyway, sorry about this, buddy. Hopefully it's over quickly.'

The Filipino opened his mouth but no words came out. Mortal fear had seized him in its icy grasp — Forrest was ashamed to admit that he had seen such terror many times before. He hadn't always been like this, but when you reach this level of the game, drastic measures are a necessity.

So he elbowed down hard on one of the Filipino's flimsy wrists, causing enough shock for the guy to release his iron grip on the railing. Forrest levered down with his other hand — still wrapped around the back of the man's neck — and forced him stomach-first into the steel bar. It knocked the breath from his lungs, allowing Forrest to manhandle him over the edge of the walkway.

Old man strength, he thought as the kid toppled ten feet, arms flailing.

A distinct *thump* resonated up through the grated flooring as the dealer hit the dirt. He might have broken a couple of bones in the fall, but those were the least of his worries.

Forrest leant over the railing so he had a clear view of the proceedings. As much as he would have preferred to look away, there were still unpleasant necessities to deal with.

The Tsavo lions materialised silently from the darkness, pumped full of testosterone, almost entirely hairless. Their rippled bodies dripped with muscle and sinew. Their eyes were savage. Primal. Focused.

Powerful goddamn beasts, Forrest thought.

Still craned halfway over the steel railing, he navigated to the camera on his smartphone, pointed it straight down at the jungle floor below, and hit *record.*

The lions fell on their prey. It was over in moments. Covered in blood and gore, the pair of carnivores dragged the fresh corpse into the tree line, the brunt of their work done.

It was time to feast.

Now, Forrest allowed himself a grimace.

Sometimes, a man has to stomp all over people so the world doesn't stomp all over him.

Will Slater was up five hundred and fifty thousand dollars for the night when he watched a little girl get snatched and bundled into a limousine.

The night was warm and humid, as most nights were in Macau. He had abandoned professionalism in favour of comfort and lost the jacket and tie, opening his dress shirt at the neck in a feeble attempt to cool down.

The suit had been custom-fit to his frame by an exclusive tailor in Zurich, but he had spent much of his time in Switzerland recuperating from a laundry list of horrific injuries, and as a result he'd lost a considerable amount of muscle mass during the stay. Now three weeks healthy, he'd packed the weight back on with a rigorous fitness routine. It meant the suit was now close to bursting at the seams. He'd need a new one. As he rummaged around in his pocket for the collection of hundred thousand dollar chips he'd left the VIP room with, he realised that wouldn't be much of a problem.

He took a long drag on the Cuaba Colección cigar gifted

to him from the VIP room's staff as a congratulatory departing present. He knew they intended to shower him with gifts in an attempt to entice him back to the tables, but he didn't mind. He would happily partake in any form of flattery Mountain Lion Casino & Resorts felt necessary to provide.

Standing motionless on the sidewalk, observing the proceedings around the base of the gargantuan towers on either side of him, Slater took a deep breath and internally searched for any twinge of phantom pain that felt the need to arise. Most of the gruelling recovery period had faded from his immediate memory, but every now and then he found himself doubled over, wracked by the traumatic memories of a stretch of time he'd spent in Yemen.

He never wanted to think about what had happened there again.

It had tested limits Slater didn't think a human body could go through. When he'd stumbled out of the war-torn country with his life hanging by a thread, he'd understood the nature of his injuries and recognised the need for a specialised kind of recovery.

Which had led to Zurich.

For two reasons.

Firstly, Slater had a lifetime's worth of government black operations money sitting in accounts with little protection from his old employers. Because they hadn't exactly parted amicably, and also because Slater didn't feel inclined to give up everything he'd made over the years in service of his country, he'd turned to the murky dealings of Swiss bankers to help funnel his millions into offshore accounts. Sure enough, just a couple of days after he'd dealt with the brunt of the problem, his private banker had informed him that there'd been an attempt to drain all his old accounts at once.

An unknown source, the man had said.

Slater knew the truth.

Simultaneously, he'd utilised a four-week program at a private stem-cell clinic on the outskirts of the city. It had taken several favours he'd earned over his career to smuggle himself into Zurich, but by the time he dragged his broken body onto the doorstep of the clinic and offered the specialist doctors hundreds of thousands of dollars to nurse him back to full health with experimental treatments, he'd been knocking at death's door.

Six weeks later, standing tall and comfortable at the lip of one of the most expensive casinos in Macau, Slater couldn't believe the rapidity of his recovery.

The stem cells had nursed him back to one hundred percent — and then some.

He hadn't mentioned it to a soul — or even vocalised it in general — but ever since he'd stepped out of the clinic, he'd felt unnatural energy and vigour coursing through his body. He'd been on a mad quest to experience the crazier side of life ever since, opting to venture into Macau and embrace all the vices that had eluded him over his career.

Making up for a lifetime of pain and deprivation, it seemed.

And now, those same traumatic experiences allowed him to recognise all the signs of an imminent snatch.

The little girl wandered across the sidewalk in front of him, her arms flapping by her sides. She couldn't have been much older than eight or nine, with soft features and a clouded expression on her face. She was frail, with silky black hair. It seemed she was half-Asian — mixed parentage, Asian and white.

Slater wouldn't have looked twice at her if he hadn't been startled by the absence of a parent. Despite Macau's grand sights, it remained a dangerous, poverty-stricken territory, and a young child wandering down the main gambling strip alone drew attention. So he afforded her a second glance, which offered him a plethora of warning signs.

He noted the foggy look in her eyes and the dilated pupils and realised she had been drugged. There seemed to be a purpose in her stride but it was hindered by the cocktail of chemicals flooding her system. She was doing her best to mask its effects, which was why Slater hadn't noticed it upon first assessment.

He weighed up the ramifications of stopping her in her tracks and seeing whether she was alright.

Then, like magic, the sidewalk became pandemonium.

Slater felt right at home amidst the madness. Faceless men in suits — security of some kind — brushed straight past him, their sights set on the little girl. A jet-black limousine with tinted windows and fat tyres screeched to a halt out the front of the left-hand skyscraper, planning to intercept the kid along her current trajectory. The rear door flew open, leading into darkness.

Waiting.

The security team congested into a spearhead, almost all of them Asian, bundling together shoulder-to-shoulder and descending on the girl in a wild flurry of movement. Slater sensed the testosterone crackling in the air — this was an important goddamn retrieval. He tasted the nerves and the sheer determination. They had converged on the sidewalk from a number of different angles, so as not to attract attention until the very last second.

Slater cast a precursory look in either direction and noted that — at this exact moment — there was barely any foot traffic in sight.

They'd been waiting for their opportunity to move.

They'd seized it.

There were six or seven of them — Slater couldn't work out an exact number in the confusion. The two in front wrenched the girl off the concrete like she weighed nothing — she probably didn't. Another pair hurried to the open limousine door and guided her straight into the vehicle. She only had a second to protest the move, and it seemed she was in shock — or the drugs made her slow to react. The other three men formed a rudimentary barrier of sorts around the interaction, shielding most of the details from view of any scrutinising eyes with their giant backs.

It all unfolded in the space of a couple of seconds — they were seasoned professionals. Even if they'd been standing in the same position, an ordinary civilian might not have seen anything. A barrage of movement meant nothing when the confusion of six or seven bodies were involved.

But Slater mirrored their professionalism, and he saw everything.

And his fast-twitch muscle fibres burst into movement, his brain making the decision to act in the half-second of opportunity he had to capitalise on the situation.

He understood live situations like no-one else. Anything that involved force and motion and adrenalin played to his strengths. He could take advantage of opportunities that not even combat veterans would sense — most of it came down to the reaction speed that had seen him recruited into the world of black operations in the first place.

Just because he had left an active career behind, it didn't mean he'd lost his touch.

So even as the last two suit-clad security were brushing past him, he fell straight into line alongside them, mimicking the urgency and pace of their steps, keeping his head low, hurrying his comrades forward. When the limousine door flew open to welcome to the party — with the drugged-up little girl hurried into their midst — Slater simply followed the procession into the cabin in a flurry of limbs and movement.

He found the darkest stretch of seat inside the booth-like interior and squashed into a corner, shoulder-to-shoulder with an Asian thug on either side of him. There was one other black man in the group, which carved out a narrow window for Slater that would make all the difference. It would take the group a brief period of time to realise that they had an extra member, and right now that was the least of their concerns.

All eyes turned to the little girl — the crucial payload. They forced her down into one of the plush leather seats and clamped a hand over her tiny mouth until the limousine door had swung shut behind them. When they were all sealed inside the vehicle, the driver stamped on the accelerator and everyone lurched in their seats, thrown around by the sudden change in momentum. Tyres squealed and the limousine shot away from the sidewalk, roaring down the road.

They left Mountain Lion Casino & Resorts behind in a flurry of tyre smoke.

Slater sat patiently, motionless, in the centre of the seats and waited for all hell to break loose.

3

Peter Forrest strode into one of the hundreds of VIP rooms dotted through both towers of Mountain Lion Casino & Resorts.

He had purpose in his stride.

With his phone clasped in one hand and his eyes fixed on the two elderly Asian businessmen still loitering around the very same table he'd caught them laundering their profits through, he advanced steadily toward them.

Neither of them would have a clue who he was.

Over his life, Forrest had made sure that — no matter what levels of success and achievement he attained — he kept his name and face out of the media. It meant that he'd managed to ascend to the status of one of the wealthiest men in Australia without so much as a single person ever stopping him in the street to ask for a photo or an autograph.

Certainly in Macau, no-one had a clue who he was. The "Mountain Lion" brand had nothing to do with Forrest on a personal level, and it meant he could move around his buildings freely, without disturbance.

He despised the concept of celebrity.

He preferred silent power.

He preferred to control things from the shadows.

So as he stepped into the free slot on the high-roller baccarat table — where bets started at 300,000 HKD — neither of the pair even looked in his direction. They had no interest in him, and nothing to bother him with apart from focusing on the table where they were likely siphoning millions of dollars of drug money into legal profits.

Forrest nodded briefly to the dealer — a young British guy, roughly the same age as the Filipino he'd just thrown to a grisly demise — and then pivoted on his heel to face the businessman on the left-hand side. The guy furrowed his brow and stared straight ahead, refusing to make eye contact.

Perhaps he thought Forrest wasn't on the man's level. Maybe few were. Maybe he was one of the many Hong Kong businessmen who ventured over with billions of dollars to throw on the tables in Macau. These men and women were the "whales", the compulsive gamblers who lost or won eight figures at a time.

They couldn't stop, and because the house always won over the long run, if Forrest and his competitors could convince the whales to continue returning to their premises — well, it spelled a literal fortune in profits and a financial disaster for the addicts.

But this man had tried to do dirty deals behind Forrest's back, which negated any potential profit the guy might earn him in future. So Forrest leaned across until he was clearly violating the man's personal space and thrust the smartphone under his nose.

The elderly Asian's brow furrowed and he flashed a look at Forrest that would wilt lesser men. Forrest stared back with equal verve and nodded once to the smartphone screen.

Wordlessly, reluctantly, the man turned his eyes to the screen.

Horror spread across his features in a change of expression like nothing Forrest had ever seen before.

He didn't blame the man. The video he'd recorded had revealed the dealer's fate in excruciating detail — only a single second of viewing would have been enough to churn even the most hardened soul's guts. Before the businessman could react any further, Forrest wheeled on the spot and pressed the screen maniacally into the second guy's face.

He reacted in similar fashion.

Neither of the two made a move — either they were too old to flee or they simply understood that Forrest would have every inch of the casino covered. There were five or six other tables in this particular VIP room, each of them bristling with whale customers. Forrest didn't feel like causing a scene and creating potentially hundreds of millions of dollars in losses over the long term, so he kept his voice low and turned his gaze from man to man while he spoke.

'You both get the fuck out of here,' he said. 'And you tell your friends that anyone who tries to leave me out of a deal will get the same result. You're lucky I let you two live. It'll be worse for anyone who tries to pull this shit again. Trust me. And if you think anyone will ever find out what happened, you're poorly mistaken. Leave my casino in ten minutes or I'll feed you to the same lions.'

His business complete, Forrest turned on his heel and left the VIP room without fanfare. He'd kept his tone barely above a whisper during the spiel as to not attract attention.

But both businessmen understood every word — he knew that much.

They wouldn't be a problem in future.

He knew broken men when he saw them.

He headed for the upper level.

~

IN A COMPARTMENTALISED ROOM tucked into one corner of the complex's upper level, the three triad members who had delivered the dealer to Peter Forrest sat watching his progress on the bank of live surveillance feeds on the desk before them.

They sat alone, their lowered voices echoing around the room in the silence. Each of them observed Forrest's reckless actions with fascination. They didn't mind the shocking violence they'd witnessed on the walkway — that sort of behaviour had become a part of their daily lives for as long as each of them could remember — but they hadn't seen an employer make such waves in quite some time.

Peter Forrest had blasted onto the Macau gaming scene with enough verve and aggression to carve out a sizeable portion of the market. He'd felt the need to utilise the services of the triad long ago, a natural response to such a dangerous industry.

They'd been with him ever since.

Now, the largest of the three leant forward so his nose rested inches from the screen. His eyes widened as he scrutinised the fuzzy surveillance footage.

'Look at the dealer,' he said in Chinese.

The other two concentrated hard on the British guy in the midst of the proceedings. They nodded in unison, recognising all the characteristics of someone scared for their life.

They were familiar with the man — the triad had been responsible for recruiting certain members of the casino's staff to ensure they would be complicit in illegal tactics — but they hadn't been expecting such a reaction.

The kid had devolved into a nervous wreck in front of Forrest and the two businessmen. Even on the grainy footage, the tallest triad member could see the blood drain from his face. His forehead turned shiny, breaking out in sweat. His eyes darted everywhere but the table in front of him, trying desperately to search for a reprieve from his terror.

He had caught a glimpse of the video on Forrest's phone.

'Could just be a natural reaction,' one of the members said. 'Maybe he got a look at his friend being eaten. The dealers would know each other.'

The taller man shook his head. 'I saw the video Forrest recorded. You can't tell who it is unless you study it. Forrest isn't angling the phone in the kid's direction.'

'So why is he that scared?'

'Because he knows what's going on. He's part of it. He's in bed with the businessmen. A two-man dealer team that they're using to hoard their profits.'

'Has Forrest realised?'

The taller man stared at the screen, watching hard. 'Not yet. He's a violent man but he's not used to this game. He's concentrating too hard on the businessmen.'

As they spoke, Forrest turned on his heel and left the VIP room as quickly as he'd arrived. The young British dealer visibly exhaled, letting out a ball of tension that had built up inside him over the course of the conversation.

He thought no-one had noticed.

But the triad had.

'What do we do?' the second man — who up to this

point hadn't uttered a word — said. 'Report it to Forrest and get in his good books?'

The tallest man paused for thought. 'We're already in his good books. I think this kid might be useful. I think he'll do anything to make sure no-one finds out about his guilt.'

'Oh...' the other two said simultaneously, realising what the tallest man intended.

'Change of plans,' the tallest man said. 'We don't involve ourselves in the ground-level work. We've got the messenger in place, but I say we use this guy to our advantage. We have more dirt on him than anything he could possibly fathom.'

'Should we go get him? Bring him up here?'

'Has the girl been released yet?' the tallest man said.

The first checked his watch. 'Ten minutes ago.'

'Then go tell him to finish his shift. We'll use him. But make sure we keep this away from Forrest. For obvious reasons.'

4

The longest twenty-two seconds of Slater's life began to tick by.

He mentally counted out each increment, breathing normally and keeping his heart rate calm and subdued. Over time he'd learned to compartmentalise as much adrenalin as possible. The situation leeched with stress, but panicking about it would only sap energy from the outburst that inevitably needed to occur.

So he sat, and waited, and stared straight ahead until someone realised he wasn't a member of their security detail.

They were fairly amateur in that regard. Each man craned their necks to stare out the tinted windows at the vast sprawl of Mountain Lion Casino & Resorts fading away in the background. They were searching the sidewalk for any sign of panic amongst the civilians. They didn't realise that one of the civilians was missing entirely.

And in the vehicle with them.

Most of them nervously shuffled on the spot, letting the heightened emotion of a live situation fade away. The little girl squirmed in her seat, her face pale and her eyes wide, clearly uncomfortable but too terrified to make a break for it. At the same time the murky fog resting over her features lingered, preventing her from reacting in any significant capacity. Slater could tell she was scared out of her mind, but her limbs refused to function properly.

She was definitely drugged.

He loosened his shoulders, relaxing any tightness and tension in his body. A fight was imminent — there was no way around it. He had seconds to compose himself. He sketched out a brief plan of attack in his mind based on the position of the security all around him, and then settled back and waited for the madness to ensue.

'How the hell did she get out?' one of the men in front of him said, staring across the interior at his two buddies on the other side of the limousine.

One of them shrugged. 'Don't know. She didn't make it far though.'

'She shouldn't have made it anywhere.'

The man to the left of Slater nodded imperceptibly in agreement, and turned his head to check whether his friend felt the same. He glanced once at Slater, then paused for a single second that felt like an eternity.

'Hang on,' he said, 'who the fuck are—'

Slater detonated an elbow off the side of his temple with enough built-up momentum to shut the lights out with a single strike. The guy's head snapped back against the partition separating the interior from the driver's cabin. An audible *thwack* rang through the limousine and the guy slumped forward, unconscious.

You have two seconds before they're on you. Cause as much damage as you can.

Adrenalin and tension had dissipated from the rest of

the men, and it would take them a period of valuable hesitation to return to combat-mode. Slater had been waiting for the opportunity to pounce for far too long — it gave him a distinct advantage.

He twisted at the waist, turning to face the man on his right, and slammed his forehead against the cartilage in the guy's nose. Blood sprayed and he went down howling.

At that point the closest man to Slater who wasn't incapacitated made a half-hearted lunge across the seats. Slater wasn't sure what exactly the man was trying to achieve, but he batted the guy's outstretched arms away and scythed an elbow from floor-to-ceiling, connecting against a sensitive portion of the man's jaw and snapping his head back with enough kinetic energy to send him sprawling to the floor between both rows of seats.

Three men down.

He wasn't moving fast enough.

Slater noticed the four remaining security detail reaching instinctively for their waists, responding to the chaos that had erupted. They were carrying firearms. Slater registered the shift of momentum in a heartbeat. Behind him, the glass partition had splintered when the first guy's head had bounced off it, creating a spider web of cracks across its surface.

It was set to fall apart.

Barely thinking, reacting out of intuition, Slater pivoted in his seat and swung a balled-up fist as hard as he could at the weakened glass. He accepted the consequences, and simply rode out the pain as his fist hammered straight through the sheet in an explosion of fragments, slicing his knuckles up. But Slater hit like a freight train, and the journey through the glass had taken barely any force out of the movement. His knuckles slammed home against the back of the driver's skull. The man hadn't yet responded to the carnage, which made his muscles loose, which added whiplash and shock to the punch. The driver's brain rattled around inside his skull and he slumped over the wheel without resistance.

The limousine picked up speed as he unconsciously leant pressure on the accelerator.

Slater was already on the move, ducking down and dragging the two unconscious men on either side of him across his torso, forming a spur-of-the-moment human shield in case any of the men across from him felt inclined to fire directly at him.

But they didn't, frozen by hesitation, understanding that the limousine was in the process of careening out of control and that half their security detail had already been dispatched.

The child screamed, responding naturally to the carnage.

Panicking, the four remaining men struggled to wrench their sidearms free from their holsters, their eyes darting back and forth between Slater and the girl.

She must be valuable, Slater thought.

One of the closest men dove across the limousine's interior, making a wild swing at Slater. His fist whistled by Slater's chin — the guy had martial arts training. There was raw power and technique behind the blow. If it had connected — lights out.

But it didn't — mostly because the guy was off-balance, but also because the occupants of the limousine were being thrown around viciously as the vehicle swerved and mounted the sidewalk a few hundred feet down the road from Mountain Lion.

Slater heaved the unconscious bodies off him, recognising what was about to happen. He reached over and snatched the girl off the seat, pulling her against his torso and locking her tiny frame in an iron grip. With the other hand, he reached desperately for a seatbelt. He didn't have time to check how close to impact they were — he simply knew a crash was imminent.

And it wouldn't be pretty.

No-one in the vehicle had bothered to secure themselves. They would be thrown around like cereal in a box.

Slater wrapped a sweaty palm around one of the polyester straps and wrenched it tight across his body.

He squashed the little girl between himself and the seat, securing her as best he could, and braced himself for the impact of a lifetime.

5

The world went completely mad.

Slater had squeezed his eyes shut before the inevitable chaos, so he didn't get a glimpse of how the destruction unfolded. He imagined he would have seen nothing but a blur as his vision dissipated from sensory overload. So he opted to bury his head into the soft upholstery of the seats and hold on for dear life.

The limousine hit something side on, crunching into an obstacle with the sound of screaming steel. Slater felt the interior warping around him, and the next thing he knew the entire car had flipped onto its roof. His stomach fell into his feet and the seatbelt cut tight across his chest, preventing him from tumbling straight into the grinder underneath him as the roof shredded against the concrete sidewalk.

The young girl screamed against his chest but he barely heard it, surrounded by a cacophony of noise. Bodies tumbled and spilled, and limbs splayed. When the limousine finally skidded to a halt — still resting upside-down on its roof — the noise died away and Slater released his white-knuckle hold on the seatbelt. He and the girl dropped a couple of feet to the surface below, landing hard on his back. He shielded her fall with his own body.

The interior lighting had understandably died, and Slater found himself in relative darkness, surrounded by coughing, spluttering security guards in the process of recovering from the mother-of-all-crashes. Surprisingly, he had come out of the ordeal relatively unscathed. He rolled in either direction to assess any immediate threats.

He spotted a gun barrel slicing through the air toward him.

He recognised the make of the weapon — it was a Beretta M9 sidearm, relatively cheap on the black market. It meant these men weren't employed in any official legal capacity, confirming his suspicions that they'd been in the process of doing something awfully sinister with the young girl.

Fight-or-flight kicked in.

Ninety-nine times out of a hundred, Slater chose fight.

The man with the firearm had likely been concussed as he'd been thrown around the limousine's interior, but he'd still kept a grip on his weapon.

Slater sensed the laborious nature of the man's movements and capitalised instantly, rolling onto his side and snatching the Beretta out of the man's grasp. The guy resisted, but a single burst of applied pressure to the guy's wrist loosened his grip, and Slater wrenched it free. He knew how to deal with leverage and power like no-one else.

He spun the weapon in a practiced motion and jammed a finger inside the trigger guard, so that the barrel ended up pointing straight back at the man who'd been clutching the gun a second earlier.

The guy's face paled, but Slater felt no inclination to spare his life.

Slater would have met the same fate if he hadn't been fast enough.

Besides, anyone he left alive had the capacity to come for the girl.

He fired once, piercingly loud in the cramped interior. The guy caught the bullet in the centre of his forehead and slumped pitifully to the floor.

Slater rolled away from him and elbowed the nearest window, utilising the added strength that came with fear. It shattered, allowing him to lever the young girl out onto the street, taking care not to drop her directly into the thin coating of glass fragments dotting the sidewalk. He scrambled straight out after her, leaving the miserable occupants of the limousine to wallow in the injuries they'd sustained. One of their crew was dead for even bothering to wave a weapon in Slater's direction, and he doubted the rest would be motivated to give pursuit after how effortlessly they'd been manhandled.

He winced as one of the pieces of glass sunk into his hand, but forced it out of his mind. The little girl had taken up position a few feet from the limousine wreck, staring wide-eyed in disbelief at the scene before her. Slater imagined she was deep in the early onset stages of shock. He figured she might have broken down entirely if not for the drugs messing with her sense of reality. He kept a tight grip on the Beretta as he wriggled free from the wreckage and stumbled to his feet alongside her, panting hard to expel some of the tension in his body.

Before he said anything, he raised the Beretta level with the opening in the side of the limousine and lingered for a few critical moments. If anyone materialised in the window frame, intent on following him out of the vehicle, he would

dot them with lead until they decided to either retreat
or die.

But no-one appeared.

They'd thought better of giving pursuit.

Nodding with satisfaction, he turned and ushered the
young girl into the lip of the nearest alleyway — a narrow
space between two towering residential complexes only a
few hundred feet away from the largest casinos in Macau.
Lights glowed in apartment windows even at this hour —
Slater figured the whales lived here, the men and women
who could afford a permanent residence in such close proximity to the largest gambling haven on the planet, a strip
that dwarfed even Las Vegas in its level of turnover.

The alley lay shrouded in darkness.

Slater wondered if anyone had come here to blow their
brains out with relative discretion after losing their entire
fortune on the tables.

'What just happened?' the girl stammered.

Slater paused, startled. Her accent was American. He'd
intuitively figured that she spoke no English.

'Don't worry,' he muttered. 'We'll have time to talk about
it later.'

'There were seven of them,' she said. 'There's only one
of you.'

Slater found himself surprised that she had the awareness to do a head count, even in such stressful circumstances.

'You should have seen what I did in Yemen.'

'What?'

He hurried her into the alleyway, under cover of
darkness.

6

At four in the morning Macau time, having been awake for nearly twenty-four hours, Peter Forrest decided to call it a day.

The penthouse atop the Mountain Lion Casino & Resorts complex had been constructed in such a way to provide him the ability to get downstairs to his offices in a heartbeat. Every waking moment he spent not working was simply an inconvenience, aside from an hour or so he carved out of each evening to unwind before he hit the sack. He slept four hours a night maximum, using the other eighteen to ascend up the financial ladder and climb the social hierarchy. He hated wasting time almost as much as he hated being broke, which had culminated in a schedule that left zero room for pleasantries.

Except for that spare hour.

The Asian woman rolled off him, both of them slick with sweat and panting with exhaustion. At ten thousand dollars a session, Forrest expected the absolute best that the prostitution industry had to offer, and he'd never come away from the sex disappointed during his entire time in Macau. They sure knew how to keep a man pleased over here.

The girl who'd been summoned to his sleeping quarters was in her twenties. She could have graced the cover of any swimsuit magazine on the planet. Her lithe frame had gyrated over him for the better part of an hour now, and Forrest had only finished inside her upon realising he needed enough sleep to function the next day. Now she disappeared into the depths of his enormous penthouse, her work complete, and he dropped his head to the satin pillow behind him to let himself cool down.

With sweat dripping off his ageing body, he stayed still for only the briefest of moments. There were endless thoughts spilling through his head, more than he could keep track of. He hated the concept of sleep. He wished something were invented to abolish the need for rest entirely. Working on his empire twenty-four hours a day would be the greatest blessing of his life.

He latched onto the most pressing thought still churning at the forefront of his mind and lifted a digital tablet off the ornate bedside table. He tapped into the casino's surveillance system and brought up a list of hundreds of different CCTV feeds. It didn't take him long to find what he was searching for. He brought up footage from earlier that night in the specific VIP room he'd stormed into and watched his work unfold on the small screen.

Propped up in the four-poster bed, he studied the surroundings for any sign that the other occupants had noticed the reason for his presence. Satisfied that everyone was keeping to themselves, he scrutinised his own actions, looking for anything that might have shown weakness.

What he found had nothing to do with him.

It had to do with a British dealer sitting a couple of feet

away from where he'd pulled to a stop, literally shaking in his seat. The kid was sweating and wide-eyed and trying his best to keep his line of sight fixed on anything but Forrest.

Forrest watched himself on the monitor. He figured he hadn't been paying attention to the dealer at the time, and as a result he'd missed the obvious.

This guy was involved, somehow, some way.

Still naked, Forrest realised he wouldn't be falling asleep any time soon. Fog had descended over his brain, brought on by a lack of sleep, but he had to keep moving. He felt a thousand strands tugging for attention in his mind, and he decided to approach them incrementally, eliminating the most pressing issue first.

Which now concerned this new kid he'd missed upon first look.

He'd sent a team of his men to deal with the other issue.

The result of the retrieval was in their hands.

He cancelled out of the surveillance footage app and brought up a catalogue of all the staff Mountain Lion Casino & Resorts employed. He found the young guy without much effort — Samuel Barnes, a twenty-two year old British expat who had applied for a job as a baccarat dealer six months ago and been granted a position in the VIP rooms after a successful job interview. The job paid almost nothing, but dealers in that setting usually received the occasional tip from a successful whale. Sometimes Forrest heard of staff getting upwards of fifty-thousand HKD in tips.

The potential was astronomical.

But maybe Samuel Barnes hadn't received a tip in quite some time, and had turned to more desperate measures in collaboration with the Filipino dealer.

In any case, Forrest was determined to figure out what

the kid knew.

He rolled off the bed and dressed in a simple collared shirt and dress slacks, grumbling to himself, close to a state of delirium. It was now four-thirty in the morning and he had a long night ahead of him.

He snatched his phone off the dresser and dialled one of the triad thugs who had fetched him the Filipino dealer. He couldn't remember the guy's name — just the giant jewelled earring hanging off his right lobe — but the man answered in seconds. 'Yes?'

'I need you to round up one of the other dealers.'

A pause. 'Who?'

'Samuel Barnes. Same room as the last guy you brought me. I need to find out—'

'What makes you interested in him?'

'He was acting shifty on the surveillance footage. I want to find out what he knows about—'

'Leave it with us.'

'I'm sorry?'

'The three of us will interrogate him. Find out what he knows. We'll report back to you.'

'I'd rather you—'

'We're on a tight schedule, sorry. Boss wants us back by the morning.'

'Then bring him up to my penthouse and I'll deal with him myself.'

Forrest could almost hear the triad thug shaking his head on the other end of the line. 'No. You need us. We'll find out what we need and pass it up to you.'

'Uh—'

The line went dead.

Forrest paused, awfully confused.

He recalled his introverted childhood and the numerous

years he'd spent caving into other people's demands. Business and entrepreneurship had forced him to come out of his shell and he'd embraced the process relentlessly, morphing from a shy kid to an outgoing, confident adult. But his experience rested in handling real estate developers and lawyers and accountants. His dual venture into illegalities hand-in-hand with the triads had taken him far out of his comfort zone. He found himself wilting during intense back-and-forth conversations with the thugs.

Once again he'd let them do as they pleased. They intimidated him, despite his penchant for violence and ability to adopt a menacing tone in front of them. He could scare dealers into submission, and even kill them, but he couldn't do much else.

He scolded himself, sweating profusely at the thought of the triad learning vital details about him and his business.

Suddenly, a sharp electronic beeping sounded throughout the penthouse.

His version of a doorbell.

Forrest froze. The only people who had access to this echelon of the complex were his most trusted advisors. That included the security detail he'd sent out to deal with another problem that had cropped up — one of what felt like hundreds that he dealt with on a daily basis.

This issue, however, carried a little more significance than most.

Which made him sprint for the front door of his lavish suite, anticipating good news. It would settle his heart rate, and ensure he remained calm throughout the rest of his dealings.

He flung the broad oak door open without even bothering to check through the peephole what might await him.

Too late, he realised his mistake.

But what he found didn't put him in danger. There was no-one waiting with a weapon, ready to put a bullet through the billionaire's head, despite what he'd been expecting.

Instead he found two of the men he'd sent downstairs to re-capture Shien, both still dressed in their official jet-black suits but missing their ties. Their shirts hung open at the collar, exposing blood across both of their chests. One of the men sported a freshly broken nose and the other was clutching his jaw in a manner that suggested serious internal injuries.

Forrest paled. 'What the hell happened?'

'She wasn't alone,' the man with the broken nose muttered — the other couldn't talk. 'A black guy ambushed us.'

'A black guy? A single guy?'

'He followed us into the limo. No-one was really paying attention, I guess...'

'Are you fucking joking or something?' Forrest said, veins on his forehead protruding, his face turning red. 'What is this bullshit?'

'He was trained, man. He fucked us all up real bad. Lau's dead.'

'Lau's dead?' Forrest rammed a fist into the front passageway's wall, gouging out a chunk of the plaster. 'This is fucked. This entire situation is fucked. The girl's gone?'

The man nodded. 'Yeah, Peter. The girl's gone.'

'You know what this means?'

The man nodded again.

Forrest bared his teeth as he spoke, flecks of saliva spraying out of the corners of his mouth.

'You round up every single person on my payroll,' he snarled. 'You get her back. Or I go down, and everyone goes down with me.'

7

S later strode all the way through to the next street, which opened into a dingy overcrowded row of apartment buildings crammed to the brim with Macau's residents. Only a hundred feet in separation between the extravagant casinos and five-star restaurants lay the grid of complexes home to the working population.

Slater understood perfectly, even as he stared out at a staggering number of apartments. He had seen the amount of staff necessary in Mountain Lion Casino alone, from dealers to cashiers to security to supervisors to the small army of surveillance staff that would no doubt be in place behind the scenes.

He couldn't imagine how many staff the entire gambling industry employed. It seemed like it made up more than half of the population of the country alone.

He and his new sidekick blended into the smattering of civilians dotting the broad sidewalks, filtering out of the structures behind them as their shifts ended and they headed for bed. Slater made sure to keep the young girl close, shielding her from view of anyone on his right side.

He'd tucked the Beretta into the inside pocket of his suit jacket back in the alleyway to prevent any unwanted attention. But he felt it there, bouncing intermittently against his torso, at the ready in case he needed to access it fast.

They walked for five minutes straight, keeping a brisk pace, before either felt the need to speak.

The young girl opened her mouth first.

'Are you going to kill me?'

'No.'

'I think you killed someone back there.'

'I think so too. You seem pretty calm about it.'

'I don't feel right.'

Slater nodded. The drugs — whatever had been administered to her — were suppressing her emotions. She was operating in a murky haze. Slater could tell by the way she moved, her steps laborious and her eyes drifting down to the concrete under her feet. She seemed entirely unconcerned with the fact that Slater had broken her out of a car filled with seven violent men minutes earlier.

'Do you know what's happening to you?'

She paused, thinking hard, wrestling with her thoughts so she could communicate effectively. 'Sort of. My brain is really fuzzy right now. I'm confused. I'm just doing what everyone tells me.'

She's suggestible, Slater thought.

'What's your name?'

'Shien. What's yours?'

'I'm Will.'

'Hi, Will.'

'Hello. Maybe I should have started with that.'

She shrugged. 'Maybe.'

'I don't talk to people in your age range much.'

'I don't talk to killers much.'

He paused and glanced down at her, a wry smile curling across his lips. It felt unnatural. He hadn't smiled in quite some time. 'Is that what you think I am?'

'You saved my life, mister.'

'Your English is very good. Are you from Macau?'

'No,' she said, shaking her head, but the silence that unfolded in the aftermath of the single syllable said everything that needed to be said.

You can't remember, Slater thought.

'I'm from Hong Kong,' she said finally, after much deliberation. 'My daddy is from Hong Kong.'

'And your mother?'

'Uh, America. Texas, actually! Are you from Texas?'

'No,' Slater said. 'I'm not from Texas.'

'Anyway, we spoke English at home ... yes, that's right. I remember now. We lived in Hong Kong at the top of a building.'

'Lived?'

'Well, I still live there. Sorry, mister, I'm very confused.'

Slater held up a hand. 'Maybe we should have this conversation later. When you're more like yourself.'

She stared at him and shrugged. 'Okay. Thanks, Will.'

'No problem, Shien.'

The tenement housing grew thick, with the squat, unimpressive apartment complexes giving way to more rundown dwellings as they continued heading for the old city. Macau's glitz and glam had fallen into the background, replaced by the cruel reality. The humidity seemed to increase in turn, as if the enormous five-star casinos and resorts had managed to alter the weather itself.

The air hung oppressively over them, to the point where Slater strongly considered stripping the suit jacket off his frame and stuffing the Beretta into his waistband. His dress shirt had soaked through with sweat — he hadn't noticed in the aftermath of the violent brawl, but the intense heat had drawn seemingly all the sweat from his pores at once. He fanned himself uselessly with his free hand, keeping the other resting gently against Shien's back.

She didn't protest.

He thought it might make her feel more secure.

He had almost no experience with kids, so he wasn't sure exactly what she was thinking.

The sidewalks changed, narrowing as they headed further into the grimy urban grid. Despite the relative hostility in the air in these parts, Slater felt right at home. He preferred to be around people, no matter how dangerous they were. They would act as a temporary smokescreen to whoever might be coming after them.

And, glancing down at Shien as she strolled unperturbed through the grimy town, he realised there might be an entire army coming after them.

He had no idea how valuable she was.

He had no idea what he'd got himself involved in.

He elected to find out.

'So,' he said, struggling to find the words that would ensure she remained calm, 'before all the craziness happened — where were you headed?'

'H204VR68,' Shien said softly, still staring straight ahead.

Slater froze. 'What?'

She turned to him, half-smiling. 'I bet you think I'm a robot, mister.'

'I don't know what you are. I don't know what I got myself into. But you were in danger.'

'That's just a string of numbers and letters,' she said.

'I know that.'

'I know two more.'

'Tell me.'

She rattled another two codes off, each an identical length and an equally random mix of letters and numbers. 'Three of them. Like I told you.'

'What are they?'

'I'm not completely sure. They're important, though.'

'Seven men tried to snatch you off the street. I bet those three codes are important. Where did you find them?'

'Um...' she said, trailing off, falling into the pit of her own mind again.

Slater gave her time.

There was no rush.

He avoided eye contact with the residents of Macau trawling the street at this hour, instead staring far into the distance, predicting the kind of urban terrain they would be headed into before it sprung up on them unannounced.

From here, it looked like more of the same.

Cramped, dingy tenement housing drowning in humidity.

Slater had learned to embrace the uncomfortable decades ago. He didn't mind the stifling conditions and the poverty and the tension. In truth, he felt more at home amongst these people than the uber-rich back in the casinos and five-star resorts. There was five-hundred thousand dollars in casino chips in his pocket, which could probably buy an entire street worth of real estate around these parts, but Slater had spent half his life with an obscene net worth on paper.

Black operations paid handsomely.

More than handsomely.

It hadn't ever stopped or faded his drive. Being worth tens of millions meant nothing. Heading into an active war zone to do good and save lives carried with it a deep sense of personal satisfaction that no amount of digits in a bank account could ever rival.

So the discomfort and violence that lay ahead if he chose to stay with the young girl barely crossed his mind.

In fact, he welcomed it.

And he needed to.

Shien opened her mouth and said, 'I just remember being kidnapped out of my Daddy's hands a couple of weeks ago.'

8

'That's all you remember?' Slater said, furrowing his brow.

He hadn't anticipated such a strong amnesiac flowing through Shien's system. If she didn't even know who her captors were, there would be few solutions to this problem. But Slater had never been one to solve issues with tender care and sensibility. Instead he hit hard and fast until everything in his path wilted and he got what he wanted.

Shien paused, then shook her head. 'There's more. There's a lot of stuff. But it's all jumbled up in my head. Whatever's in my system isn't good for me at all, mister.'

'I don't like mister. Call me Will.'

'Sorry, Will.'

'Those three codes,' Slater said. 'You can easily remember them, right?'

'Yes.'

She rattled them off again, one by one, in the exact same order she'd uttered them last time. Then a sharp look of realisation spread across her face, and she added a final detail to the spiel. 'Beco da Perola.'

'What's that?' Slater said.

She scrunched up her features. 'A road. Near here. With a dead end. We're on Taipa, right?'

One of the islands of Macau, connected to the neighbouring island of Coloane with man-made landfill. Slater had arrived at Macau International Airport on the east side of Taipa just over a week previously. From there, it had been a short trip to Mountain Lion Casino & Resorts, where he'd spent the duration of his stay.

He got the sense he wouldn't be returning to the gigantic complex anytime soon.

He nodded, confirming Shien's question. 'Yes, we're on Taipa. Do you know your way around?'

'Sort of. I've been to Macau a few times. Daddy likes to visit the big buildings.'

'The casinos?'

'Uh, yeah. I think so. He doesn't like to talk about it. Anyway, there's a bunch of apartments along this street. Like the ones on either side of us now.'

Tenement housing, Slater thought. *Just what I was looking forward to.*

'Who told you this? Who released you?'

She paused. 'This part's hard. For some reason I can't remember faces and names, but I can remember those codes and that address easily. They must have repeated it to me so many times...'

'It's okay,' Slater said, reassuring her. 'You're doing great. We have plenty of time — it'll come back to you. I don't have anywhere to be, so I'll look after you as long as it takes to sort this out.'

She looked up at him, her eyes narrowed in suspicion but her face somewhat hopeful at the same time. 'Why, miste— uh, Will?'

'Why what?'

'Why did you follow me into the car and beat up all those men?'

He sighed. 'That's just what I do, Shien. Don't ask me to explain it. I don't know what the protocol is for talking to kids.'

'You can talk to me.'

He glanced down at her, taking his eyes off the path ahead for a brief moment. 'You're switched on for a kid. How old are you?'

'Nine. Daddy says I'm very smart for my age.'

'You sure are. Do you speak other languages?'

She nodded. 'My school in Hong Kong teaches us English, but I've been learning Portuguese and Chinese on the side. Daddy says they speak those languages here in Macau and he wants me to be flexible with where I want to work in the future.'

Slater couldn't fathom how to respond to that. He tried to remember what he was doing when he was nine years old.

Not much.

That conjured up a fresh wave of dark memories from those years, and he felt the inklings of rage bubbling to the surface. Fury and unease were palpable in his mind, and he once again suppressed his childhood from memory. He had let it come back to him once — the details of how his mother died came flooding back when he'd encountered a similar situation in Corsica, and by the end of his rage-fuelled frenzy an entire boatload of mercenaries were dead by his own hand.

He had to control that side of himself for as long as it would take to find the proper counselling and psychological evaluation that he knew he needed. A career in black operations had been compartmentalised through sheer willpower, and in later years Slater knew it would take some serious elbow grease to unpack.

He left that for another day, though.

Just as he always did.

'You've gone quiet,' Shien noted. 'Are you thinking about something?'

'Sure am, Shien,' he muttered. 'Nothing I want to talk about though.'

'I want to talk about what's been happening to me. I just wish I could remember everything properly. Can I try?'

'Of course you can try. You don't need to ask me to do that.'

'Three men,' she said suddenly. 'I was being kept in a small room with no windows. Then three men showed up and hurried me through all these dark corridors. There wasn't much light around. That's what I remember most. Everything was in the shadows. The three of them took me to a very bright room and told me those codes over and over again. Yes ... that's right ... now I'm getting it. Then they finished with the address.'

'Did they say anything else?'

'It's all really blurry. Like trying to remember a dream that you can't put your finger on. Uhh...'

'Take your time, Shien.'

'There'll be a man waiting for me,' Shien said, her eyes widening as more details came back to her. 'At Beco da Perola. One of the apartments is theirs. They have every-thing ready.'

'You're a messenger,' Slater muttered under his breath. 'Why aren't they doing it themselves?'

'Are the codes for bad things?'

'Maybe,' Slater said, then reflected on every dangerous

situation he'd ever been involved in. 'Actually — almost definitely.'

'Well, then,' Shien said, deep in thought, 'maybe they want whoever I'm supposed to share the codes with to take the blame. You know, pretend he did it when they might be forcing him to do it. Then none of this would involve them and maybe only the apartment guy and me would show up on any security cameras. Cause there's lots of those around Taipa. Oh ... and you would show up, too.'

Slater couldn't take his eyes off the little girl trotting alongside him, staring innocently into space as she unloaded all the thoughts bubbling around in her mind.

'You know what, Shien,' he said, 'I think you might have nailed it.'

9

Thanks to the wonders of digital web mapping services, Slater found Beco da Perola within seconds of searching. The application on his phone located the dead-end street, dropped a destination pin over it, and provided him with crystal clear instructions on how to reach the area as fast as possible on foot.

Slater gulped involuntarily.

He wasn't sure if he wanted to.

He didn't fear what might be waiting for them in a rundown apartment complex buried in the depths of Beco da Perola. In fact, that portion of the coming hours invigorated him with such intensity that he fully recognised it as an unhealthy character trait. His life had been pain and misery for so long that he couldn't detach himself from it. If there was a fight on the horizon, he would welcome it with open arms.

Briefly, he wondered if intervening in this situation had been worth the hassle.

Then he looked down at the brilliant young girl by his side, and realised that even if he had to give his life to make sure she survived unscathed, he would probably do it.

That thought sent him down a much darker tunnel in his psyche.

He'd experienced almost everything he wanted out of life. He'd served his country with reckless abandon and saved thousands of lives in the process. He'd ended lives too, hundreds of them, most of which he felt satisfied with. He didn't often retaliate unless someone provoked him, and in his previous line of work there was seldom good reason to provoke Will Slater. He had been sent into the worst hell-holes on the planet and made it out relatively intact. At the same time, the millions of dollars he'd earned in exchange for his services had allowed him the ability to purchase the best experiences money could buy.

But there was one thing money couldn't buy.

Family.

Slater had been alone for as long as he could remember, and preferred to keep it that way. No-one in close proximity to him had ever benefitted from it, and he wanted it to remain that way out of personal preference.

He would help Shien with whatever she needed, and then he would be on his way.

They stepped into the dead-end street at close to four-thirty in the morning. Despite the hour, an odd murmuring ran through the grimy streets like soft discharges of electricity. The air crackled with crime and desperation and opportunity. This was clearly one of the most dangerous parts of Macau, and a hot trickle of anger filtered through Slater's veins as he thought of Shien wandering into these streets alone, drugged to the eyeballs and searching for refuge.

How dare those motherfuckers send her off like that.

He considered leaving her in a safe place and returning

to Mountain Lion Casino & Resorts to knock heads together until someone told him who was responsible. He considered himself supremely effective at getting what he wanted by applying force, but he was reluctant to leave Shien alone. Even if he could hide her away, there was no guaranteeing what she would do once the drugs wore off.

Would she be a different person, and decide to venture out into the unknown in search of her father?

So he reached down and took her hand as a low rumble resonated through the black sky overhead, signifying an incoming storm. As if on cue the humidity heightened, the Macau air bearing down on them hot and thick. Slater coughed as they made their way down the street, dwarfed by the tenement buildings on either side of them.

The complexes loomed, blocking out the sky, dilapidated and rundown and teeming with thousands of residents. Some were out of bed at this hour, roaming the streets in drug-addled states or simply sitting on damp concrete steps and staring out at the world with hollow, sunken faces.

It boggled Slater's mind that they had crossed over to these conditions so quickly. It felt like minutes ago he'd been sitting in one of the most lavish VIP rooms he'd ever laid eyes on, being served complementary fifteen-year-old scotch and throwing hundreds of thousands of dollars at the gambling tables in an attempt to distract himself from the past.

Now he led Shien to the very end of Beco da Perola, where a great grey slab of tiny apartments speared across the end of the street like a vast wall. Slater gazed up at the dwellings, hundreds of balconies poised in the gloom. Another thunderclap tore across the sky, and he hurried Shien toward the ground floor of the building. They crossed a cracked footpath overflowing with weeds and ducked into the apartment complex's lobby.

'Is this the place?' Slater said.

'I don't know. I think so.'

They stepped into a long stretch of decrepit corridor that smelled of sourness and old age. Slater wondered if the entire building would cave in on their heads, but pressed on regardless. He approached an elderly man with caramel skin and deep wrinkles etched into his forehead, perched behind a simple wooden desk that offered no security to its owner.

'You the landlord?' Slater said gruffly.

The man simply raised his head and looked deep into Slater's eyes, narrowing his gaze as he studied the new arrival. Slater felt suddenly vulnerable, as if the man could see into his soul. He stepped back instinctively, and Shien in turn stepped forward.

'I think he's Portuguese,' Slater muttered. 'Do your best.'

Shien fell into natural conversation with the elderly man. He responded with single syllables, grunting his replies, darting his gaze from the girl up to Slater, then back to the girl. He pointed directly at Slater and shook his head, muttering a string of Portuguese.

Shien shook her head in turn, crossed her arms, and pouted.

Finally, after an elongated period of silence, the man shrugged. Relenting, he handed over a key and gestured to the stairwell at the far end of the corridor, just as dilapidated as the rest of the complex.

The landlord shot daggers at Slater the entire time they stayed within eyesight.

When they reached the damp stairwell and began to

ascend into the foul centre of the structure, Shien finally decided to speak.

'He was expecting me to come alone. I had to convince him you were added security.'

'So whoever set you loose called this place in advance.'

'It's all been set up for me,' Shien said.

Slater peered up into the dark abyss. 'Let's see where it leads.'

10

The single key given to Shien by the old man unlocked a nondescript door made of rotting wood on the sixth floor of the complex. Tucked into the core of the building, there were no windows or fresh air in sight. The humidity had reached near unbearable levels, and Slater found himself choking on the heavy atmosphere as he prised the key out of Shien's tiny hand and slipped it into the requisite lock.

The handle turned.

Slater ushered Shien behind him and withdrew the Beretta from his jacket pocket. He took a moment to assess his outfit and realised it was likely the sole reason he'd made it past the landlord. He looked like typical security detail, which must have helped convince the guy to let him through.

But as he steadily swung the door open — the wood omitted a low creak as it moved on its hinges — he realised he needn't have bothered acting like security in the first place.

There was no-one home.

As soon as he realised the apartment was empty, he ushered Shien straight through, shielding her from the dangers of standing alone in the hallway. He imagined there were any number of drug-addled residents along these corridors, and he didn't want her out in public for any longer than necessary.

He swung the door shut behind them, took a deep breath of hot rancid air, and soaked in their surroundings.

They had been gifted a single-room dwelling with a tiny kitchenette falling apart at the seams and a single yellowing mattress with no linen thrown on the floor. The beige carpet had been torn up in a dozen different places, exposing the cheap wood underneath. There were no windows, and no decorations on the rotting plaster walls.

'They gave you an expensive suite, that's for sure,' Slater said.

'There's no mattress for you,' Shien said, staring absent-mindedly at her surroundings.

The conversation with the landlord had clearly drained her of energy.

'I'm not supposed to be here, remember?'

'Oh. Yes. That's right.'

'Are you tired?'

'Yes. I've been very scared these past few days.'

'You said you were kidnapped two weeks ago — is that right?'

'Yes. I remember that clearly. And I've been held in different rooms since then. There were always clocks on the walls, so I could count the days. Otherwise there was no way to tell how long it had been. The three men who rescued me were the first people I'd seen in a while.'

Slater crossed to the sink and poured himself a dirty glass of water. He washed it back, his throat parched from the all-out slugfest he'd taken part in earlier that night in the limousine. He took a deep breath, stripped his jacket off, rolled up his sleeves, and rested his massive hands on the kitchen countertop.

'I don't think they were rescuing you, Shien,' he said, bowing his head.

A bead of sweat dripped off his bald skull, splashing against the rim of the sink. He ran the cold water tap, splashed some of the soothing liquid across his face, and took another breath.

'Okay,' he muttered. 'One step at a time.'

'What was that all about?' Shien said. 'Why are you talking to yourself?'

Slater turned to check on her — she'd curled up in a ball at one end of the mattress, tucking her knees to her chest and resting her head against the flaking wall behind her.

'I think some very bad people are coming for us, Shien,' he said. 'I don't know what exactly it is you know, but I don't think whoever captured you had any intention of letting you go. I think that was something else. And if the original kidnap had anything to do with Mountain Lion, then that's billions of dollars we're dealing with. There's a lot of moving parts in a business that big and I wouldn't put it past them to be dealing in illegal things. I think you were kidnapped for a reason, but I need to find out for myself.'

'You seem angry, Will,' Shien said quietly.

'Because I have an idea of why you might have been captured. And if it's true, I'll become a different person. And I don't want you to see me like that.'

Shien's eyes widened. 'See you like what?'

'I have ... some personal issues. Let's just keep it at that. Something happened to a family member, decades ago, and whenever I see anything to do with it I lose it. I don't want you to see me lose it, Shien. So I'll sort this mess out, but I'll return you to wherever you need to go first.'

'Will. Why are you doing this?'

'To help you.'

'Yes, but why?'

'That's just what I do. I already said that. I get wrapped up in situations like this. Maybe I enjoy it — I don't know.'

Shien shrank into herself, tucking her knees tighter. 'I don't enjoy this.'

'I know you don't. Trust me, it won't be long before it's all over. I promise.'

'What do we do now? I thought I was supposed to meet someone. That's what we were talking about.'

'I feel like this is just one stop on a wild ride,' Slater said. 'These guys are professionals. This is just a holding cell, if you think of it like that. If I could guess, there'll be another address coming. When they have their man in place...'

'I don't understand,' Shien said.

'I don't expect you to. Try to get some sleep, okay?'

'Okay. Thanks again, Will.'

She slid down the wall and adopted the foetal position, keeping her arms wrapped tight around her tiny legs. Slater watched strands of jet black hair fall across her face, masking her features. Within a half-minute she was asleep, breathing deeply, aided along the journey by the drugs coursing through her system. Slater had little experience with sedation, but he hoped some of the effects would wear off by the time she woke up.

He needed her awake and alert.

He needed details.

He stood frozen in the centre of the claustrophobic apartment, sweating freely from all his pores, breathing deep, trying to compose himself in the midst of chaos. There were dozens of variables at play, and he wasn't sure who would come for them first.

He didn't know who had sent Shien on this wild journey, and what motives they had.

But someone, somewhere, knew they were here. The landlord had expected Shien's solo arrival, and Slater's presence had almost certainly startled him into passing the information up the food chain.

So Slater made sure the Beretta M9 in his right hand was live — ready to fire at a moment's notice — and he sat down with his back against one of the kitchen cabinets, staring at the apartment's only entrance door with unblinking eyes. He had learned the subtleties of keeping watch a decade earlier, and he had enough confidence in his abilities to know he wouldn't falter.

It didn't matter how tired he was.

He would sit in this cramped, sticky apartment on a shiny patch of cheap linoleum and wait for someone to come barging in through the front door with guns blazing, as he assumed they would.

In the end, he didn't have long to wait.

S later's watch displayed a time of 6:42am when he heard movement on the other side of the door.

There were no adjustments to make, seeing that he'd maintained a state of readiness for the full two hours he'd been perched on the kitchenette's floor. Shien had spent the entire time dozing peacefully on the other side of the room — which, in this case, rested a distance of less than six feet away.

Slater sensed the presence of a hostile body before he properly heard the man.

Despite the intruder's best efforts to remain silent, one of his footfalls sent a muffled, imperceptible noise trickling underneath the gap below the door.

Slater gave the man zero time to prepare for an assault.

At the exact millisecond his brain registered the noise, he shot to his feet and hurled himself two feet through the air, hitting the flimsy rotting surface of the door with his shoulder, driving kinetic energy and power and momentum into the wood.

The weak material simply snapped off its hinges and the entire door frame tipped straight out into the hallway.

Slater made sure to pull back from the initial charge so that he didn't sprawl head-over-heels into the corridor, instead leaping over the door and ramming straight into the frozen suit-clad man on the other side. The guy had taken some of the impact to the top of his head, darting out of the way of the falling door at the last second. The explosion of noise and movement had shocked him into hesitation, and Slater had the Beretta trained on the guy's forehead within a half-second of stepping out into the corridor.

He looked to be in his thirties, with bronze-coloured skin and Asian features. Slater guessed Filipino and Chinese, or some similar mix. His hair was jet black and close-cropped, and an ugly neck tattoo speared above his collar, reaching for his chin. Some kind of dragon. A massive jewelled earring rested in his right lobe.

He looked tough, and angry as all hell.

He stared at Slater with venom in his eyes, as if he were offended by the mere prospect of Slater being present.

'Don't move,' Slater said, noticing the chunky pistol resting in the guy's palm out of the corner of his eye.

He didn't dare glance down at the weapon, at risk of being placed at a tactical disadvantage. Instead he kept his eyes locked on the man's in a deadly stalemate, both of them standing silently in the creaky hallway.

Nearby, fetid water dripped from cracks in the ceiling.

More sweat began to flow from Slater's forehead.

He felt hot and sticky and awful.

And, on top of everything, his heart had started to pound mercilessly against his chest wall as the adrenalin of a standoff took hold.

The guy had his gun pointed at the floor, but Slater

figured there was a language barrier, and he had no way of knowing what the man might try. The safest option would be to blow the guy's brains across the far wall, but he felt inclined to keep the man alive for the time being.

He wanted answers.

He'd jumped into a murky situation that he needed to understand better, and this guy would be the first piece of the puzzle.

Slater gestured with the Beretta, instructing the man to head straight through the open doorway. He planned to interrogate the guy in the privacy of their own place, using Shien as a translator if necessary.

'Will...' a soft voice called from inside the apartment. 'You okay?'

Slater cocked his head ever so slightly in the direction of the noise — either a fatherly reaction, or a simple natural response to someone he knew — but the man in front of him decided to try and capitalise on it. Before Slater could protest, or tell the man what a fool he was, the guy attempted to swing the gun barrel up to meet Slater's face.

Slater didn't even have time to cry out.

He simply pumped the trigger once, clinically, and blasted a cylindrical hole through the guy's forehead. The man's jewelled earring sparkled as he fell to the complex floor and the gunshot tore up and down the empty corridor, echoing off the walls far in the distance.

Shien screamed.

Slater needed to obscure the body from view of any curious residents. Before the guy had even finished kicking in his death throes, Slater reached down and wrapped a hand around the upper portion of his tie, yanking him by the throat through the open doorway of the apartment.

Shien wasn't used to seeing dead bodies — and the sight

of Slater dragging a corpse would no doubt be grotesque — but Slater thought he heard a distinct sigh of relief as she saw him materialise, alive and safe, in the doorway.

'I thought you got shot,' she said quietly.

Slater barely heard it.

The unsuppressed gunshot at such close range had set off the uncomfortable whining in his ears, a noise eerily similar to tinnitus. He waited for the sensation to dissipate, taking the time to dump the corpse in the foot of the hallway and prop the apartment door loosely back into place.

'You killed that man, too,' Shien said after a beat of hesitation.

Slater looked to her, then to the body. 'Yes, Shien, I know that.'

'Was he coming to kill me?'

'He looked rattled. I don't think so. He wasn't supposed to show himself. He's one of the men behind this, and he was meant to keep in the shadows. But they couldn't resist sending a man down here when they got word that you weren't alone.'

'I think I recognise him,' Shien said.

Reluctantly, Slater reached down and propped the body into a seated position. 'Ignore the blood. Look at his face. You know him?'

She cast her eyes up to the bloody mess that used to be his forehead, scrutinised his features for a single instant, then turned away in disgust. 'Yes. That's one of the three men that rescued me.'

'You've got to stop saying "rescued",' Slater said. 'These men have bad intentions. They're keeping themselves out of this for a reason. You're the scapegoat.'

'I don't know what that means.'

'You're the one who'll pay the price if you get caught.'

'Caught by who?'

'I don't know.'

'What if I just do as they say?'

'You think they're good people?'

'I don't know. You don't either.'

'Well, this one tried to shoot me,' Slater said, motioning to the corpse. 'Whatever you think about the others, he got what he deserved. I'll try my best to take it easy on anyone else we run into.'

Sarcasm laced his tone, and Shien noticed. She pouted and turned away, burrowing back into one corner of the mattress. Slater scolded himself for talking openly about murder and flaunting a corpse in her presence. He realised the drugs were still in her system — otherwise she would have broken down long ago.

He doubted a nine-year-old would have much experience being around the dead.

'Shien,' he said. 'I'm sorry. Just try to relax, okay.'

'How am I supposed to relax?' she said.

'I think it's time I tried to get in touch with your parents.'

All the blood drained from her face as she turned white as a ghost. 'No.'

12

The reaction threw Slater for a loop.

Shien withdrew into herself, narrowing her eyes and sliding steadily down the wall. She became groggy and unresponsive all at once, yet Slater knew it was all an act. For nine years old she had talent, but the transition had been too abrupt to have been real. She simply didn't want to talk about her parents. The thought of getting in contact with them had terrified her.

Slater grew suspicious, and sat down at the other end of the grimy mattress.

'You can talk to me,' he said.

'Mmm,' Shien mumbled.

'Shien. You were perfectly fine ten seconds ago. I know you're faking it.'

'Not faking it,' she grumbled, slipping even further into the charade.

'If you don't talk to me about it, I'll leave you here to work things out for yourself.'

Instantly, she became alert. A cross expression fell over

her features, complete with a furrowed brow and an icy glare. 'You wouldn't...'

'No — I wouldn't — but it made you give up your performance, didn't it?'

She folded her arms across her chest and shifted restlessly. 'I hate you.'

'That's not very nice.'

'It's the truth.'

'I don't think you do.'

'You don't know what I'm thinking.'

'I have an idea. It has something to do with your parents. Do you think they're involved with this?'

That brought about a fresh wave of emotions, each of which rolled over Shien with fervour. She made no attempt to hide them. First shock, then realisation that she'd let her feelings show, then anger at herself.

'No,' she demanded firmly, harsh enough for Slater to discern she was telling the truth. 'Definitely not. Daddy's not like that. He'd do anything to get me back. It's just...'

'Just what?'

There was no going back. The second she'd opened her mouth, Shien tumbled down a hole she couldn't escape from. If she wanted Slater's help, she would have to share what was on her mind, and he watched that realisation take hold in the form of an irritated twitch in her left eye.

'We didn't come to Macau for good reasons,' she said. 'Daddy was angry. It feels like he only comes here when he's angry, and he had to bring me along because Mummy is back in Texas visiting family.'

'Does she go there often?'

'No.'

'What does she do?'

'Nothing now. She is very pretty and Daddy is very rich.'

'I see.'

'She won Miss Texas. Back in the day. At least that's what she tells me.'

'I see. Do you get on well?'

'Who?'

'You and your mother.'

'I don't see her much. I don't really have a mother...'

'What does your dad do for work?'

'He's a businessman.'

'Do you know what type of business?'

'No. Nothing bad, though.'

'Are you sure?'

'Yes.'

'Do you have security around all the time? Back in Hong Kong?'

Shien nodded. 'But not because he does bad things. Daddy is worth a lot of money. He gives loans to people. I think that's how it works.'

'He's an investor?'

'I don't know what that means.'

'Did he come here to get his money back?'

Shien frowned, her brain moving fast in an effort to keep up. 'I don't know. It seemed like it, but he never talks to me about those things. He just said we were going on another trip. He was very mad.'

'At you?'

'No. Never. Just in general.'

'Where were you staying?'

'A hotel. I ... can't remember what it was called.'

'Fancy place?'

'Of course.'

'Was your dad around much while you were here?'

'No. He was always out. Doing his business.'

'Were there men protecting you here?'

'Less than usual,' Shien said. 'Daddy has a whole army back in Hong Kong. Well, not really, but I like to pretend they're our private army. They just keep us safe.'

'How many were with you in Macau?'

'A couple.'

'Were they around when you got kidnapped the first time?'

'I don't remember it,' she said. 'Someone pushed something in my face — like a cloth or something — and that's all I remember. Then I was kept in rooms for days and days. I never saw anyone, and they kept putting these needles in me to keep me like this. Then those three men let me go, and everything went crazy when you showed up.'

'That usually happens with me,' Slater muttered. 'These men who let you go — did they say anything else?'

'No,' Shien said, then hesitated. 'Well, maybe. That part's still foggy. I just remember the codes and the address.'

'Is your memory good, Shien?'

'Yes, I think so.'

'Very good?'

'I don't know. I was in advanced classes.'

'If they knew that, they might have realised they could use you as a messenger. If they knew with absolute certainty that you'd remember the numbers and letters they told you.'

'But I still feel foggy. I'm surprised I remember.'

'There's ways to embed things in people's heads,' Slater said.

'I don't like the sound of that.'

'You shouldn't.'

'How do you know that?'

'I used to do things for my country that weren't legal.

There's a lot I know about that you wouldn't like the sound of.'

'Can you tell me?'

'Not now. Probably not ever. Right now I need to know if there's anything else you can remember the three men telling you. You're obviously important to them. Think, Shien. Where were we supposed to go from here? We need to figure it out on our own now, because there's no way we can pretend to go along with the plan anymore. They know I'm protecting you. They won't help you.'

'The tap.'

Slater froze. The statement had come out of nowhere — one second Shien had been uniformly mute, the next she'd blurted out the two words as if mid-epiphany.

'What?' he said.

'They told me to stay here overnight. And then check the tap. How did I forget that?'

'Obviously they didn't repeat it as much as the codes,' Slater muttered.

He shot to his feet and crossed to the kitchenette. On the way he glanced into the front hallway and caught a glimpse of the dead man near the door, slumped against the wall and sitting in a puddle of his own blood. The bullet hole in his forehead refused to stop bleeding, along with the gruesome exit wound in the back of his skull.

Slater studied the rusting metal tap on the way over to the sink, spending little time wondering where the information would be.

He thought he knew.

Spurred on by the ticking clock counting down to when the next armed killer would show up, he wrapped one bloody palm around the tap and wrenched it free from the wall, simply tearing it out of the damp plaster around its base. With a groan of crumpling supports it dropped into the sink, flakes of rust falling off its surface. The feat must have looked superhuman, but Slater realised Shien could have probably made the same actions with half the effort.

The tap had been deliberately weakened — or already removed previously.

Slater peered into the narrow hole in the wall, where the pipeline disappeared fast into the darkness, and spotted the murky glint of a dirty key a couple of inches inside. It had been secured to the side of the pipe with a single piece of scotch tape, ensuring it didn't detach when the flow of water rushed past it.

Slater ripped the key out of the pipe and twirled it over and over between his fingers, studying the tag that came attached with it.

It read 516.

'Shien,' he said. 'What's our room number?'

He heard her rustling around the floor beside the mattress, retrieving the key that had let them into this pitiful residence.

'502,' she said softly.

'This is just down the hall,' Slater muttered. 'When are we supposed to—'

'Midday, today. They told me that too.'

'You just remembered that now?'

'Yes.'

'Is this coming back to you by chance, or were you supposed to remember it?'

'I don't know.'

Slater checked his Rolex — it was just after seven in the morning. 'So they need until twelve. I guess they're putting someone in place, and they need time to do it. You hungry?'

13

At ten in the morning — Shien had requested another couple of hours sleep — they found themselves at a thriving eatery tucked into the ground floor of one of the sprawling buildings lining the nearby streets. Slater had ushered Shien quickly out of their complex in case they were being watched, but he quickly realised the density of the neighbourhood would prevent any kind of tail from following them.

There were thousands of people on the streets, floating between markets and laundromats and shooting past on motorised scooters. It seemed that the humidity intensified during the daytime — up to this point, Slater had spent most of his days in air-conditioned luxury, tucked deep in the bowels of Macau's five-star resorts and casinos.

The heat reminded him of Yemen.

A place he would do good to forget.

They sat at a cramped booth in a long, narrow room packed with dozens of paying customers. Rickety fans blasted overhead, switched to the highest possible setting, but they did little to combat the weather. The temperature compounded with the body heat of the civilians packing the steaming room to create a sweltering atmosphere that Slater was still acclimatising to.

It seemed Shien was used to the conditions.

She munched on a plate of *minchi,* a traditional Macanese dish made of minced beef. A young waitress with a glistening forehead brought over two tall glasses of room-temperature water and Slater drained his glass in a couple of seconds, relishing the brief reprieve from the dry throat that had plagued him for the last twelve hours.

Combat and tension stressed him out, which wreaked havoc on his body.

Nothing he wasn't used to, though.

Stress had become normal long ago.

'You never answered my question this morning,' Slater said when Shien had polished off the last few kernels of rice on her plate.

She swallowed and frowned at him. 'What are you talking about?'

'Why don't you want me to contact your parents?'

Her cheeks flushed red — she couldn't help it. 'I just don't want Daddy to be put in danger.'

'That's not the reason.'

'Will...'

'I get you don't want to talk about it, but I'm risking my neck here. At least spare me that much.'

She paused, tapping her fingers incessantly against the lip of the empty plate in front of her. 'Fine.'

'When you're ready.'

'I think it has something to do with my Daddy. And, despite what you might think, he's a good person. He doesn't do anything illegal. You might not believe me and that's fine. But I know the truth. And if I try to get back to him, they might kill him. I'm scared... I don't know what to do.'

'How do you know he's not dead now?'

Wrong fucking choice of words, he thought.

She made to respond but the breath caught in her throat, an emotional reaction to a terrifying hypothetical. Slater gulped back unease and lifted a palm in apology, shaking his head. 'It's unlikely. There's all the chance in the world you've been kidnapped to extort money out of him.'

Shien managed to restrain herself, massaging her temples with her tiny fingers. 'I hope he's okay.'

'I'm sure he's fine.'

'But — what do we do from here? If I can't go back to him, where do I go? What do we do?'

Slater wished he had answers.

'Let's take care of what we can control,' he said. 'I'll find out what the deal is with this second apartment we're supposed to visit. You won't be in any danger. I'll make sure of that.'

'What was all that about anyway? The first apartment....'

'I think it was a holding room. Whoever released you needs time to get things in place.'

'Why?'

'I don't know everything, Shien.'

Suddenly, seemingly out of nowhere, her upper lip started to quiver and she stared at Slater with a certain apprehension that hadn't been there before. Slater shifted uncomfortably in his seat — he could violently subdue hired killers all day long, but dealing with the emotions of a vulnerable child took him far out of his comfort zone. 'What's wrong?'

'Y-you killed that man back there, Will. He's dead.'

'I know.'

He realised his own foolishness. Sooner or later, the effects of the suppressive drugs in her system would abate entirely and she'd be free to consider everything she'd witnessed. So far it seemed she'd barely been affected by the chaos all around her — in his inexperience with children, Slater had chalked it up to a simple tough morale.

But no kid could handle what Shien was going through.

The drugs were artificially helping her compartmentalise the dead bodies she'd seen and the carnage that had unfolded all around her.

Now, her emotions were beginning to catch up to her.

Slater pondered the best course of action before reaching across and placing a hand on Shien's wrist. His fingers dwarfed her forearm, but she managed to compose herself.

'This is an awful situation,' he whispered. 'But it's going to be okay. I'll get you back to your dad.'

'You can't do that unless he's going to be safe,' Shien said, pouting. 'And there's no way to tell whether he's safe.'

'I'm fairly talented at dealing with situations like this. I have experience with this kind of thing.'

'You don't even know what the situation is.'

'That was part of my job description. I dealt with unique threats.'

'What did you do?'

'That's not something I like talking about.'

'You can talk to me about it.'

'Actually, I think you're the last person I should talk to about it.'

She yanked her wrist out of his grasp, staring at him with all the intensity she could muster.

The drugs were certainly fading.

Her emotions were heightened.

'Will,' she said. 'I know I'm nine, but I'm not stupid. My Daddy is not a bad man, but he deals with bad men. I think he gives them money, and expects it back. So I'm very young but I've seen a lot of things and I know how the world works. I know people do bad things. I don't care if you used to do bad things. I—'

She trailed off mid-sentence, furrowing her brow. For such a youthful kid the speech had taken a great deal of concentration, and finally the burden had become too great. Slater saw the fogginess draping back over her in brief flashes — the remnants of the stuff in her system battling for control.

The speech itself had shocked him. He hadn't antici-pated it — his gut reaction told him to shield Shien from any kind of exposure to violence and suffering. He'd slipped up by handling the corpse around her back at the apart-ment, and before they'd trekked to the eatery he'd silently promised himself to keep her as distant as possible.

But maybe she needed to know certain details.

For her own sanity.

It would mess with her head if Slater kept himself solemn and mute for the rest of their time together. Perhaps she'd live in fear of what he might do to her.

'Look,' he said, 'I was in the military. That's all I'm comfortable telling you.'

'A soldier?'

'A special kind of soldier.'

'Like a superhero?'

He bowed his head to mask a smirk. 'Something like that, Shien.'

14

Shien had explicitly told him midday, but Slater decided to make the journey back to the apartment complex's fifth floor twenty minutes before the allotted time slot. He had to roughly maintain the schedule they expected of him, but adjust it just enough to throw them off their game. Maybe whoever was expecting them wouldn't be prepared for an early arrival.

He could catch them off their guard.

He passed the same Filipino landlord they'd encountered earlier, hurrying Shien through the lobby as fast as he could. He mustered his best menacing expression and shot daggers at the elderly man. The guy wilted under Slater's glare, hunching forward and staring straight at the ground between his feet. He must have informed Shien's captors of the presence of a stranger, which had sent the thug with the jewelled earring to check on them.

He must have seen the man go up the stairwell, four hours earlier.

He wouldn't have seen him come down, for the thug was lying dead in their apartment.

So the landlord knew what Slater was capable of, and would try his best to stay out of their hair.

It was in his own best interests.

When they made it past the elderly man, Shien felt it safe to speak. 'I'm scared, Will.'

'That's only natural. I'm scared too.'

'You don't look scared.'

'The fear never really goes away. You just get better at hiding it.'

'So why do you keep doing these things over and over?'

'It's what I've always done, Shien,' he muttered.

They climbed the same stairwell, inhaling the abhorrent combination of dampness and rot that had needled its way into Slater's brain over the last twelve hours. The five-star suites were a thing of the past. Despite the less-than-favourable conditions, something about the dingy surroundings felt familiar to him.

It felt like home.

He had no idea what to expect from 516. They'd been given a key, which gave them direct access to the apartment, which eliminated privacy from the equation. Whoever resided in the flat wouldn't be able to prevent them from entering. It made Slater think that whoever they'd be meeting wasn't in bed with Shien's captors.

Another scapegoat, perhaps.

A chain of people thrust into a difficult situation to separate the men responsible from any guilt.

He kept that in the back of his mind as they strode out into the familiar fifth-floor corridor. Slater pressed a hand instinctively to Shien's shoulder, holding her back while he checked whether the coast was clear. The hallway lay empty — he guessed the residents were either drugged to the eyeballs or at work. He glanced at the carpet outside room

502 — the bloodstain where the thug with the jewelled earring had collapsed was barely noticeable amidst the surrounding filth.

In retrospect, he couldn't have picked a better location to shoot a man dead.

It seemed like the event had barely registered in this place. No-one had responded with panic to the gunshot — in fact, nobody appeared at all.

A fully unsuppressed blast from a Beretta M9 must be considered relatively normal around these parts.

It sent a shiver down his spine. If he or Shien wound up dead in one of these apartments, no-one would ever know. Their bodies would be tucked away and left to rot, without anyone realising.

Everything stank of rot around here.

He wondered how long it would take for someone to find the dead thug in room 502.

Weeks, he imagined.

From their position in the lip of the stairwell, he had a perfect view of the door to apartment number 516. It sat in a shadowy corner of the decrepit corridor, unimpressive and unnoticeable. He remained frozen in the middle of the hallway, listening for signs of anything suspicious. Finding nothing, he released his hold on Shien and withdrew the Beretta from his suit jacket.

'I want you to knock on the door and stand in front of it,' he muttered, keeping his voice low.

'Why?' she whispered back. 'We have a key.'

'I don't want to barge in. They might be preparing for that.'

'Who?'

'Anyone's guess. None of this makes any sense if I'm

being honest. But if they see you standing out here alone, they might drop their guard. I can force my way in.'

'Are you going to kill more people?' Shien said, her voice stammering.

She was terrified of the possibility.

'I honestly don't know,' he said. 'I can't promise you anything. It depends who answers the door.'

Her eyes turned to the Beretta in his right palm, and she shivered involuntarily.

'Can you do this for me, Shien?' he said. 'I need your help if I'm going to sort this out.'

'Okay.'

Nothing about her response signalled confidence, but Slater didn't need her to be confident.

He just needed her to knock.

They slunk down the corridor, their shoes squelching against the damp carpet. Slater tuned the disgusting surroundings out of his conscious thought and narrowed his vision on the door with 516 inscribed in the wooden surface. He guided Shien into position and retreated to the far side of the hallway, keeping low, searching for somewhere he could take cover while maintaining line of sight.

He noticed a narrow doorway embedded in the wall opposite 516, leading to a secondary stairwell in even scummier condition than the first. Slater could barely make out the dark space through the fingerprint-stained window set into the door, but a smattering of faded warning signs indicated that the stairwell was some kind of fire escape. He nudged the swinging door open a foot and retreated into the shadows, taking care not to inhale at risk of passing out from the horrific stench.

And there he waited, crouched like a phantom in the darkness, Beretta clutched in a sweaty palm, leaning against the door with his back to a dark, musty stairwell. He whispered, 'Now,' to Shien and she reached a closed fist up and rapped it twice on the door to apartment number 516.

Slater poised like a tensed coil, ready for anything.

The door swung open.

15

If the movements of the man who answered the door had been hostile in any manner, Slater would have charged across the corridor like a bat out of hell. But he came across something entirely different — the door peeped open a crack and a nervous voice with a thick British accent stammered, 'A-are you alone?'

'Yes,' Shien said, remaining remarkably composed in the face of such a volatile situation.

Slater couldn't get a good look at the guy due to the angle of the door, but he seemed scared as shit. Slater was forced into a spur-of-the-moment decision — stay out of sight and let Shien venture into the apartment alone, or present himself and terrify the British guy into resistance.

In the end, Slater couldn't imagine the guy posed much of a threat, and he needed answers.

He opted to wait.

A few seconds more.

Just to see how things transpired.

'I ... I was told you had company,' the British guy said.

'No,' Shien said. 'Just me.'

'Um, I'm supposed to get some codes off you. Do you know what I'm talking about?'

'Yes.' Shien made an act out of glancing in either direction down the hallway. 'You sure you want to do the exchange out here? Maybe I could come in.'

'Oh. Yeah. That's a good idea. Sorry, I'm just nervous — y-you sure there's no-one with you?'

'Why would there be anyone with me?'

'I don't know — that's just what I was told.'

'Just me,' Shien repeated.

Slater couldn't help himself — he was damn impressed. Often in sensitive circumstances people who were nervous unloaded everything in their brains all at once. Shien could have easily started trying to justify the reasons why she was alone, all of which would only serve to give the British guy time to think and grow more suspicious. By keeping her responses to a minimum, the onus fell onto the guy to make conversation — something he was struggling with given his level of nerves. Instead of asking what had happened to the man who was supposed to be accompanying Shien, he was forced onto the back foot.

'Uh, yeah, okay. Come in.'

He opened the door a little wider, and Shien stepped forward.

As soon as she started to disappear from sight, Slater's natural instincts kicked in. He couldn't leave her alone in an apartment with a complete stranger — no matter how nervous the guy was or whether or not he'd been forced into the position. It still left all kinds of variables he wasn't comfortable with, so he tightened his grip on the Beretta and began to move out of the shadows to intercept the British guy as Shien brushed past him.

Shien moved through the doorway into the apartment, and the door started to swing close.

Slater pressed faster.

Then a vicious burst of kinetic movement sounded behind him, tearing his attention away from the task at hand. He froze and spun on his heel, pivoting to get a proper look at what was unfolding.

He saw three people in the gloom — all of them had made their way silently up the stairwell behind him, planning to step out onto the fifth floor undetected. Slater's presence had frightened them — maybe they hadn't seen him crouched in the doorway. When he'd burst out into the open they'd sprinted up behind him to try and catch him off-guard.

All three were Asian, and all three were armed with sidearms and dressed in tactical combat gear.

Their guns swept up through the air, on trajectory to aim at Slater's face, but no-one had fired a shot yet.

They were hesitant to make noise and startle the natural flow of things.

Maybe they had been sent to retrieve Shien.

Either way, Slater didn't give a shit about making noise.

He flicked the Beretta up to shoulder height and blasted the closest thug's face apart with a single unsuppressed round.

16

The corridor turned to bedlam.

Slater guessed the British guy had slammed the door in panic, sealing he and Shien inside the apartment, but he had no way of knowing for sure. His hearing had been destroyed by the close-range gunshot, and he had no time to turn and look before the first thug's corpse pitched forward and crashed into him, carried by the momentum of the guy's charge.

Slater couldn't help himself — he instinctively recoiled. Blood from the dead man's forehead splattered across him and he naturally stepped away from it.

A grave error.

The guy was heavyset — thick and big-boned. He had the stocky build of a powerhouse and when his dead body-weight collapsed against Slater's chest it sent him stumbling off his feet, zigzagging uncontrollably across the corridor. He slammed back-first into the wall next to apartment number 516 and the damp plaster caved in under his weight, sending him reeling back into the foundations themselves.

Rancid water splashed down over him, disrupted by the gaping hole in the wall. Slater had no time to pull himself out of the half-seated position inside the wood — the dead thug's trajectory carried him straight down on top of Slater, his mass sprawling against Slater's torso.

Slater grunted with frustration, then instinctively pulled the dead man in front of him as the other two fired.

Twin gunshots roared down the hallway, and the dead man on top of Slater jerked unnaturally as he took two bullets to the torso. Thankfully, his weight meant that the lead remained embedded in his ribcage instead of blasting straight through and sinking into Slater.

There was a beat of hesitation as the two remaining thugs realised they'd just fired on their own man.

In the chaos and confusion, they hadn't been able to tell if Slater's bullet had killed their friend. They might have thought the man lost his balance and simply stumbled into Slater — which would add the mental torment that they might have possibly just murdered their comrade.

Slater used it to his advantage.

Still gripping the Beretta — which had become sandwiched between his stomach and the dead man's body mass — he found purchase on the damp carpet and levered himself out of the hole in the wall, heaving the corpse upright at the same time. As soon as he'd wrenched himself free from the torn wood and sprung to his feet, he thundered a front kick into the dead guy's stomach, sending his bodyweight hurtling back in the other direction.

The corpse slumped uselessly against the other two men.

They mimicked Slater's previous actions, recoiling away from the body. This was their close friend, a man who had been alive and functioning seconds previously — now he was bleeding from the forehead and the torso, stone dead and slumping in gruesome fashion across them. They stepped back, throwing themselves off-balance in the process.

A terrible move.

It opened up the slightest window of opportunity for Slater to act.

He raised the Beretta and fired twice, slicing his aim from forehead to forehead, clinical in his movements. Twin explosions of gunshot reports resonated down the hallway, and blood arced from the exit wounds that blasted out the back of both men's skulls.

They dropped like rag dolls, hitting the ground in unison with the first guy, who had been thrust from man to man like a hot potato. The trio of corpses made a collective thump as they splayed out across the filthy carpet, each sporting a neat bullet hole in the centre of their foreheads. The first guy had a pair of rounds embedded in the meat of his back — Slater identified that as the source of all the blood.

He stood panting in the middle of the hallway, surrounded by dead men, shocked by the rapidity with which the situation had escalated. Now that the massive bolt of adrenalin had run its course he felt warmth across his upper back. He reached one hand over the opposite shoulder and winced as he ran his fingers over wooden splinters embedded in his skin.

They'd effortlessly torn through his suit jacket.

'I just bought this fucking thing,' he muttered, disgruntled.

The tailored fit had cost him several thousand dollars.

With the shock of the sudden ambush wearing off, he

picked up signs of commotion all the way along the hallway. Five gunshots in quick succession had disturbed the peace, no matter whether the residents were accustomed to violence or not. Slater stared down at the three corpses — a whole lot of bodyweight — and grunted a realisation that he couldn't hide them in the same way he'd dealt with the first guy's corpse earlier that morning.

Shien.

He pivoted on his heel, tearing his attention away from the dead men, and searched for the door to apartment number 516. In the panic he'd lost his bearings, but it didn't take him long to locate the flimsy panel of wood with the corresponding number engraved on its surface. As he suspected, the British guy had become terrified by the sudden onslaught of noise and locked the door behind him.

There was no sign of Shien.

She was in there.

A deeper, darker instinct took hold and Slater shouldered his whole weight into the centre of the wooden door. The material heaved and groaned, and gave way a half-second later. He wasn't sure whether he was going to crash straight through the door or simply burst the lock open — either way, he was on course to barrel his way into the apartment at a blistering rate.

Exactly what he was accustomed to.

The hinges gave way before the lock did, and the entire door simply crashed into the front hallway in a burst of tearing wood. Slater powered straight over the top of the falling panel, storming straight into 516.

First, he noticed that the filthy room had the same layout as the first apartment they'd entered in the early hours of the morning — an unimpressive windowless room with a kitchenette and a bed.

Second, Slater noticed the British guy huddled in one corner of the room, holding Shien in front of him.

He noticed her shaking where she stood, pale and sweating and horrified.

There was a gun to her head.

17

'I'd put that fucking thing down if I were you,' Slater snarled.

He meant it.

He recognised all the features of abject terror on the British guy's face, and he understood the dynamic the man was working with — the guy had no knowledge of who Slater was and what kind of threat he posed, and had elected to use whatever he could to try and protect himself from harm.

But he'd chosen the wrong person to hold hostage.

'L-look, buddy, I don't know who you are, but leave me alone!' the British guy said. 'Just leave. I don't know what's going on. I'm following orders. I'm not trying to hurt anyone. Please, just—'

Slater stayed deathly still in the lip of the hallway, keeping the Beretta pointed squarely at the floor. He wasn't going to aim it at the British guy's head — he was trying his best to prevent any kind of knee jerk reaction to getting a weapon aimed at one's temple.

'Put. The. Gun. Down.'

'Who are you?' the British guy said, and his voice changed pitch drastically, cracking in the face of fear. 'What do you want?'

Slater realised he was young and impressionable and inexperienced. He had something to work with. He didn't take his eyes off the guy. He could sense Shien just a foot below, in his peripheral vision, staring at him silently with pleading, watering eyes.

Get this gun off the side of my head, Will, her eyes were saying. *I'm scared.*

'What's your name, kid?' Slater said.

'Samuel Barnes.'

'Samuel Barnes, I don't really want to have to kill you. That girl you're holding is with me, and it's my responsibility to keep her alive. Take the fucking weapon away from her temple and we'll talk.'

'How do I know you're not going to kill me?'

'Samuel...'

'Look, man, I can't take your word for—'

'*Put it down!*' Slater roared at the top of his lungs, shockingly loud in the claustrophobic space.

Samuel visibly jolted, and fresh tears spilled down Shien's face. Slater could sense the raw, unbridled terror in the air — she thought she was about to die.

The pistol — an archaic Polish P-64 likely purchased dirt cheap on the black market — faltered as Samuel wilted under the stress. He bowed his head and began to let the barrel fall toward the floor.

'Please, just don't kill me, man,' he muttered as he started to cave in.

Slater took no chances. As soon as the weapon was pointed away from Shien, he burst across the room like a raging bull and hurled her onto the bed, throwing her away from Samuel with enough force to knock the breath from her lungs. Shien bounced off the mattress and came to a halt, breathless but out of harm's way.

Slater grabbed two handfuls of Samuel's shirt and kneed him in the stomach with the force of a seasoned Muay Thai practitioner. The kid crumpled as the breath exploded out of his lips. He spluttered and coughed and slid down the musty wall, ending up in a pathetic heap in the corner of the room.

Slater ripped the P-64 sidearm out of his grip and hurled it across the room.

'What were you thinking, kid?' he said.

Samuel winced in pain as the secondary effects of the knee began to take hold. Slater knew exactly what the guy was going through. The searing pain would work its way up his mid-section, agonising enough to teach him a lesson. However, Slater had thrown the strike with enough restraint to ensure he didn't cause any damage that wouldn't fade in minutes. He easily could have broken ribs or torn muscles against such a vulnerable opponent.

'I was trying to save my own skin,' Samuel muttered.

'If I was almost anyone else I would have killed you for that. You think the gangsters around here would have tolerated that shit? They're probably all triad. They would have strung you up by your throat.'

Feebly, Samuel shook his head. 'No, they wouldn't have.'

'And why's that?'

'Because it's the triad telling me what to do.'

Slater paused. 'You work for them.'

Samuel looked up, disbelief flooding his face. 'Hell no, man! You think a guy like me would work for them?'

'You never know. Looks can be deceiving.'

'Well, I'm exactly what I look like. I'm about to pass out from all this stress.'

'I want to know everything,' Slater said. 'I've got a young kid here who's been held against her will for two weeks. Tell me everything you know, and you'd better not hold anything back.'

Samuel flicked a glance in Shien's direction. 'I don't know anything about no kid, man.'

'You were expecting her.'

'I was just told to meet a little girl and a black man at this location.'

'And?'

'Uh—'

He was hesitating. Slater feigned another strike and Samuel winced involuntarily, bracing for another painful impact. Slater pulled back on his punch at the last moment. 'Samuel. Tell me everything.'

Samuel sighed and bowed his head. 'Can you tell me who you are first? I don't want to get myself killed for saying the wrong thing.'

'I'm a guy with no affiliation to anyone. I couldn't give a shit what you've done. I just want to know the truth, so I can piece all this together.'

Samuel ran both hands through his curly hair, stressed to the eyeballs. 'Okay, man. Okay. The triad are hanging threats over my head. I fucked up. I need to do whatever they say or I'm going to be in deep shit.'

'What did you do?'

'I work at Mountain Lion Casino & Resorts. As a baccarat dealer in one of the VIP rooms. I—'

'Seems like this all revolves around Mountain Lion,' Slater muttered. 'I was just there.'

'Doing what?'

'Minding my own business until I got wrapped up in all this shit. Continue.'

'Right, so, there's a form of money laundering where two players work with each other to place bets on opposite sides of the table over and over again. Their collective total remains the same, but they're technically "gambling" the money. You get me? They can use creative accounting to avoid taxes.'

'I'm following,' Slater said.

'Well, there's a small army of wealthy businessmen who use the tactic, but the owner of Mountain Lion takes a cut for allowing the service to take place on the premises.'

'Uh-huh.'

'He's very tight with money.'

'The owner?'

'Yeah. He doesn't tolerate anyone trying to siphon money away from him.'

'What's his name?'

'Peter Forrest.'

'And I take it that's exactly what you did? Siphoned money away from Peter Forrest?'

'Me and my friend. We're both baccarat dealers. We figured he couldn't watch every VIP room at the same time. We could run the scam and take the casino's cut for ourselves.'

'How much money are we talking?'

'The equivalent of two hundred thousand British pounds.'

'That's a lot of money for a service fee.'

'They're laundering tens of millions. It's a drop in the bucket.'

'And life-changing money for the two of you.'

'Yeah. But Forrest found out, and he killed the other

dealer. But he thinks the other guy was working as a one-man-show. He doesn't know I'm involved.'

Slater pieced it all together. 'Which is what the triad are hanging over your head.'

Samuel nodded. 'They found out, somehow. They'll tell Forrest I was involved if I don't do their dirty work.'

'This is their dirty work? Whatever the two of you are doing?'

Samuel nodded again. 'Man, I can't tell you what they're doing, though. Please don't ask. I need this all to go ahead or they'll kill me. Just let me do my thing and then I'll be on my way. I need three codes.'

Shien piped up, having previously stayed silent. 'I know three codes!'

Slater shot her a dark look, as if to say, *Be quiet,* and turned back to Samuel. 'Do you know what the triad are doing?'

'All I know is that they're stealing a shitload of money.'

'From who?'

'I don't know. They're not going to tell me their entire plan. They just need me to initiate the transfer from this apartment. So there's no paper trail back to them.'

'That's what I figured was going on,' Slater said.

A messy pile of thoughts fought for the upper hand in Slater's head — Shien's dad, Mountain Lion Casino & Resorts, Peter Forrest, Samuel Barnes, the triad, an exorbitant amount of money.

'You said you're doing it from this apartment?' Slater said.

'Yes,' Samuel said. 'I've got a laptop — and experience as a programmer. I know how to use the software they're conducting the transfer with.'

'How much money?'

'I don't know. I'll know when it goes through. I'm just the guy who executes it.'

'I think you're about to bankrupt Peter Forrest,' Slater said. 'I think this all comes back to him. The triad are sensing an opportunity and capitalising on it. You two are the middlemen.'

'Maybe,' Samuel said. 'No way to tell for sure, man. But if I don't go through with it, I'm a dead man walking. Please — let me do this transfer. It doesn't affect you either way.'

'How many triad guys have you been in contact with?'

'It's a three-man team. I think they're working alone.'

'Did one of them have a jewelled earring?'

'Yes.'

'I killed him this morning. Around seven.'

'They roped me into all of this about five a.m. when I finished my shift. One of them must have gone to check on you two afterwards.'

'You sure they don't have help?'

Samuel shook his head. 'They seemed paranoid. Like a rogue unit. Like they were trying to do all this in secrecy and get away with it and carry on with their lives.'

Slater shifted uncomfortably, heating up in the cramped apartment. At the same time, a cold shiver ran down the back of his neck. His hairs stood on end.

He motioned to the open doorway leading out into the corridor. 'I just killed three guys out there. Who the hell are they?'

Samuel paused, deep in thought, then his eyes widened. 'Forrest's men?'

'I fucking hope not,' Slater said. 'That means he found us. He'll have an unlimited supply of hired guns.'

'Wait, so—'

Samuel paused mid-sentence, his eyes darting to the

open laptop resting on the kitchenette. Beads of sweat had broken out across his forehead as he mentally rolled through a list of consequences if he were caught red-handed with the information capable of stripping money out of Peter Forrest's accounts.

Slater made to respond when discordant shouts cut through the corridor outside.

He wheeled on the spot, close to hyperventilating.

There were multiple voices, all male, all eliciting what sounded like battlecries. From the way their voices rang into the apartment, Slater had to guess there were close to five or six men bundling into the tight space.

They had seen their dead comrades.

'More of Forrest's men,' he muttered.

Out of the corner of his eye, he noticed the blood drain from Samuel's face.

'Stay with the girl,' Slater said.

He sprinted for the doorway.

All-out offence was the only way he could feasibly see himself standing a chance against such an overwhelming number of hostiles.

18

I n Hollywood films, when frantic, close-quarters combat occurs, time slows down as the hero makes split-second decisions that eventually save his life.

Slater had always found that reality worked quite the opposite.

His brain flooded with cortisol — an acute sensation that heightened his reflexes and set his conscious thought into overdrive. But the ability to react faster didn't slow down his thoughts. He sunk into a state of total focus and simply let his limbs follow his brain's commands.

He glimpsed the congestion in the corridor outside — there were men in suits everywhere, all in the process of studying the three corpses on the floor between them. Slater realised he had a couple of seconds to act and — still sprinting full-pelt — reached down and heaved the entire front door off the ground.

It was heavy, but Slater tapped into decades of power-lifting training and the added benefit of an adrenalin spike to hurl the entire wooden plank into a vertical position and charge straight out into the hallway, carrying the door in front of him while gripping the Beretta awkwardly between two fingers.

There were two men directly opposite the doorway to apartment number 516.

Slater had no clear view of them, because his vision had been obscured by the door, but he remembered their last position and sprinted straight at it.

He felt the other side of the wooden plank slam into the two bodies, bundling them into the opposite wall through a mixture of momentum and sheer weight. Crushing them against the damp plaster opposite would impede them for a couple of seconds — anything to buy him more time.

Slater had made sure to bounce off the door with his right shoulder when it crushed into the two men, which thrust him awkwardly back into the centre of the corridor. Refusing to hesitate, he raised the Beretta and blasted four shots into the crowd of men milling around the bodies — screams rose and bodies ducked for any kind of cover they could find.

Enemy weapons raised in his direction, but Slater didn't even give them a fraction of a second to squeeze off return fire.

He finished unloading his volley of shots and — still moving — hurled himself back into the open doorway, out of sight.

As soon as he ducked back inside the apartment he flattened himself to the floor and twisted to aim through the space he'd just disappeared from. Gunfire cracked from semiautomatic pistols but Slater was no longer there. Across the hallway, he watched the two men he'd crushed with the door manage to hurl it off themselves. They were rattled, thrown off, reaching for their weapons but slow to react due to getting bundled so effortlessly into the disgusting plaster.

Slater let his breath out, went still, and fired another two rounds with the Beretta.

Twin headshots.

The two thugs went down in a tangle of limbs directly on top of the door.

Slater heard grunts of confusion as the rest of the party tried to compose themselves. They'd been thrown into disarray by the sudden onslaught — some were injured by Slater's bullets, some were dead, and all of them were likely wondering exactly what the hell they'd got themselves into.

Behind Slater, back in the depths of the single-room apartment, Shien screamed.

The high-pitched whine seized the attention of the men outside — they quietened, recognising the noise for what it was. Their target rested inside the apartment.

They had come to collect Shien by any means necessary.

Suddenly, Slater heard retreating footsteps. He tuned his ears to the sound — refusing to let his guard drop until he was certain they were safe — but his senses weren't deceiving him. The rest of the hit team were retreating, accompanied by grunts of agony and the distinct limp of a couple of members. Slater had hit a handful of them in debilitating spots — legs, arms, stomachs. They were all heading fast for the distant stairwell.

Regrouping.

Several of their outfit were dead, and they hadn't anticipated such carnage when they'd been sent to retrieve a young child. All the devastation had occurred in a narrow timeframe, and Forrest likely had no idea of Slater's capabilities.

The hallway emptied out. Just as quickly as the gunfight had initiated, it was over. His ears rang and his body ached from the exertion, but he was otherwise unharmed.

He lay there, flat on his stomach, and felt the raging fire of adrenalin dissipate along with the threat.

In that moment Slater realised the gravity of the situation — it hit him like a freight train.

He couldn't protect everyone. These attacks would continue, unceasing, until Forrest ran out of men or Slater succumbed to sheer overwhelming numbers. Eventually his ammunition would run out and he would be cornered in the stifling apartment complex. Shien would be recaptured and Slater would die knowing he had uniformly failed on his final task.

He couldn't let that happen.

He had no personal attachment to Samuel — he pitied the man's predicament, but the obligation to help Shien vastly outweighed any kind of inclination to protect the baccarat dealer. If Slater stretched himself too thin over the coming hours, he would fail everything at once.

He needed to focus on a sole purpose, or he'd lose his mind trying to juggle every problem in Macau all at once.

With that knowledge in the back of his head, he picked himself up and stumbled back into the main section of the apartment. Samuel and Shien cowered in one corner, both of them visibly shaking. As Slater went through the simple act of putting one foot in front of the other he winced — sharp pain shot through the outside of his knee.

That was the worst part of all-out combat — injuries poured on without any awareness. He'd probably twisted his knee as he powered across the corridor with the weight of a door on his body, but it hadn't even registered until the combat had dissipated. If he hadn't sprinted around on a bad leg for those vital seconds, he might have saved himself from serious injury.

Now that he noticed the damage, his brain concentrated

solely on it. Every tiny morsel of pain amplified, compounding in his mind, convincing him he might never walk again.

He broke out in sweat, slid down the closest wall, and stared at Samuel across the room.

'I'm hurt,' he said matter-of-factly. 'And it's only going to get worse. I can't do this forever.'

Samuel stared at him, flabbergasted. 'What do you mean? Man, you just saved ... you just saved my life. Thank you.'

'You're welcome. Now you're on your own.'

'W-what?'

With great difficulty, Slater picked himself up and reached into his pocket. He withdrew a single casino chip from the depths and tossed it across the room. It landed at Samuel's feet. The dealer stared down at the mauve-coloured chip, in shock.

'That's not real, is it?'

'You'll find out. Mountain Lion scans every chip of that magnitude when you cash out. But it's legit.'

'Why are you doing this?'

'Because I'm leaving you here, and I'm taking your laptop — two things which I know you won't be happy about.'

Samuel glared up at him, reeling. 'You can't, man. They'll kill me.'

'So hide. You're a hundred grand richer. Go cash in your profits and start a new life somewhere. There's nothing else I can do for you.'

'You think I've got any chance cashing this in at Mountain Lion? They'll round me up within seconds of walking through the door.'

'It's a big complex. Get in and out fast. You'll be okay.'

'I don't know, man.'

'Your call. Don't cash it in, stay here, do whatever the hell you think's best. But I can't stay with you. I've got enough on my plate.'

Before Samuel had the chance to respond, Slater limped across the room and snatched the chunky Dell laptop off the kitchen countertop — he slammed the screen closed and tucked it under the crook of his armpit. He motioned to Shien, who ran straight over to him, tearing herself free from Samuel's grasp.

He dropped the Beretta — it was nearly empty anyway — and took Shien by the hand. With a single nod of farewell to Samuel Barnes, Slater turned on his heel and hobbled awkwardly out of the apartment.

Deep down, something told him he had just sentenced the young baccarat dealer to death.

He hoped like all hell that Samuel had the initiative to figure things out for himself.

'Lay low,' Slater called as they walked out through the open doorway, stepping into a minefield of corpses in the hallway outside. 'Good luck.'

'T-thank you?' Samuel called.

Slater fetched an identical Beretta M9 off one of the dead hostiles and ushered Shien down the length of the corridor.

Keep moving, at all costs.

19

Mountain Lion Casino & Resorts was an impossibly large complex, with thousands of staff and tens of thousands of customers each and every day. The twin skyscrapers held enough resources to create what amounted to a miniature civilisation, a world in which high-net-worth gamblers and greedy tourists could get sucked into a hedonistic labyrinth for days and weeks on end.

Time didn't exist in casinos.

Neither did laws.

The two triad thugs sauntered through a dingy sub-level of the left-hand tower, taking their time so they could talk before they reached their intended destination.

They needed all the time they could get.

'Any word from Jin?'

'None.'

'It's been five hours.'

'We need to operate under the assumption that he's dead.'

The first man bit his lip to suppress a wave of emotion

— something that could readily get him killed in the world he lived in. 'Ten years, Tak. Ten fucking years we've been in this business. The three of us grew up together. He can't be dead. He can't. He just went to check on the goddamn girl.'

Tak — the older of the pair, with a decade more experience handling trials and tribulations — seized the other man's wrist. 'We're in too deep. You can't falter now — not at this hour. We can't afford it. Antoine, look at me...'

Antoine wasn't the second man's real name, but he had disposed of his birth name when he'd first dipped his toe in the business of the triads. It had been a transformational experience — he'd been forced to shed his old life like a snakeskin and leave the dirty slums of Singapore behind for a better existence.

Antoine's existence.

'When is Forrest expecting us back?' he said.

'He wants this wrapped up in ten minutes. But I'm taking five more. This is our only chance to talk.'

Antoine cocked his head. 'We can talk above ground, surely.'

'Forrest has surveillance fucking everywhere,' Tak hissed. 'No cameras or microphones down here. For obvious reasons.'

'Why are we doing his dirty work?'

'Because if shit hits the fan I don't want him to suspect us.'

'Why don't we just kill him?'

Tak furrowed his brow. 'I thought you were smarter than that, my friend.'

'It's an option.'

'No, it's not. Do you know what a billion dollars can buy you? The allegiance of all organised crime in the country.

That's why we started working for him in the first place, you fool. We kill him and it's a death sentence.'

'We can go somewhere else if we get this money,' Antoine said, persisting.

Tak suddenly stopped in his tracks and seized Antoine by the throat. He slammed the young man against the closest wall and kept him pinned there, clenching his teeth and riding out a wave of fury. This section of Mountain Lion was shrouded in shadow, off-limits to all but a handful of staff, all of who were up to their necks in corruption. It seethed with debauchery and illegality.

It was Tak's only chance to say what was on his mind.

'You are inexperienced,' he hissed in Antoine's ear. 'And you don't know how the world works. If we successfully get this money it will take months to launder it through the proper channels and actually gain access to it. What do you expect we do until then? Every triad member in Asia will be hunting for us if we kill their highest-paying, most reckless customer. The plan all along was to siphon money away from him and pin it on a foolish worker and a young kid. We don't change that. Not now. Not ever. You got it?'

'Uh-huh,' Antoine muttered.

'Until then, we do every damn thing Forrest wants us to do. Even if that means doing his dirty work. Like telling paying customers their purchase won't arrive.'

'Isn't it ironic, though?'

'What?'

'This guy is waiting for the girl we set free.'

Tak sighed and tightened his grip on Antoine's throat. 'There's no cameras down here, but if I hear you even whisper that again, I'll kill you. Never mention that again.'

'Okay.'

'Ready to take care of business?'

'Yes,' Antoine said, wheezing, turning red.

Tak released his hold. 'Let's go, then. Pull yourself together. I don't need you falling apart the first time you face adversity in your life. Everything's been easy for you up to this point. You're about to learn what hard work looks like.'

'Don't talk down to me like that,' Antoine snarled, adjusting his collar. 'My life hasn't been easy.'

'It has in comparison to some. Imagine I wasn't there to help you up the bottom rungs of the triad. You're young and impressionable and dumb. You're not even thirty. You would have been bounced around and exploited until you quit or got yourself killed.'

Antoine said nothing.

'This is a new level. We have enemies everywhere. Pay attention to what you say. Pay attention to who's listening.'

'Yeah, got it. Relax. Let's get this done.'

Tak nodded. 'Want me to do the talking?'

'I guess.'

'Watch and learn. I have a feeling this guy won't be happy. It's a sick world down here. You might not be used to this either. Throw your morals out the window.'

Antoine scoffed. 'What morals? We threw them out when we got into this business.'

'True. But this is a slightly darker level. You ever dealt with the people who pay for this shit?'

'No. I just knew what was going on.'

'Then get ready.'

They set off down the corridor again, surrounded by lavish decor yet draped in a darkness that seemed to indicate all was not as it seemed in this section of the casino complex. Doorways along the hall led to plush rooms with hundred-thousand dollar carpets and designer furniture imported from European villages, but it all seemed like a front to mask a pit of degradation.

They reached a closed metal door at the end of the hallway and Tak gently pushed it open, stepping through into a smaller room.

Antoine followed suit.

A plump European man with a greasy comb-over sat on one of the couches, the armpits of his collared shirt sporting yellow pit stains and a line of sweat dotting his brow. He reeked of a desperation that Tak despised — but Tak didn't let his feelings show.

A steely haze settled over his features and he sat down on the couch opposite, gesturing for Antoine to follow suit.

'You don't have what I paid for,' the European man said in English, his Spanish accent thick but his words clear. He was conversing in the only common language they shared.

Tak had no problem speaking English.

'No. We don't. That's what we're here to talk about.'

'Where is she?'

'We've run into some difficulties. She won't be around for some time. We apologise on behalf of Mr. Forrest for the delay.'

And we were the ones to cause the difficulties, Tak thought.

But what Forrest, along with the man in front of them, didn't know wouldn't hurt them.

'I paid a lot of money to be here,' the guy said, sweating harder.

'Like I said, we apologise. Stay another day. We'll see what we can do.'

'That's not good enough,' the man demanded.

He started to lean forward.

Tak burst off the couch and swung an uppercut into the underside of the guy's jaw, knocking a couple of teeth loose and sending him splaying back across the cushions with a bloody mouth and watering eyes. He crumpled under the force of the blow, stunned by pain and surprise. Tak continued to his feet, looming down over the man.

'It's going to have to be good enough,' he said.

Inwardly, he scolded himself for allowing his emotions to break through the hardened exterior. Long ago Tak had succumbed to the reality of the world, and that meant killing people who sometimes didn't deserve it — but this was just sick. He found it tough to put up with such a morally depraved situation, even if it was in the interests of Peter Forrest's bottom line to do so.

The fat man spat blood across the expensive upholstery and shrank away from Tak, cowering on the couch. 'Just wait until I tell Peter what—'

Tak backhanded him across the cheek, putting enough weight into the slap for a resounding *crack* to echo through the otherwise-empty room. The guy let out a feeble cry of protest and touched a hand to his face. One side of it was already swelling.

'Just wait until I track down your family and friends and tell them all in explicit detail exactly what you're doing here at Mountain Lion.'

'You can't do that. You don't know me, and I was promised total—'

'Don't tell me what I can and can't do, Marco.'

The guy stiffened at the sound of his real name. 'How…?'

'You will put up with any delays we need, and you won't say a fucking word to Peter Forrest about any of this. And if you do, I'll simply pay him to let me do what I want to you. You know as well as I do that money is Forrest's game, and I've got plenty of it.'

'I'll outbid you.'

'By the time you try, I'll have already cut your balls off and fed them to you. Go back to your hotel room and stay there until I tell you otherwise.'

'Do you need my room number?'

'Already got it. Clean yourself up.'

20

As they hurried down the second stairwell, Slater stared at the new Beretta in his palm and started to align the information he'd received into a somewhat cohesive picture.

'Outside Mountain Lion,' he said to Shien, 'I think Peter Forrest was trying to get you back.'

'When all those men grabbed me?' she said, her voice hollow in the space yet still timid.

'Yeah. The triad let you go to do this. Forrest wants you back. So the question is — what were you doing in his possession in the first place?'

She shrugged. 'I don't know, Will. They put a lot of bad things in my arm to keep me drowsy. I don't remember much.'

'You said you were kept in a room.'

'Different rooms. I kept getting moved, but it's all so blurry.'

'Did you see anyone?'

'No. I feel like they were preparing me for something.'

'Like what?'

'I don't know.'

Slater froze on one of the steps and clamped a hand down on Shien's shoulder. 'Hang on.'

They went still in the gloom, surrounded by leaking walls and a curving, rusting banister. Slater guessed there were two or three more floors to go before they reached ground level, but something had set him on edge — he sensed some kind of hostile presence on the landing below. It wasn't anything palpable, but after this much experience in the field there were certain subtle cues that triggered his survival instinct and caused his awareness levels to skyrocket.

'Hold this,' Slater whispered to Shien, and passed her the bulky laptop.

She took it in her arms.

The landing several steps below them opened out into a third-floor corridor, eerily similar to the hallway they'd just come from. It was complete with damp walls and flickering lights and all manner of features to indicate nothing had been spent on renovations for decades. Slater crouched low, taking the Beretta in a double-handed grip, and slunk down to the landing.

The ground levelled out, providing him a clear view down the hallway. To the side the stairwell twisted away, continuing on its path to ground level. Slater was milliseconds away from telling Shien the coast was clear when he spotted the doorway a dozen feet into the corridor, open just a crack.

Slater stared hard into the darkness beyond, and thought he saw the subtlest shift of movement.

One of the thugs hanging back?

He wasted no time. Hesitation led to the deaths of talented men, so instead he fired a shot directly through the wooden door, sending splinters flying and creating a noise loud enough to shock even the most battle-tested veterans. From there he took off down the corridor, closing the gap like a raging bull. The pain in his damaged knee was nowhere to be found. Once again, adrenalin and determination masked all superficial injuries.

When unsure, resort to the usual tactics.

Speed.

Aggression.

All-out assault.

The guy on the other side of the door didn't have time to shut it completely — he was too busy recoiling from the noise of the gunshot. Slater barged the door open. It slammed directly into the body on the other side, halting Slater in his tracks. He reared back and shouldered into it again, then a third time.

Finally, the person on the other side shrank away, refusing to take a fourth dose of blunt force trauma. Slater bundled his way inside...

... and a fist crashed into the sweet spot above his left ear.

He bit his lip in an attempt to ride out the sudden disorientation. A timid voice in the back of his head begged for retreat — he was badly hurt, and the sooner he accepted that, the greater his chance of survival.

But retreat would send he and Shien back into the heights of the apartment complex. From there they would be sitting ducks, cornered at every turn, cordoned into certain sections and pinned down in the disgusting corridors until they were overpowered and overwhelmed.

So Slater pressed forward in the face of adversity, even though in all likelihood it would spell a death wish. He narrowly avoided a second swinging punch — knuckles scythed through the air toward the bridge of his nose but he hurled himself away from the blow at an unnatural angle.

He crashed into the opposite wall of the interior hallway, rolled off the surface, and got his bearings.

An Asian man stood across from him, dressed in khakis and a loose-fitting long-sleeved cotton shirt. His skin was dark bronze, and judging by the force with which he'd rattled Slater with the punch, he guessed the man was from Thailand. Despite having landed a decent blow, the guy looked similarly disoriented — it was then that Slater noticed the Beretta handgun lying between them, smashed out of the man's grip by the force of the door slamming into him three consecutive times.

For a moment Slater thought it was his own weapon, but he glanced down and noticed his own Beretta still resting firmly in his palm — a palm slick with cold sweat. If he'd been operating at full capacity, Slater would have fired a round through the man's temple in the blink of an eye, but the overbearing ramifications of the concussive blow were revealing themselves.

Move! he screamed at himself.

He couldn't.

He started to raise his arm to line up a shot but his limbs moved horrendously slow, failing to respond to his commands in time. His vision wobbled as he lifted the Beretta, and it felt as if he were moving through quicksand. Mentally exhausted from the strain, he kept the gun scything upward in an arc that would bring the barrel up to aim between the man's eyes.

Too late.

The Asian guy threw a twisting side kick that caught Slater in the wrist, crunching his fingers against the Beretta's trigger guard and sending the gun twisting out of his palm.

Slater made to squeeze off a wild shot even as the kick crashed into him but he simply couldn't find the trigger in time. The Beretta cascaded away, and Slater stumbled back as the force of the lashing boot transferred into him.

Definitely from Thailand, he thought.

As if all his problems were bubbling to the surface at once, his knee decided to give out as he leant away from a follow-up kick. He lost function in his right leg as it buckled, sending him careening awkwardly into the plaster wall behind him.

Thankfully, it held.

Plunging straight through the damp material would have placed him in a predicament he wouldn't have been able to come back from, so he silently thanked the heavens as he bounced back into range.

Which proved a ridiculous thing to thank anyone for, because it allowed the Thai man to size up another kick and lash the same lead leg through the air, aiming for Slater's throat.

It would have caved his larynx in if it had connected, leaving him to suffocate, but Slater tapped into ten years worth of mixed martial arts training and employed all the tools he had available.

He changed levels, leaning the majority of his weight on his good leg to ensure he didn't buckle at the worst possible moment. By dropping into a crouch he avoided the man's shin bone, sensing the air displaced above his head as the kick whistled through empty space with the speed of a seasoned practitioner.

From there Slater shot into range and seized hold of a single-leg takedown, wrapping both arms around the sole limb the man had on the ground. It was a simple enough procedure to lever his weight through to the leg and throw the guy off-balance.

Together, the pair sprawled to the grimy carpet.

Your stand-up's good, Slater thought. *What about your ground game?*

Slater had a third-degree black belt in Brazilian jiu-jitsu, and he savoured the moments in no-holds-barred, hand to hand combat when he sensed weakness in an opponent. If they weren't well-rounded, he would crush them.

And a knee injury meant nothing on the ground.

Like a true amateur, the Asian guy rolled onto his stomach in an attempt to lever himself to his feet as fast as possible. In theory it made sense, but Slater needed the slightest opportunity to capitalise, and the man gave it to him on a silver platter.

He pounced on the guy's back, wrapped both legs around his waist, and wrenched a meaty forearm around the man's throat. The guy had left his neck exposed, failing to tuck his chin or employ any kind of defence against the hold.

He'd sentenced himself to death by failing to defend himself for a fraction of a second.

The way life goes, Slater thought.

There was nothing left to do but squeeze. The outcome was inevitable, and as he applied a vicious barrage of pressure to the guy's throat he realised that too. The guy somehow managed to get to his feet — still wearing Slater like a backpack — and used momentum to twist on the spot, smashing Slater side-on into the nearest wall.

It hurt, but Slater wasn't letting go of the choke unless someone severed his arms at their sockets.

He would take anything this guy could dish out, because

the man's consciousness was rapidly fading and in seconds he would be completely out.

Next, the guy scrabbled at Slater's forearm, digging his nails into the skin and attempting to peel the arm off his neck.

Not a chance.

The man succumbed to the lure of unconsciousness in messy fashion, refusing to submit until the final moments. His legs turned heavy and Slater sensed him about to drop as his senses faded. With one foot, Slater reached back and pushed off the wall, so the momentum carried the guy to the ground stomach-first. He slammed into the carpet, twitching and kicking but ultimately out cold.

Slater saw no need for unnecessary suffering, so he tightened his grip up a notch, tapping into the reserves of energy one could only locate in times of maximum exertion. Nothing tested his mental resolve like this — doing what would minimise suffering over what felt like the right thing to do. If he left the man alive it would only be a matter of time before he came awake and made another attempt on Slater's life. Besides, all was fair in these scenarios — the man had tried to kill Slater, so Slater found himself unburdened by the thought of finishing the job.

Just the nature of the beast, he thought.

He kept pressure on the throat for a long sixty seconds before the unconscious man underneath him turned to a corpse. There was a subtle shift in the atmosphere — Slater had enough experience in the field to understand what it meant — and he released his grip on the guy's neck to find his breathing had ceased entirely.

It had been a relatively painless death. The transition from alertness to unconsciousness had only taken a couple of seconds, and the man would have been blissfully ignorant to anything beyond that.

Slater peeled himself off the body and shook out his arm. Operating at one hundred percent capacity for over a minute, all the muscles in his forearm had effectively died. Feeling would return in a matter of minutes accompanied by sharp pins and needles, but until then Slater was left dangling one limb uselessly by his side.

With his good hand, he snatched the Asian man by the collar and dragged him into the adjoining bathroom. The lights were out, and Slater kept them that way.

Shien had witnessed enough death for the time being.

He pulled the door shut, hiding the body from sight, and called the young girl into the apartment.

21

S hien pottered into the room, her eyes darting in seemingly every direction at once. There was no doubt that she'd heard the commotion — violent fights to the death left no room for imagination — but she seemed surprised by Slater's half-hearted attempt to hide the body.

'Where is he?' she muttered as she brushed past him.

'Out of sight.'

'Will,' she said, her tone far too condescending for someone of her age and inexperience. 'You've already killed people in front of me. I think I can handle one more.'

'Are you always like this?' Slater said. 'You're the only nine-year-old I know who wouldn't be shitting their pants in a situation like this.'

She cocked her head to one side. 'Is it not showing?'

'What?'

'I'm scared out of my mind.'

'You still feeling groggy?'

'A bit.'

'I think whatever they pumped into your system for two weeks straight is still suppressing some things.'

'I hope not.'

'A kid doesn't belong in this world, Shien.'

She shrugged. 'I've been around it for a while. I haven't seen anything up close, but I'm smart enough to work it out for myself. I'm not stupid.'

'I thought you said your father wasn't a bad man.'

'He's not. But he works in a bad world. I know that much.'

They lapsed into silence and pressed further into the apartment. With a sigh of relief, Slater realised this particular room had some semblance of natural light. For hours the stifling nature of the complex had weighed down on him, to the point where he was growing increasingly desperate for any kind of glimpse of the outside world.

Everything in here was hot and rancid and horrific.

But a narrow rectangular window ran across the opposite wall — directly alongside this apartment's kitchenette — and Slater raised himself onto his toes to catch a glance outward. The day was heating up. A heavy layer of cloud hung low in the sky, draped over everything in sight, suppressing any kind of joy one could find in these slums.

They were positioned along the front of the complex, facing out over Beco da Perola and the hundreds of civilians hustling along the narrow sidewalks a few floors below. Urgency was palpable in the air — all these people had places to be, measly dollars to make, children to feed.

Slater glanced back into the apartment and realised he faced a similar predicament — caring for a young kid.

Possibly for the first time in his life.

'You hungry?' he said.

Shien said, 'We just ate.'

He glanced at his watch, and once again found himself fascinated by the nature of the human brain. It felt like he'd been fighting for his life for hours on end, but they'd only spent a total of sixteen minutes in the apartment complex upon returning to its bowels. He brushed off the strange sensation and spotted Shien still clutching the laptop tight between her small fingers.

'Give me that,' he said.

She handed it over, happy to be free from its possession. Maybe she considered it a bad omen. 'What are you going to do with it?'

'He had the program up on the screen,' Slater explained. 'That Samuel guy. He was eager to get this over and done with. Almost too eager. I think we can go through with all this without him.'

Shien froze. 'Why do we want to do that?'

Slater paused.

Actually, he hadn't quite considered the reasoning yet. He'd simply been reacting, capitalising on openings he found in the situation, seizing opportunities. Stealing money from a billionaire casino owner meant nothing in the long term — especially since Slater had no control over where the funds were deposited.

He would never see it. He would simply make the triad wealthier.

But, deep down, he knew why it was important.

The triad were looking to cause anarchy by tearing profits away from a man whose entire existence revolved around profits.

Slater thrived in chaos.

He was no closer to remedying the situation with Shien, and if she felt unsafe returning to her father he had no ability to convince her otherwise.

He had to demolish anyone who felt it necessary to threaten her life.

And, simultaneously, get to the bottom of what exactly she'd been doing in the possession of Peter Forrest.

Something told him he wouldn't like what he found.

But the first step to any semblance of success would involve flushing Forrest or the triad thugs out of their private hiding places. To do that he would need to throw their dealings into disarray — cause confrontation, instigate conflict, generally implement chaos.

So he slammed the laptop down on the kitchen countertop and flipped the screen open, ignoring the sweat dripping off his forehead. He wiped a cuff across his eyebrows to try and clear his vision — combat drew out perspiration in a way that few other events could. Recreational sports were challenging, but there was a natural limit one could reach when pushing themselves to the next level. A life-or-death fight eliminated those barriers, to the point where people could do things they'd previously considered impossible.

All the fighting had sapped the energy out of Slater entirely.

He hunched over the screen, studying the algorithms and symbols in front of him. Amidst all the technological jargon were three rectangular boxes for entering information.

They lay empty.

In fact, the mouse cursor hovered over the first box, as if Samuel Barnes had been preparing nervously in anticipation of Shien's arrival. He'd been planning to approve the transfer within seconds of her showing up at the door.

No wonder Slater's presence had terrified him so completely.

He was a nervous kid.

Briefly, Slater glanced skyward and wondered how Barnes was faring up there.

He regretted leaving him already.

It was in his nature to protect people.

'You're thinking you shouldn't have left Samuel in the apartment.'

Once again, Shien proved herself deceptively attuned to the finer details of Slater's expressions. He tried to mask his surprise, but it proved useless.

'Don't bother,' she said. 'I've been doing this kind of thing for years.'

Slater cocked his head. 'How so?'

'My Daddy gives money to people, which apparently is very sensitive to talk about. People don't like talking about money. And I don't think he gives money to nice people. Not usually. But he expects it back, which means he has to be careful about what he talks about around me. It took me a while but now I can almost tell what he's thinking because he's always trying to hide things. Just like you're trying to do now.'

'I'm not trying to hide anything from you, Shien,' Slater said. 'In fact I can't even believe I've been so honest with a nine-year-old myself.'

'But you don't want to talk about who you are. I asked you a couple of times and you keep pretending like I never said anything.'

'That has nothing to do with you. Who I am isn't something anyone should be interested in.'

'You've saved my life about a hundred times, so I'm pretty interested.'

Slater paused. 'Maybe later. And don't push it — this is unheard of from me. You're not old enough to know the details anyway.'

'I'm old enough to get kidnapped and drugged and nearly killed,' she said, her face twisting in an attempt to mask her tears. 'I'm sure some words won't hurt me.'

'You deserve a better life than this.'

'So do you, Will.'

The words hung in the air, striking Slater in such a way that made it difficult to form a response. The breath caught in his throat and he paused, composing himself, horrified at the thought of showing any emotion in front of this little girl.

'And what's worse is that you chose to be here,' Shien said, hammering her point home. 'You hate it but you can't stop doing it. I can tell by your face. You think you need to help everyone. That's why you're so scared about Samuel. Even though it's none of your business.'

Slater reached down and gripped the edge of the countertop with white knuckles, riding out a sickening wave of nausea. At the same time a pang of acute pain rang up the side of his leg, reminding him of his condition. The sweat continued to flow from his pores.

'You're damn good at reading people.'

'Thanks.'

'What were the odds I'd run into a kid as smart as you? You've got to be one in a million.'

'I could say the same.'

Despite everything, Slater smirked. 'You're a good kid.'

'I don't know if you're a good person, but you've been one to me, and that's really all that matters I guess.'

'I don't know either, Shien,' Slater said. 'Now hold on while I bankrupt this Peter Forrest guy.'

22

Slater had limited experience with computer programming or anything of the sort, but from what he could deduce it seemed Samuel Barnes had done the majority of the necessary grunt work.

'Give me that first code again, Shien,' he said.

'H204VR68,' she said calmly.

Slater punched each key in rapid succession, his fingers flying over the keyboard. When he finished he tabbed to the second empty box and stared expectantly at Shien for the remaining two codes.

She rattled them off, one by one, barely pausing between digits. She had no trouble reciting them — it seemed almost automatic, just as the "Beco da Perola" location had materialised in her mind. He wondered if there were certain techniques to implant information in someone's head to ensure they'd remember it even under the foggy haze of a drug-addled state.

If there were, he imagined the triad had utilised them.

'You sure all three of those are right?'

'Yes.'

'No doubt whatsoever?'

'I don't know how, but I can remember them so easily.'

Slater stared at the screen — all three boxes had been filled with Shien's codes — and took a deep breath. 'Well, here goes nothing. Let's hope this kicks up a storm.'

He scrolled to the bottom of the page and clicked *PROCEED*.

A fresh page loaded instantly, the command executing in milliseconds, going through as soon as he placed pressure on the mouse pad.

Horrifyingly simple, given the ramifications of what he had done.

Slater's eyes darted over the rapidly materialising information.

Account numbers.

Digits.

Hong Kong dollar signs.

HK$1,117,300,405.

HK$904,077,030.

HK$755,000,000.

HK$620,400,306.

Slater roughly added the four obscene numbers displayed on the screen, siphoned into four separate accounts, and came up with close to HK$3,400,000,000.

Three-point-four billion.

He ran through calculations in his head — something that had always come effortlessly to him — and landed on the equivalent of $435 million USD.

An unfathomable amount of money.

Money that he'd just sucked dry from four of Peter Forrest's accounts.

Sitting in the dingy, humid apartment within a complex that rested in one of the more rundown sections of Macau,

Slater felt a sudden surge of raw power that came with causing devastation to a titan's finances. He had no way of working out where the money was headed, or what the triad planned to do with it, but he had to imagine there were further steps Samuel had been planning to take to ensure anonymity.

Slater had no idea what to do next, so he simply left the laptop where it was and smirked as he considered the consequences.

It wouldn't be complicated to trace the source of the transfer, and Slater didn't intend to try and hide it.

Let them come, he thought.

By then he'd be long gone. And there would be enough evidence left lying around to trace the source of the heist to the triad, at which point Forrest would be forced into an uncomfortable decision.

The more uncomfortable the man was, the more mistakes he would make.

Mistakes Slater fully intended to exploit.

'What happened?' Shien said, breaking the dead silence.

Slater realised he'd entered a trance-like state, staring at the numbers on the screen without any awareness of his surroundings. If anyone — from the triad thugs to Forrest's hitmen — had chosen that time to barge into the apartment, both he and Shien would have been history.

He forcibly dragged himself back to the present moment, despite his fascination with the amount he'd just ripped from Peter Forrest's holdings.

'The man who kidnapped you,' Slater said. 'I think I just made him very mad.'

'I never met him,' Shien noted. 'He can't be a nice guy, though, if he's doing things like that. How did you make him mad?'

'I just stole almost half a billion dollars from him.'

Shien's eyes narrowed in an effort to concentrate and tap into her memories. 'Wow. That's a lot of money. Isn't that what Samuel was going to do? Is that what my codes were for?'

'Yes.'

'Why did you go through with it? This has nothing to do with you.'

'You're right. It doesn't.'

'You want to make the bad man angry?'

'Exactly.'

'Why? Then he'll just send more people after us.'

'I can deal with that if we get out of here right now. He'll make mistakes if he gets angry. I can take advantage of that.'

'Are you going to kill him?'

'I think you're very important to him and his reputation. You were kidnapped for a reason, Shien, and I don't want to even consider what that might have been. That's what I was talking about before. You might see me angry if I find out exactly why you were there.'

Shien glanced instinctively toward the bathroom, where the dead man rested silently in his makeshift burial chamber. 'I've seen you angry.'

'No,' Slater said. 'You haven't. Not *truly* angry.'

'I don't think I want to see that.'

'I won't be able to help it if I find out the truth.'

'What truth? You keep hinting at something but I don't understand. Why was I kidnapped?'

Slater thought of the darkest period of his life, a time where his own mother had left the house to go to work and hadn't returned. A time where revelations had presented themselves about the true nature of her work. A time Slater could link to nothing but pain and torment. From that point onward, he'd vowed to transform himself into a monster, so that the sheer helplessness he'd felt in his earlier years could never be repeated. He'd wanted the ability to destroy anyone capable of causing that kind of pain.

He knew the men that had taken his mother. He knew what they'd done to her beforehand. He knew where she'd been headed, and understood the torment she would have undergone before she'd eventually succumbed to death.

The product never survived the sex slavery pipeline.

Never.

'I'm willing to talk to you about almost anything, Shien,' he said. 'But not that.'

She frowned. 'Why not?'

'Because I could be grasping at straws.'

'What does that mean?'

'I have no way to tell if my hunch is accurate or not.'

She pouted, recognising that Slater wouldn't be elaborating. He could almost see the gears whirring behind her eyes, working with what little information she had. Once again, he found himself astonished by her capabilities.

'If you find out you were right,' she said. 'What will you do?'

'Very bad things.' He gestured to their surroundings, summing up everything that had transpired within the complex's walls. 'This will look like nothing in comparison.'

'Have you gone off like that before?'

'Once.'

'Did people get hurt?'

'Yes.'

'Will you hurt me if you go down that path?'

'No.'

'You sure.'

'Positive.'

She shrugged. 'Okay, then. I can't get anything else out of you. Where are we headed?'

Slater glanced at the laptop. The required work had been done. 'Far away from here.'

'We taking that thing?' Shien said.

'Definitely not. They'll be tracing it as we speak.'

'Does that mean more bad guys?'

'Sure does, Shien. We won't be here, though.'

'Where will we be?'

Slater gazed around at the filth they'd spent the last twelve hours in. The sweat and the humidity and the claustrophobia and the dark corners and the flickering lights and the stench of tension all culminated together into a disgusting cocktail of unpleasantness. None of it fazed him — he'd spent half his life in similar settings — but at this moment their predicament was easily resolved. His own discomfort didn't bother him whatsoever, but he glanced down at Shien and noticed the unbridled fear on her face. She was surprisingly composed for such a small child, but the atmosphere was getting to her. Her skin was slick with sweat and her previously untarnished hair now rested in wet, matted knots.

'How about an upgrade?' Slater said, twirling the hundred-thousand dollar chips in his pants pocket.

23

'What the *fuck?!*' Forrest roared at the top of his lungs.

Emotion overwhelmed him. Unable to help himself, he launched the chair underneath him away from the grand oak dining table, letting it tumble across the floor. His veins surging with fury, he sprinted to the nearest wall of the lavish penthouse and gouged three consecutive holes in the plaster with the toe of his trainer. Teeth clenched, forehead sweating, his horror reached a boiling point and he smashed his temple into the wall, over and over again, beating the anger out of himself the only way he knew how.

When his fit of destruction had ceased, he stumbled away from the stretch of wall, panting with exertion, disoriented but still seething. Three of his most trusted members of security stood on the other side of the table, their hands clasped behind their backs, their faces white in reaction to the sudden outburst.

They knew that Forrest had his limits regarding how far

he was willing to take things, but they also knew those limits melted away when his fury took hold.

By now, the anger had reached a previously unseen level.

'How the fuck is this possible?' Forrest demanded, his voice shaking as he struggled to control his tone.

He raised a finger and pointed accusingly to the laptop still resting on the broad wooden table's surface. Its screen displayed a listing of secure accounts — accounts that had been acting as his personal safety net for as long as he could remember.

Accounts that now lay uniformly empty.

He deliberately conducted all his illegal business dealings in the safety of these accounts, which had cost him a small fortune to set up in a jurisdiction with effective bank secrecy laws.

Over the years they had slowly compounded in value as the extent of his dirty work magnified — as he'd realised earlier, the corruption had single-handedly taken over his life by this point. He was knee-deep in shit, and the hundreds of millions of dollars that his efforts had produced were now wiped off the face of the planet.

Even thinking about the house of cards his entire empire was perched on had him considering going straight for his bedroom dresser and blowing his brains out with the 9mm resting within.

No safety net meant no ability to make repayments. The financial demands were coming from everywhere at once, and Forrest had been dangerously close to tapping into the reserves he'd never previously touched.

Now, he had nothing to fall back on.

Mountain Lion — and everything he'd ever worked for — would crumble unless he got that money back.

'We don't know,' one of the men said. He was a small Filipino man — scared out of his mind at what Forrest might do. They'd heard rumours of his temperament. Now they were seeing it in the flesh.

'Who could have done this?' Forrest said. 'I'm the only one with encrypted information about those accounts, but there's only a handful of people who would even know the right place to look.'

'I—' one of the other men started.

But Forrest's mind had taken off, racing through potential scenarios. 'Look, there's no point hiding the existence of those accounts anymore. I need that money. I need to take risks. I'll deal with the accounting later — that's a fucking breeze if you have the right people. But I need that money back. I want you to put the casino's entire tech team on this. They're the best of the best. Trace literally everything. You got it?'

'Sir, are you sure that's the best idea?'

'Of course it's not. But what's the alternative? I take too much care and the entire payload slips away. This is a time sensitive situation, you dumb fucks. Get everyone on it. Find where the transfer took place.'

'We can do that ... but then everyone in Mountain Lion's backrooms knows about those accounts. It's not hard to work out you didn't get half a billion dollars in reserves by any legal measures.'

'Fuck it. I don't get that money back and I'm toast. Like I said, creative accounting fixes everything. Nothing gets fixed if I'm too sensitive about this.'

'How bad is it, boss?' the third guy on the end said.

Forrest's life had become so chaotic that he couldn't remember the names of the men and women who worked for him. There were literally thousands of workers on his payroll, and the people who reported directly to him — regarding both legitimate and illegitimate business dealings — had by this point blurred into a constant string of concerned faces.

It seemed, in this business, no notable news was ever good.

But Forrest remembered this man.

He was as short as his comrades — no more than five foot six, with a skinny, hunched posture and skin the colour of caramel. Another Filipino guy, but Forrest always remembered him for the bags underneath his eyes and his unwavering loyalty to the job. He rarely asked questions, and when he did, it was because every atom of his being was desperate for information. Underneath the timid exterior, he was concerned for his employer.

Forrest allowed him a response, opening up for one of the first times in his life.

'It's bad,' he said. 'I borrowed far too much money to pay for this place, and I'm scared no amount of revenue is going to get me ahead. I was going to tap into those accounts to buy me time to pay back my debtors, but now that I have nothing they're going to come for my head. This isn't even considering all the legal ramifications. Mountain Lion will close, but I'll be murdered long before that. I need this fucking money, boys. I need time. To make everything right.'

'Using the tech team is a bold move, sir. I don't know what they can do, in any case. These accounts are next-level.'

'Some of them will have answers. I studied all their backgrounds before I hired them. I remember it. Some of them were dangerous goddamn people. I hired them because I don't ordinarily give a shit about that kind of thing, but there's enough ability in that unit to track the trail of bread crumbs and find out exactly what happened.'

'Who knows about the accounts?'

'No-one knows the details.'

'But who knows of their existence?'

Forrest paused, thinking hard. There were certain members of his entourage who were in the madness just as deep as he was. He must have mentioned it to a handful of them, somewhere in the maze of illegalities they discussed on a daily basis. If the conversation moved from drugs to guns to girls, who was he to assume he'd never mentioned where those profits ended up?

Suddenly, he remembered a certain encounter. Only hours ago. Any kind of odd behaviour came roaring to the forefront of his mind and he recalled a phone conversation with two certain triad members who he'd never heard sound so panicked when he'd asked them to quiz a certain baccarat dealer. He hadn't realised it at the time, but now it stood out like nothing else.

He'd been talking to them about the accounts just days earlier, he realised. He hadn't mentioned anything concrete, but they would have understood that he had hundreds of millions of dollars piled in a single online location. No matter how many loopholes they might have had to jump through, and no matter what level of resources they had to utilise, they could have thrown caution to the wind and simply gone for it.

Could it be possible?

Dark emotions forming in the pit of his stomach, he said, 'Where the fuck are Tak and Antoine?'

If anything came back to imply their guilt, it would be

their heads on the chopping block. He didn't give a shit who they worked for.

The whole triad can get it, he thought, enraged.

In that moment, Peter Forrest was ready to take on the whole world.

24

S later made it to the twenty-second floor of the luxury hotel complex in a thickly-carpeted elevator before he realised he couldn't even remember the name of the place he'd booked a room at. He hadn't bothered to check, instead simply trawling the streets with Shien in a state of delirium until they came across a glowing aura of opulence and strode straight into a marble lobby the size of a warehouse.

With his adrenalin reserves depleted and his body dangerously close to shutting down after sweating out a few pounds in water weight, Slater had reached a temporary limit. Fighting to the pinnacle of one's abilities required a journey into an untapped reserve of energy — and experience had taught him time and time again that rest was crucial.

So he booked the most expensive available suite that money could buy and ushered Shien into one of the elevators, desperate for a much-needed handful of hours to recuperate. She sported a wide-eyed expression the entire time — even though her old life probably consisted of non-stop visits to five-star hotels given the nature of her father's business, Slater imagined it was a shock to return to such comforts after a couple of weeks in the hands of hostile parties.

'We can clean ourselves up in the room,' he said.

'We're not going back to the slums?'

'No. Not unless we have to.'

'What are we doing here?'

'Resting.'

'And then?'

'Then I'll go searching for anything that will lead me to Peter Forrest. Or the triad. Or anyone. And I'll sort all this out.'

'You don't need to do this for me, Will.'

'Yes I do.'

'You should just leave me in this room and book it for a few days. That'll give time for everything to cool down and then I can try and find my Daddy.'

Slater considered all the information he'd received so far regarding Shien's father. 'I wouldn't count on that.'

'What do you mean?'

'How long did you say you've been gone?'

'About two weeks.'

'There's no way I'm leaving you until I find out you have someone to go back to.'

Once again, not the most poignant statement to make in such a tense situation.

Shien's upper lip began to quiver — Slater noticed it out of the corner of his eye. He swallowed back unease and silently thanked the elevator for electing to arrive at their floor at that exact moment. It gave them something to do other than stand in awkward silence, contemplating just how drastically Shien's life had been turned on its head.

Slater had been in hundreds of luxury hotels over his life — his previous occupation had provided an undisclosed salary that more than afforded the odd journey into the land of the mega-wealthy. By now everything had blurred together into an amalgamation of plush carpets, ornate decorations and the permeating scent of perfume and opulence. He'd seen it all before.

So had Shien, evidently.

They made their way down a luxurious corridor set at the optimal room temperature. Slater felt the cool touch of the artificially-adjusted air on his skin and breathed in a sigh of relief. It had taken them thirty minutes on foot to make the journey from the slums of Macau to the unrivalled luxury of the casinos and accompanying resorts — but this place was a world away from the crummy apartment complex they'd come from.

In terms of comfort, and safety.

Up here, no-one was waiting around the corner to take their heads off.

This establishment offered a little more security than the previous building.

Slater unlocked the door to the presidential suite at the end of the hallway with an electronic keycard and ushered Shien through. The ceiling towered far above their heads, and the suite consisted of a living area, kitchen, dining room, and entertainment room all rolled into one wholly impressive space. There was enough room to house six or seven people at minimum — the hotel had taken no short-cuts in an attempt to cut down on space. The air-condi-tioning had been preset to a certain temperature, draping the entire room in a cool aura.

The most stunning feature of the presidential suite was the array of floor-to-ceiling windows looking out over

Macau's skyline — deliberately facing the aesthetic glow of the towering skyscrapers and casinos instead of the slums and darkened neighbourhoods on the other side of the building. If Slater hadn't been trawling through the humid, poverty-stricken boroughs less than an hour earlier, he might have forgotten such sights existed in this artificial pleasure centre.

'You need a shower?' Slater said.

Shien nodded. 'This place is amazing. Can we stay here for a while?'

'You can stay here for as long as you need. No-one knows you're here.'

'Will. You're not leaving me here, are you?'

Slater stripped off his suit jacket to provide some semblance of reprieve from the now-sticky clothing and shoved his hands in his pockets, staring inquisitively out at the Macau skyline.

Mountain Lion Casino & Resorts dwarfed every building in sight, towering over the other complexes like the alpha male of an extravagant wonderland. Its upside-down U shape looked stunning from a distance away — Slater imagined that was the effect its owner had been going for when he commissioned its construction. The colour palette had been soaked in a soft neon green, covering the exterior of the complex in deliberate fashion. The lighting — spooling out of well-positioned floodlights and aiming at certain angles to highlight the complex's most prominent features — accentuated the shadows even in the daytime, making Mountain Lion appear larger than it actually was.

Atop the rectangular slab connecting both skyscrapers rested the gargantuan "ML" logo spearing into the sky, a clear attempt to kick off a similar brand of structures across the world.

Even from half a mile away, Slater could recognise ambition when he saw it.

Peter Forrest had taken brazen steps to build this monolith.

He would take brazen steps to protect it from falling to pieces.

Slater realised he'd been silent for quite some time. He glanced down at himself, noting the blood and sweat and dirt caked thick across his dress shirt. He turned to Shien and noticed she was in a similar state of disrepair.

It had been an arduous night.

'Go have a shower, Shien,' he said. 'We'll talk about it when we're both cleaned up.'

25

For the first time in over four days, Peter Forrest exited Mountain Lion Casino & Resorts.

It was close to midday, and he couldn't remember the last time he had slept. His life had devolved into instinctual reactions, rolling with the punches, trying to keep his head above water for long enough to survive another day. There were so many facets of his business he needed to deal with that his brain had almost shut down on itself, giving up after working on overdrive for close to forty-eight hours.

As he slipped into a limousine that had been patiently anticipating his arrival for close to thirty minutes, he realised his heart had started to beat uncomfortably hard against his chest wall. He touched a hand to his left pectoral, concern spreading across his face as he scooted his rear across a soft row of leather seats.

Two of his hired guns followed him into the limousine.

'You're certain Tak and Antoine are nowhere to be found?' Forrest snarled.

He'd brought the small, loyal Filipino man with him,

along with a larger Asian guy who dwarfed both of them. The second man was by all definitions a stranger — close to six-foot-five and resolutely silent, crammed into his tailored suit in such a fashion that could only prove horrifically uncomfortable. He'd barely said a word to Forrest the entire time he'd served in the man's employment. But he showed up when required, and he looked intimidating as all hell.

That was all that mattered.

Forrest would need him to hold his own in the coming hours.

He had a lot of talking to do, and a giant hole to dig himself out of.

The large Asian man shut the door and the limousine's interior lapsed into silence. Forrest bowed his head, massaging his temples in a pathetic attempt to alleviate some of the stress, but it proved worthless. He felt the vehicle moving underneath him, which leant him a morsel of relief — if they were on the move, then Forrest had the internal satisfaction that he was making an attempt to salvage the situation.

'Sir, are you sure this is the best idea?' the small Filipino man said. 'The triad are dangerous people.'

'I know they are,' Forrest muttered through gritted teeth, his head still resting in his hands. 'But I pay them good money to lend me workers, and as of this moment those three workers they gave me are the prime suspects for stealing all my money. You follow?'

'Yes, yes, of course I follow, sir,' the man said, careful not to antagonise Forrest. 'But I don't know how much you will achieve by going into their territory. You lose every advantage that way.'

'That's why I brought him,' Forrest said, gesturing to the solemn Asian brute in the corner of the limousine.

As usual, the man said nothing.

'I see that,' the Filipino guy said, 'but — no offence, sir — I don't know how well one man can protect us.'

'If they decide to kill me, then I'm a dead man. We're all dead men. I just want to look somewhat intimidating so they elect not to. That's all.'

'You should have brought them to Mountain Lion. The heads of the triad. Then you could have presented the evidence on your terms.'

'What evidence?' Forrest said, laughing pathetically at his misfortune. 'I'm grasping at straws. I have nothing. I just need powerful people to rely on. If I can convince them not to turn on me before Tak and Antoine and Jin feed them lies, then I can buy myself time. That's all I'm trying to do right now. Buy myself time...'

'Sir, I don't want to overwhelm you,' the Filipino man said. 'But before all this — you were worried about a girl? Have you cleared that up?'

Tension arced through Forrest — how the hell could he have forgotten? In the midst of the chaos he'd ignored Shien entirely. An attempt had been made to retrieve her, but it had failed spectacularly. He was racing through a million new problems, and that debacle had shifted to the rear view mirror.

Now it came roaring back to the surface.

If she managed to somehow find her way back to her father, shit would hit the fan. Forrest could imagine the man piecing the reasons for her kidnap together and storming Mountain Lion with a small army of his hired guns.

He shouldn't have fucked with a man's child.

Especially a man with that kind of power.

Her father, Jang, was a Hong Kong businessman with a complex web of illegal dealings and a fortune comparable to the GDP of a small country. He'd leant Forrest tens of millions of dollars to fund Mountain Lion's additional construction costs. Forrest had promised the repayments in monthly instalments, but had come up short on the first payment last month.

When Jang had made the journey to Macau two weeks earlier to demand repayments, Forrest had quietly seized his daughter.

It had been a bold move, but it seemed Peter Forrest's life had devolved into a series of brazen acts. Trying to keep his head above water had proved daring.

The kidnap had ended up benefitting Forrest in two ways.

First, Jang had melted into the shadows, preoccupied with trying to work out what happened to his little girl and forgetting about the money Forrest owed him.

Second, Forrest realised he could make a profit off her.

That hadn't always been the plan. Two weeks ago, Forrest had been a better man. He'd planned to hold the girl until he had enough money to make the first repayment, and then conveniently release her into the streets where she would find her way back to her father. Jang would never know who had taken her, or why, and Forrest would have bought himself time to collect revenue to make the repayments.

All would have ended perfectly.

But then he got greedy. He'd recently opened a new venture — a dark venture — in an industry he never thought he would dip his toes into. Now he was knee-deep in it, making money hand over fist, and reluctant to stop. If he shut down the operation — which took place deep in the bowels of the Mountain Lion complex — he would lose an important cash pipeline and find himself in even murkier financial waters.

No.

The operation had to continue.

Which is why he'd decided to make Shien a piece of merchandise. He'd been days away from sending her onto paying customers when she'd slipped out of his grasp.

As always, he'd become greedy.

Now, the consequences were slamming home all at once.

Twenty minutes slipped by — Forrest sunk deep into his own thoughts, mulling over what the future might hold. The limousine twisted and turned through the slums, its windows tinted to prevent anyone from getting a glimpse of its occupants. It burst out the other side into a rarely visited section of Macau, home to empty lots and generally abandoned streets. Junkyards and dormant industrial estates sprawled across the surroundings.

Out here, Forrest felt exposed.

And, tucked into the corner of the most unimpressive section of the land, lay a collection of the most powerful men in Macau's most powerful triad.

Forrest swallowed a ball of tension that had caught in his throat and wondered — for a split second — whether Jang had been successful in working out where his daughter had been taken.

If he had, it wasn't the smartest move for Forrest to have left the relative safety of the Mountain Lion complex.

What if? he wondered.

A moment later, the view out the window lurched sharply to the right. A horrific jolt threw Forrest across the cabin, cracking his head against the nearest window, and the sound of screaming metal roared in his ears. He recognised that something had rammed the vehicle from the left-hand side, but he could do nothing but snatch for a hand-hold as the limousine pitched off the road and entered a brutal barrel roll down the side of a shallow embankment.

When the wild ride came to a bone-shattering conclusion, the limousine finished its descent upside-down in a filthy layer of sewage, wedged into the crevasse formed by two dirt slopes. The engine died and Forrest spat blood — a tooth followed the crimson liquid out of his mouth.

He crawled pathetically for the nearest window, desperate to get out of the vehicle.

He had no idea where the other two men were — or the driver. He didn't know which way was up. His head pounded incessantly and a cold chill snaked its way up his spine.

He knew what was happening.

He was helpless to prevent it.

Movement materialised all around the limousine — Forrest heard car doors slamming and heavy footfalls on the dirt. With his vision swimming, he glanced at the thin sliver of natural light spearing in through one of the destroyed window frames and spotted combat boots thumping into the dirt, standing directly next to the limousine, bearing down on him from all sides.

He heard raised voices.

Shouting. Madness. Chaos.

He searched desperately for his giant Asian bodyguard.

As soon as he craned his neck to try and locate his comrades, a hand reached into the limousine and grabbed him forcefully by the collar. It yanked him out of the relative safety of the vehicle, dragging him through muck and filth into daylight. Despite the cloudy weather, Forrest hadn't been outside in days on end, and the bright light made him squint as hands snatched at him and hauled him in five different directions at once.

Amidst the chaos, he reached down for the holster at his waist.

A feeble, desperate attempt.

'Gun!' someone roared in Chinese.

Still blind to what was happening, Forrest's eardrums exploded as a gunshot rang close by. Unsuppressed, abhorrently loud, it came accompanied by a burst of pain across his forearm. He yelped and jolted in shock as he realised he'd been hit. Hands snatched at his waist and tore his gun free, disarming him in the space of a second.

As his eyes adjusted to the daylight, he spotted a crimson sheet flooding down his forearm, blood dripping off his fingers. The bullet had sliced a trail of skin off his upper wrist. He was surrounded by stern-faced Asian men in suits — well-dressed mercenaries, no doubt. They were in the process of establishing control over the scene. Bodies dove inside the wrecked limousine in search of Forrest's accomplices.

One of the men holding Forrest by the throat slammed him back against the side of the limousine, knocking all the breath from his lungs as the chassis crumpled. He coughed and wheezed for breath — it had been some time since he'd been manhandled like this, and it was hard getting used to the feeling.

If these men wanted to, they could kill him right now and no-one would be any wiser.

The small Filipino man came crawling from the wreckage, hurled out into the open by two of the thugs. Another pair wrestled the big Asian guy out of the vehicle in turn. Both were badly hurt, blood covering their features and some of their limbs twisted at awkward angles. Forrest grimaced, desperate to maintain order but slowly losing his cool.

'Relax, boys,' he told his men. 'I'll get us out of—'

One of the mercenaries wrenched a cumbersome Desert Eagle handgun from a giant holster at his waist and rammed the barrel into the side of the giant Asian bodyguard's head. He pumped the trigger once, sending the guy's brains across the crumpled limousine chassis.

Without hesitating a beat, he wheeled his aim to the Filipino man and sent a second round through the guy's forehead. Both gunshots deafened Forrest temporarily, but he barely noticed. His knees gave out and he slumped to the ground as he watched his men die, helpless to prevent it.

A third gunshot sounded, and in his hazy state of mind Forrest realised the driver had been killed.

The reality of the situation sunk in.

He was alone in the middle of nowhere, surrounded by waste and degradation, all his men shot dead, in the hands of an unknown party who could do as they pleased.

Sweating, hyperventilating, panicking, surrounded by his dead workers and a dozen faceless, ruthless mercenaries, Peter Forrest wished they would just put a bullet in his brain and bring all his troubles to an end.

Then he noticed a newcomer descending the slope ahead — in his sixties, Asian, with a whisper of grey hair and a suit that looked like it cost five figures.

Jang.

The old man was staring at Forrest with venom in his eyes.

The venom of a father trying to get his child back.

'Oh, fuck,' Forrest whispered, his skin turning white as a ghost.

26

'Like I said, my Daddy isn't a bad man. I hope he's okay.'

Slater didn't want to voice his opinion at risk of offending Shien, but he seriously doubted her father operated in this world and had even a shred of nobility. 'I'm sure he's fine.'

They sat at either end of the sectional eight-seater couch in the centre of the lavish living quarters, facing each other across a distance the same size as the cramped apartment they'd stayed the previous night in. Both of them had taken long showers to wash the filth of the slums out of their skin, and Slater had ducked down to the luxury department stores on the ground floor to purchase a fresh set of clothes for both of them. He had an ulterior goal in mind when browsing outfits — he realised he might be needing to look presentable at a later time.

So now he sat in absolute comfort, feet stretched out across one of the couch's sections, dressed in pale blue slim-fit jeans and a thousand-dollar woollen jumper he'd picked up from a designer outlet.

That would satisfy any dress code he felt inclined to meet.

Some colour had returned to Shien's face — it seemed the shower and the change of clothes had refreshed her enough to wash further traces of the drugs out of her system. She still glanced around every room she entered, but a level of alertness had returned to her features. Slater watched her dozing across the couch and realised he'd inadvertently formed a bond that would be hard to break.

Despite everything, he considered her a temporary daughter.

It was his responsibility to make sure she made it through this turbulent time in one piece.

Trouble was, he had no idea what to do next.

He burrowed his head into his hands, taking deep breaths to combat the exhaustion churning his guts. He knew he had to utilise this downtime to rest up, but he had gone without sleep for over seventy-two hours in the past and lived to tell the tale. He'd felt it prudent to focus one-hundred percent of his time on the task back then...

...and he felt the same now.

As he considered the next best move, a soft noise resonated through the massive suite. He looked up and saw Shien stirring, shifting restlessly, her tiny frame wrapped in the chaise cushion. She opened her eyes and stared back at Slater.

'Can't sleep,' she muttered.

'Try to get some rest.'

'You should be doing the same.'

'Can't sleep,' he said with a smirk.

She sat up, crossing her legs and straightening her back, as if carrying out a combination of moves a teacher had taught her to present herself better.

'I want to talk,' she said.

'About what?'

'You said you'd tell me about yourself when we have time. Now we've got time.'

'Shien...'

'Don't tell me you were lying to me, Will.'

'It's not something you should be hearing.'

She gestured all around her. 'I'm a big girl. I can cope.'

'You're not a big girl. And I know you can cope, but I don't know if I can.'

'Why's that?'

'I spent some time in Yemen. A couple of months ago. I don't think it's healthy to dwell on those memories.'

'Did you do bad things?'

'To bad people.'

'Do you feel guilty about it?'

'No.'

'Then why don't you want to think about it?'

Slater paused. He couldn't discuss Yemen without bringing up something else, something that had been plaguing the recesses of his mind for his entire adult life.

Something he'd sworn he wouldn't talk about with Shien.

Sitting alone in the enormous presidential suite, feeling alone in the world, he realised he had to eventually talk about it with someone.

Why not her?

'Shien, I need to tell you something about my childhood. About a time when I was around your age.'

She paused. 'I can't picture you as a kid. You're too tough and strong.'

Slater smirked. 'I was a kid. A skinny one, too. Thirteen years old. I couldn't hold my own in a fight. I was shy.

Painfully shy. And my home life was horrible. My mother was never around, and she never told me what she did. My father didn't care about me — he took drugs almost everyday.'

'Like what was in my system?'

Slater paused. Heroin was strangely comparable to what Shien had been through.

'Almost exactly like that.'

'I didn't like that feeling,' she said. 'I was confused all the time.'

'If your life is bad enough, sometimes you turn to that kind of feeling to feel relief.' He paused. 'I don't expect you to understand.'

'No, no, I understand. My life has been pretty good. There's terrible people out there. I saw that before...'

Her voice dropped off a cliff as she stifled emotions. Slater watched the angst run across her face — she had seen men die earlier that morning, and the reality was finally sinking home as the drugs flowed out of her veins.

'Yeah,' Slater said, trying to take her mind off the immediate sensation. 'So Dad turned to drugs. We barely ever spoke. And my mother went off and ... did things.'

'What kind of things?'

'She sold herself for money.'

Shien paused. 'I don't get it.'

'Shien, I will tell you every single part of this story, but you shouldn't ask about what I just said. It's not something you want to know about until you're older.'

She sensed the deathly serious nature of his tone, and nodded accordingly. 'Okay, Will. Got it.'

'One day, she just didn't come home. Dad searched for a couple of days, then gave up. I managed to figure out what happened — I was old enough to piece it together. She'd been meeting with bad men who paid her to do what she did. Very bad men.'

'Like the people we ran into earlier?'

'Sort of. These men were called pimps. They sold my mother to another country, and they shipped her off. I never saw her again.'

Shien froze, her brain whirring a million miles an hour. 'Why did another country want her?'

'They wanted to hurt her.'

'Like punch her? And kick her?'

'And other things...'

Shien realised Slater wouldn't budge, and she clammed up.

'My Dad killed himself a year later.'

'That's called suicide, isn't it?'

'Yeah. It left me without parents. I had to grow up fast. And I always had that feeling deep inside me the entire time — that I couldn't do anything to save my mother, even though I knew the people who took her.'

'Why couldn't you do anything?'

'They would have killed me.'

'But... you can kill anyone now. I've seen it.'

'Now I can.'

'What happened?'

'I joined the military.'

'You became a soldier?'

'A certain kind of soldier. I retired a few months ago.'

'Did you go back to try and find the men who hurt your Mummy? After you became dangerous, I mean.'

'They were long gone.'

'But you tried to find them.'

'Of course I tried.'

'But that feeling's still there?'

He nodded. 'That feeling's always going to be there. For as long as I live. It's the kind of anger that I can't control, and it only comes up when I find situations like what happened to my mother.'

Shien paused. 'You think those men who took me were going to hurt me too? In the way I don't understand?'

'I think so, Shien.'

'I hope they weren't. I hope they were good people.'

'I think it's been proven that they're not good people by this point.'

The colour that had slowly started to return to her face disappeared again. She was paling, sweating, frightened. 'What were they going to do to me, Will?'

'Hopefully nothing. But that's why I need to hang around. Now I can fix problems — if I had these abilities when my mother disappeared, I would have torn the whole world apart to find her. So if you were going to be in a similar situation, I'll tear the whole world apart to make sure you stay safe.'

'You don't have to do that. You might die. Those were scary people who took me.'

'I'm a scary guy,' Slater said. 'You just can't see it. Because I'm on your side.'

She paused, reflecting. 'No — I can see it. But that's a good thing because you want to help me.'

'I could walk away right now and you'd stay safe. I could even get you back to your parents, more than likely. But then the people who took you will carry on doing what they're doing. And that's something I can't allow.'

'Because of what happened to your Mummy?'

'Yes, Shien. So that's why I'm going back to Mountain Lion.'

'Is that where I've been staying the past two weeks?'

'Yes.'

'I don't like that place much.'

'Neither do I.'

'Are you going to hurt the men who wanted to hurt me?'

'If I find them.'

She sighed and settled back in the giant cushion, letting it envelop her frame once again. 'Now I understand. Thanks, Will. I mean it.'

Slater watched her eyes flicker shut and she sank deeper and deeper into slumber, her mind finally satiated by a handful of answers that had been eluding her. It clearly gave her just enough respite to allow tiredness to take over, and a minute later she was peacefully asleep.

Left alone in the massive suite, Slater had time to compose his thoughts. He stared at the giant complex in the distance and began to formulate the initial steps for a plan of attack. There was four-hundred thousand USD worth of casino chips in his pocket, after all, and there was very little in Macau that such an obscene bankroll couldn't purchase.

He was known in the VIP rooms. He'd spent time there before.

He would flash his wealth — tapping into his Zurich accounts if need be — until someone confirmed whether or not Peter Forrest was running a sex slavery ring out of the casino's seedy underbelly.

If his hunch was right, he didn't want to know what he would unleash.

But the billionaire owner of Mountain Lion would wish he'd never been born.

27

A   s a fresh layer of thick clouds filtered across the sky, darkening the already grimy day, Forrest's insides turned to mush.

Jang had found him, cornered him, eliminated his forces, and pinned him down.

On top of that, from the dark look in the man's glare, Forrest knew the Hong Kong businessman knew the truth.

Forrest was the reason his daughter had been missing for more than two weeks.

Forrest gulped back apprehension as two of the suit-clad mercenaries held him firmly against the jagged chassis of the overturned limousine. Even worse than the fact that Jang knew was the reality that he himself had no idea where Shien was.

Jang wouldn't believe it for an instant.

Forrest was doomed.

'Jang,' he gasped as one of the mercenaries slammed a fist into his gut, almost bringing up the meagre meal he'd forced down his throat earlier that morning. 'I swear, man, I can explain.'

Jang said nothing, steadily advancing down the slope. Forrest knew that meant the worst — based on the businessman's track record, he knew the next portion of his life would involve greater pain than he'd ever experienced.

Jang wasn't a man of words.

He was a man of action.

Forrest watched in abject horror as the businessman reached into his jacket pocket and withdrew a serrated switchblade, flipping the blade itself into sight with a simple press of a button.

'*No!*' Forrest screamed.

He bucked and writhed, to no avail. The mercenaries kept him pinned helplessly in place, and one of them rammed a follow-up punch into his exposed neck for the trouble of being made to work to keep him in position.

Forrest's breath caught in his throat and he sucked in air, spluttering and wheezing and wondering what he'd done to get himself into this kind of situation.

About a hundred things, his brain told him.

Before he had time to compose himself — in reality, there was no way to prepare for what was about to happen — Jang seized hold of Forrest's bloody wrist and forced it flat against the limousine's chassis like a makeshift chopping block. Forrest stifled a squeal of protest — then, almost in fast motion, Jang lashed out with the switchblade and severed his pinky finger with a single attack.

The finger fell into the dirt amidst a spray of blood and Forrest roared, his nerve endings firing and sweat pouring off his frame uncontrollably. As soon as he opened his mouth to yell, Jang backhanded him across the face, knocking a tooth loose.

Forrest lost all resistance, and couldn't help himself

when his natural instincts kicked in. Tears sprung out of their ducts — he was helpless to prevent it.

He hunched over, a snivelling cowering mess, and waited for more trauma that he knew would soon follow.

But Jang's destructive outburst ceased instantly, and the man simply stood and stared at Forrest in the ditch. The only sound came from the heavy breathing of all the men involved in the confrontation, Forrest included.

Adrenalin leeched from every pore in the vicinity.

When Jang finally spoke, enough silence had built up to turn the tension in the air palpable.

'I will ask you where my daughter is,' he said, his English perfect. 'I will give you three seconds to answer and then I will cut off another finger. We'll repeat this until I get what I want, and then I'll start with toes. Then other, more unpleasant areas.'

Forrest flapped his lips like a dying fish, struggling to find the necessary words in the face of unrivalled terror.

'Look, Jang—'

'Where is my daughter?'

'Can we discuss this like men instead of resorting to some kind of sick and twisted—'

'That's three seconds.'

As lackadaisically as if he were simply taking out the trash, Jang wrapped the same vice-like grip around Forrest's crimson wrist and forced it back to the same surface area on the limousine. It triggered a fresh wave of terror. Forrest writhed on the spot, moaning and pleading and...

Jang smashed the point of the knife into the base of Forrest's fourth finger.

It separated from his hand just as the previous digit had.

Forrest let out a blood-curdling scream, and for a moment

his vision faltered, his consciousness threatening to leave him in the face of abject horror. He couldn't see a way out of the situation, and it crippled him inwardly. Things were only going to get worse from here — he had underestimated the determination and sheer passion of a man who had lost his daughter and would go to the ends of the earth to get her back.

All because Forrest got greedy and wanted to add her to his bottom line of revenue...

He whimpered, starting to double over in pain before the two henchmen thrust him upright again, keeping him clamped in place as effectively as if he were bound with rope. A long string of saliva dangled from his lips, tinged with the blood flowing from his now-empty gum where Jang had dislodged his tooth.

He wished to the heavens for Jang to overcommit on one of his attacks and accidentally sever an artery.

That way, Forrest could depart this planet as quickly as possible.

Anything else would only prolong the suffering...

Then the world went utterly mad.

Automatic gunfire blared from everywhere at once and Jang's henchmen dropped like flies. One after the other they contorted and twisted on their feet, locked in the macabre dance of death, before face planting the mud at the bottom of the ditch and lying still, their arterial blood mixing with the mud.

Jang wheeled on the spot, horrified, searching for the source of the fresh commotion.

A heavy bullet caught him full in the face, and suddenly Jang ceased to exist.

His half-headless corpse dropped to the dirt at Forrest's feet, and the two henchmen — previously holding Forrest with fervour against the side of the limousine — slackened their grip out of panic.

Forrest didn't take the opportunity lightly.

He'd been in shootouts before. Long, long ago.

He knew what to do.

He clasped one hand to either side of his head, dropped to the mud, and curled into a ball. He squeezed his eyes shut — ignoring the pain creasing across his face and the blood pumping out of the two stumps on his right hand where his fingers used to sit — and simply waited for the carnage to reach its conclusion.

It didn't take long. Three or four seconds after Forrest cowered away from the action, the gunfire ceased and the high-pitched whining of tinnitus settled over his hearing. Gunshots were horrifying sounds in person — Forrest had slowly come to understand real life wasn't similar to the movies.

He wouldn't forget what had just unfolded for the rest of his life.

However long that lasted.

When a strange kind of silence descended over the ditch — the kind of silence that signalled everyone nearby was dead — Forrest lifted his head out of the mud and stared through swimming vision at the top of the slope.

A figure had materialised against the grimy horizon.

No, multiple figures.

Advancing steadily toward him.

The only survivors of the firefight.

He whimpered again, succumbing to instinct, unable to save face. It didn't matter who would find him like this — whether they wanted to help or wanted him dead, they would find a broken man.

When Forrest tentatively sat up and squinted in an

attempt to make out who was descending toward him, he realised in that moment he almost didn't care whether he lived or died.

But the middle-aged Asian man with the strong build and the expensive suit descending toward him was a familiar face.

Forrest didn't know whether to sigh with relief, or curse his luck.

Maybe he would have been better in the hands of Jang.

Now he would have to explain to the most dangerous triad in Macau that he suspected three of their men of stealing from him.

All while thanking them for saving his life.

The middle-aged guy crouched down by Forrest's pathetic form, studying him with the patient reservedness of a confident man.

'Mr. Forrest,' he said. 'Seems you ran into trouble on your way to us.'

'Uh, yes,' Forrest stammered. 'Yes, I did.'

'Unfortunately for these men, they decided to confront you on our territory. Glad we were here to take care of it.'

'So am I.'

'Will these men pose a problem for us?' the man said, gesturing to the graveyard all around them.

Through a mask of blood, Forrest shook his head. 'No, sir. They're from Hong Kong. They know nothing about Macau.'

'Of course they know nothing. They tried to jump you on triad grounds.'

Forrest made to respond but nothing came out of his mouth. A searing burst of pain ran through his hand and he drew the mangled limb to his chest, unable to prevent himself from breaking down in tears.

It was all too much.

Despite everything, the triad member grunted in frustration. 'You would do good not to show weakness around these men, Mr. Forrest. They are hungry, and they feed on weakness.'

'Sorry,' Forrest said. 'Thank you for saving me.'

'Of course. It's our own reputation we need to uphold. Now why don't we get you fixed up and have a chat about why you came here today?'

That did nothing to quash any of the tension in Forrest's gut — in fact, it only made things worse. He had been saved before long-term damage had been inflicted, but the pain was dulling his senses and making him woozy with unease. On top of that, he was on his own, in the possession of a triad he knew very little about.

Soon, he would have to justify his reason for the visit.

As the middle-aged man helped him steadily to his feet, he battled down all kinds of hesitation and elected to simply press on for as long as he could.

He wasn't sure how long it would last.

28

S later stepped off the road, up onto the sidewalk, moving into the vast shadow that the Mountain Lion complex cast over everything in sight. The enormous towers dwarfed him, stirring a sense of insignificance in his gut. There were thousands and thousands of customers between the two skyscrapers, but that played directly to his advantage.

There was only so many people a security team could keep track of.

Besides, he imagined he wasn't the only black guy staying at Mountain Lion.

If they suspected him as Shien's rescuer, it would take them some time to piece it together, rallying any of the injured staff who were battered down by Slater and lived to tell the tale. They would identify him as the man who saved Shien, but by then Slater expected to be deep in the maze of Mountain Lion's underbelly.

One way or another, he was going to have to force his way out.

It would simply depend on what level of resistance he faced when he had to burst out of the belly of the beast.

Worming his way into a sex slavery ring only left one option when they realised he wasn't actually interested in the product — confrontation. As Slater realised its inevitability, a fresh burst of energy surged through him. He strode straight through to the grand lobby of the left-hand tower — which compromised most of the VIP rooms running out of the Mountain Lion complex — and a beaming concierge instantly greeted him by name.

Slater had left Shien back in the hotel suite — between the options of leaving her there or bringing her with him, the choice had become obvious. He'd instructed her to answer the door for no-one and, if need be, to hide underneath one of the beds in the rare event of someone forcing their way in.

That would have to be enough.

She couldn't see what was about to transpire.

The concierge was short and rotund but painfully welcoming — Slater imagined he would follow through with any request one could think of. His dark black hair had been slicked back with gel, and he stood patiently by the entrance with his hands clasped behind his back, scanning each fresh arrival for any sign of wealth.

Slater decided to test his luck.

'Welcome back, William,' the concierge said, flashing a pristine row of bright white teeth.

'Good to see you again,' Slater said, lacing his tone with warmth.

He loitered by the entrance, signalling that he had some kind of intention in mind with his visit. He wasn't simply here to pick up some designer clothing or a gourmet meal.

'Are you interested in returning to the same room you were using previously?' the man said.

Slater nodded slowly. 'Thought I'd try my luck one more time. Your casino has been good to me so far.'

The concierge beamed — Slater wondered if he received kickbacks for feeding whales to the high-stakes gambling rooms. 'Of course, sir. We're happy to help you. Let me make the call and once you're approved you can head right on up. It should only take a moment.'

Slater nodded, acting mightily satisfied, and clasped his hands behind his back while the concierge skirted around a small desk and raised a landline phone to his ear.

While he waited, he took the time to assess how he was feeling. He'd been involved in multiple fights to the death earlier that day, and with that knowledge in the back of his mind he found himself pleasantly surprised by his condition. Upon further assessment he didn't think the ligaments in his knee were damaged too badly — he could walk, and apply pressure on it to an extent. Squatting or levering it in any way spelled trouble, but as long as Slater could move freely he could ignore the injury until chaos broke out and the comfortable flood of adrenalin suppressed anything he might be feeling.

The concierge spent a moment listening patiently to a spiel on the other end of the line. He lifted the receiver away from his ear and stared at Slater with his head cocked to one side.

He wanted to know something.

'Yes?' Slater said.

'May I ask if you're still in possession of the bankroll you left here with? Have you gambled any of the money away at other locations? Macau can be awfully luring, after all...'

Slater paused for just a moment. He weighed up the

risks associated with both forging an explanation for the missing fifth or simply stating that he still had the full amount. In all likelihood they would ask for visual proof of the five-hundred thousand, so there was no use lying.

'I lost a hundred thousand at the Parisian,' Slater said, grimacing as if he were embarrassed to disclose the information. 'Hope that's alright.'

The concierge muttered something into the phone, listened for a beat, then nodded in turn. He returned the receiver to its cradle and turned to Slater with a reassuring smile.

'You've been accepted again,' the man said. 'As I said, much faster than the first time, yes?'

Slater had to concur. His first trip into the VIP rooms had taken some time to burst through the initial period of resistance — he was an unknown stranger with an undisclosed net worth, whereas the usual whales Mountain Lion targeted were well-known local businessmen or titans from nearby Hong Kong or China. His sudden appearance and insistence to be allowed to gamble on the high-stakes table had taken some time to grow accustomed to, but after a few days of spending his money lavishly in the resort and retail sections of the complex, they had deduced he had the funds to back up his talk and let him through to the VIP rooms.

The initial waiting period had long since been taken care of.

So the concierge gestured for Slater to follow his lead, and he led the way through a marble lobby that stretched dozens of feet above their heads, complete with ornate jungle decor and a statue of a puma erected in the centre of the sweeping floor. Its lips were curved into a snarl and it sat surrounded by riches — chests of gold, fat diamonds, ancient artefacts. There was nothing to denote what the time or date was — time didn't exist in these establishments. One could gamble for days on end — weeks even.

The VIP rooms encouraged it.

The concierge led Slater past hordes of tourists from mainland China and almost every other continent on the planet, through to a narrow passageway that curved between two marble walls, deceptively hidden from public view. He swiped a keycard against a broad set of oak doors and pushed them inward when a sharp beeping authenticated his safe passage through.

In any other situation, Slater would have remained wary.

But there was four-hundred thousand dollars in his pocket and fresh clothes on his frame and significant progress being made with tracing Shien's footsteps through the dark underbelly. He realised he hadn't felt like this in quite some time — and he realised why.

He had a purpose.

Aimless wandering and gambling and chasing cheap thrills did nothing for him. He was in a hostile environment where one of Forrest's thugs could identify him on the cameras at any moment, surrounded by men who would happily murder him without giving it a second thought, searching for a dark truth in a complex larger than he could possibly fathom.

And he was loving every second of it.

As the concierge ushered him into a private elevator with thick carpet flooring and a gold-plated interface, he took a deep breath and released every ounce of tension in his bones. He could calm himself in almost any situation where he wasn't fighting for his life — and this, thankfully, was one of those times.

The concierge nodded farewell, and the doors whispered closed.

A floor had already been preset into the digital interface — level 22, the same floor he'd been visiting for the last two weeks. As the numbers ticked by and the elevator pressed up into the heart of the skyscraper, he composed himself for the hours ahead.

It would take a marathon of gambling and subtle conversational cues to imbue the notion in the staff's heads that he wanted more than just a high-stakes betting streak. He would have to hint at a darker side, a side that didn't exist, and all the while cover his true intentions.

If they offered him a trip into the seedier, off-limits areas of Mountain Lion — which, by this point, he was almost certain existed — he would run with it. He would follow the trail into the bowels of the casino, until he stumbled across whatever it was Peter Forrest had intended to use Shien for.

Then he would unleash hell.

The elevator's digital interface ticked over to "22" and Slater felt the cable car decelerate, coming to a halt with barely a whisper of noise.

The doors sliced open, and a suit-clad security guard with a stocky frame and short, close-cropped hair offered a hand to greet the newcomer.

Slater reached out intuitively to complete the handshake.

Simultaneously, their gazes lifted to make direct eye contact.

Slater spotted the swollen cheek and the handful of cuts across the guy's forehead.

It was one of the men from the limousine.

The heavyset guard recognised him a split second later.

29

Blood soaked through the gauze bandage wrapped tight around Forrest's mangled hand. The treatment so far had been the very definition of rudimentary, but it was only a temporary measure until the triad could usher him away from the crime scene and into the heart of their territory.

He went along with the rough treatment, realising that apart from the pleasantries exchanged with the head of the triad, he was in a similar predicament than if Jang had whisked him away to an undisclosed location.

His guards were dead.

His driver was dead.

He was on his own, in the middle of nowhere, far from the safety and power of his empire. Out here, in this desolate wasteland, the triad could do as they pleased. They always would have been able to — he scolded himself for making a gesture as foolish as willingly venturing into their land.

Now he sat in the back of a nondescript grey sedan, so dull and uncharismatic that it seemed to become unnoticeable amidst the junkyards and rundown neighbourhoods. Forrest stared silently out the window, unsure whether to cry or moan in agony. The middle-aged triad leader sat across the rear seats, staring straight ahead, his posture rigid and his gaze unflinching.

Suddenly, he turned and looked at Forrest. 'I hope you don't mind that we delay our business talk until we reach the residence. Just tradition.'

Forrest nodded. *What the hell else am I supposed to do? Protest?*

But he didn't say that, because he might have received a bullet for his troubles. Instead he said, 'We met briefly, when I asked for some help running my casino. I don't think I ever caught your name, though.'

'Jerome.'

Forrest stared at him. 'That's not your real name.'

'No. But it is what you will call me.'

'Something you go by often?'

'Something I go by when I don't exactly trust the man I am talking with.'

'You don't trust me?'

'Consider it a professional gesture. I simply don't know what you came here to say. You must understand?'

Forrest nodded and gulped back apprehension. In truth he wanted nothing more than to high-tail it back to Mountain Lion and crawl under the covers — then he could ignore his problems until the front door to the penthouse burst down and his enemies slaughtered him where he cowered.

The latter end of the mental image turned his stomach, so he forced it from his mind and doubled down on the situation at hand. 'Yes, of course I understand. I'm sure you will be more than receptive of what I came here to say.'

'I hope so, Mr. Forrest. I hope so.'

The sedan turned sharply as the trail narrowed, condensing to a single laneway that curved through embankments teaming with trash and waste. In truth, Forrest hadn't realised this section of Macau existed. He didn't quite know where he was, either. The limousine crash had inflicted blunt force trauma on his skull, enough to fog his memory and rattle him. He'd lost track of time and space.

They could be in China, for all he knew.

His attentiveness ebbed and flowed as it pleased.

In his degraded state, he simply sat and waited with his shoulders hunched and his head bowed as the sedan turned onto a claustrophobic driveway complete with overbearing trees and rough gravel under the tyres. The branches hung thick over everything, masking what lay beyond the driveway to anyone passing by. Forrest wasn't sure, but he thought he spotted silhouettes ghosting through the trees, clutching automatic weapons at the ready, prepared for any unwanted visitors.

He chalked it up to his muddied proprioception and stared straight ahead, trying his hardest not to sweat.

They pulled up to a rundown, weatherboard house bordered by two literal trash heaps. The entire place stank of grime and filth — even in Forrest's semi-coherent state he could smell the putrid rot all around them. He climbed out of the sedan as it pulled to a stop near the front terrace, and gazed around with a certain trepidation.

'This is your place?' he said, trying his best not to sound condescending.

'You wouldn't expect it to be,' Jerome said. 'Which is exactly why it is.'

Sudden agony burned in Forrest's hand — he raised it to

his chest again and winced, shifting from foot to foot to try and ride out the sensation.

Jerome noticed.

'I have people who can take care of that for you.'

'I have my own people,' Forrest said, a semblance of his confidence trickling back. He'd made it this far — why couldn't he salvage this situation? He'd doubted himself for long enough. It was time to act. 'I'd prefer it if we had our talk and you dropped me back at Mountain Lion. I have urgent business to attend to.'

'You should have asked us to come to you,' Jerome said, his eyes wide. 'That would have been perfectly acceptable.'

I know I should have, Forrest thought. *I haven't been thinking straight for days.*

'It's unexpected business,' he said. 'I'm sure you understand.'

'Of course. Let us talk first, though. I hope you didn't come all this way for nothing, given … the slight problem you ran into.'

'How did you know to find me there?' Forrest said as they sauntered toward the unimpressive residence.

'Where?'

'That must have been a mile away from here.'

'It's where our territory begins,' Jerome explained matter-of-factly. 'Unofficially, of course. But you'd need a death wish to disobey us. No-one conducts business like that on our grounds. We were out there to intercept you, anyway.'

'Intercept me?'

'We would have ordered your driver and bodyguards to stay where they were while we brought you here for a private conversation. So, I guess, everything worked out the way we intended anyway. You simply won't be getting your men back at the end.'

Forrest bit back a retort as they stepped onto the front terrace and a solemn-faced Asian man pushed open the front door, inviting them inside. He had considered his two guards allies — even if he hadn't known their names, they had served him well. It sent fury through his chest to hear Jerome mention their deaths so dismissively.

As if they meant nothing.

Then Forrest realised he was simply looking for a fight.

He disposed of his own men all the time.

That thought sent a shiver down his spine as he stepped into a dingy entranceway with dim lighting and shadows flickering across the walls. How far had he fallen since he'd first arrived in Macau? He almost hadn't paid any attention to his descent — life had been moving impossibly fast for as long as he could remember.

Now's not the best time for an existential crisis, he thought.

There were almost a dozen of Jerome's henchmen in the house, Forrest realised. It was a cramped, single-storey dwelling with little space for movement. He noticed silhouettes moving through countless doorways in his peripheral vision, not daring to look in case anyone took offence to his behaviour. He wished to cause as little trouble as possible, and then get on his way.

'Not much room to move around here,' he muttered. 'How do you get anything done?'

Jerome froze alongside Forrest, adopting a demeanour that could only be described as menacing. 'We have underground quarters.'

'Oh.'

'All the important work is carried out down there.'

'I see.'

'Don't worry, Mr. Forrest. I have no intention of taking you down there.'

Forrest realised the thinly veiled threats had been designed to slowly implement control over the course of their time together. Jerome wanted Forrest to know that he owned him. Whether the concussion was wearing off or he simply felt the urge to assert himself, he decided to retort.

'I certainly hope not. That wouldn't bode well for you.'

'Oh?' Jerome said with a smirk, raising an eyebrow. 'Maybe it is time we had our talk. If you would, please...'

He gestured into an adjoining room consisting of a pair of well-worn couches and an old-fashioned desk lamp resting on an ornate table between them.

'Our meeting room,' he explained.

There was barely any unnecessary furnishings in the entire place, Forrest realised. The entire house had the aura of a hospital — sterile and soulless. He wondered how much blood had been spilt on the premises. Trying not to let his fear show, he stepped into the room and sat on one of the couches.

Jerome sat opposite. 'Now — after all that pain you went through — what is it you came here for, Mr. Forrest?'

Forrest composed himself. An icy determination settled over him. He reminded himself of the need to retrieve the money — it was paramount to his survival.

'Your three men,' he started. 'Tak. Antoine. Jin. They've been working for me for months, now, and they've been doing their job excellently. They've been involved in some of my most brutal work — I'm sure you can understand that my business sometimes requires tough responses.'

Jerome nodded. 'Of course. And I have also been under the impression that they have carried out their work with the utmost professionalism. You pay them handsomely, after all.'

Forrest nodded back. 'Not handsomely enough, it seems. I'm afraid I placed too much trust in them after we went through so much together. I firmly believe they are the perpetrators in the theft of nearly five hundred million U.S. Dollars of my personal money. They were the only people who knew enough about my accounts to successfully complete the transfer. And they have alibis during the time the transfer took place, which means they used scapegoats. This was all planned out with precision. Would I be correct in assuming they were operating of their own accord, and that this behaviour wasn't endorsed by you and your organisation?'

The words hung in the air — it seemed as if Jerome were tasting them, rolling the accusations through his mind and contemplating how to respond. He clasped his knotted hands together — hands that had no doubt been used to inflict untold trauma — and pursed his lips as he composed a response.

'You are correct,' he said. 'My organisation had nothing to do with this.'

'That's good to hear.'

'Five hundred million dollars is an awful lot of money, Mr. Forrest.'

'I understand that — which is why I'm asking for your discretion. I wish to do business with you long into the future. I hope you can work with me to return my money to me, and I'm sure you will be handsomely rewarded.'

'And what of my men? Jin. Tak. Antoine.'

'I never want to see them again. What you do with them is your business. But, if I were you, I would consider the situation wholly unacceptable. They shouldn't be conducting business like that without your knowledge.'

Forrest trailed off, even though he had a lot more to say. Amidst his tireless rant, an insidious flicker of doubt had started in the back of his mind. He realised he'd been in such a hurry to get the money back that he hadn't considered the ramifications of revealing all to Jerome.

Why doesn't he just send me on my way, and get the money off his men later?

Fuck.

It seemed Jerome had realised this near the beginning of the conversation. He had all the control — Forrest sat in his house, surrounded by his men and his guns. Mountain Lion was an enormous complex, but Peter Forrest was not a gangster.

As much as he tried to be.

Jerome crossed one leg over the other and tried to stifle a smirk. Despite the attempt, a half-smile crossed his face. 'Mr. Forrest, I think you can consider your debt repaid.'

'I'm sorry?'

'I saved your life in that ditch.'

'Y-you did.'

'How much did Mountain Lion cost you?'

'I'm sorry?'

'How much did your casino cost you?'

'Billions.'

'Did you use your own fortune to pay for it?'

'For the most part. Some loans were necessary, but it was mostly me.'

'So you are worth billions?'

Forrest nodded. He knew where this was headed.

'So by receiving five hundred million dollars in exchange for saving your life, I'm actually being extorted...'

'Jerome—'

'That's quite a low price to pay for protecting someone as valuable as yourself, Mr. Forrest.'

'I need that money.'

'What money? The gift you offered me in exchange for protection? It's rude to take back a gift.'

'I—'

'You should leave, Peter. And consider yourself lucky I didn't take offence to a sum as measly as five hundred million. My men will guide you to the car.'

Forrest said nothing. The blood had drained from his face — he was powerless, and he knew it.

As he got to his feet and shuffled toward the door, Jerome said, 'There's always a bigger fish, my friend.'

30

S later's fast-twitch muscle fibres fired and he realised — in the half-second it took to connect the dots and place the guard from the night before — that everything he'd fought to accomplish since he'd rescued Shien from that limousine came down to how fast he could react.

He spotted a congestion of silhouettes at the very end of the corridor, over one of the guard's shoulders. There was no time to discern where they were looking, or who they were — Slater simply recognised them as potential witnesses and burst off the mark, acting out of impulse.

His fingers were halfway through the act of wrapping around the guard's instinctive, involuntary handshake. In one motion he tightened his grip with every ounce of strength in his bones, and crushed the guard's hand to ensure the guy wouldn't manage to slip out of his grip. Then he yanked the guard into the elevator, wrenching the man forward, throwing his balance off and making him stumble wildly across the threshold and into the cable car.

At the same time, Slater reached out blindly with his

other hand and smashed his palm against the "close doors" button — once, twice, three times.

A little more than a single second had unfolded by the time the steel elevator doors responded in prompt fashion to Slater's command and whisked closed.

The interior of the cable car turned to madness, but Slater could deal with madness.

He couldn't deal with detection.

There hadn't been any time to check whether any of the guests in the corridor had spotted the abrupt series of gestures, but as the doors touched together and sealed the cable car's occupants off from the outside world, Slater unleashed hell.

The guard had seized a moment of capitalisation as Slater fumbled with the control panel, taking the chance to swing a wild haymaker at his face. Slater noticed the punch coming and shot away from the majority of the impact, side-stepping to allow the fist to crash against his head at the peak of its trajectory.

As a result, very little power was transferred through to Slater's skull.

Nerve endings fired across his temple — nothing adrenalin couldn't deal with. He shrugged off the non-concussive strike and darted back into range, bundling the guy into the opposite wall.

My turn, he thought.

He stayed as calm as possible — given the fact that one wrong move could result in a knockout punch and allow the guard to beat him to death with his bare hands. He reached up with both hands and looped them around the back of the guard's head, clasping his fingers together at the base of his neck.

In Muay Thai, it was called seizing the clinch.

In the heat of the moment it seemed idiotic — reaching for a favourable hold instead of letting punches fly seemed like a short-term disaster. It allowed the security guard to hammer a couple of punches into Slater's mid-section, but he'd been prepared for that. His core muscles were tense, hard as rocks, ready to take anything the guy could throw at them in the split second he had to try his luck.

If the guy hit Slater in the liver, the fight would be over and Slater would go down involuntarily in a crumpled heap.

But he didn't. The liver left a narrow opening that only a highly skilled combatant could find in a no-holds-barred brawl. Instead, a couple of glancing shots rang off Slater's abdomen, stinging like hell but achieving little else.

By then, Slater had seized hold of the guy's neck.

From there, there was no reprieve.

The guy squirmed, trying to break free from Slater's grasp, but he'd made a fatal mistake, and he only realised it when it was too late. Slater levered all the weight in his arms and wrenched the guy's head down — he was helpless to resist. He smashed a kneecap into the guy's face, bone to nose, dealing serious damage.

The guy's hands slackened ever so slightly, faltering as he recoiled away from the devastating knee.

But he had nowhere to go.

Slater maintained a vice-like grip on the back of the guy's neck. When the man reared away from the knee, Slater simply manoeuvred his bodyweight again and brought the guy's head back to the exact same position. He fired off one knee after the other.

Bang. Bang. Bang.

Blood sprayed and the guy's strength sapped even more. His legs gave out, and he started to fall to the elevator carpet, bleeding from both nostrils at once.

On the way down, Slater released the hold on his neck and delivered a final jumping knee, surging into range and catching the guy on the chin as he slumped to the floor. The momentum behind the attack sent the man's head clattering back into the wood-panelled wall. With the sound of a bowling ball bouncing off multiple surfaces at once, he hit the ground in a crumpled heap.

Slater took a deep breath, composing himself, recognising that social interaction would be required in the next few moments and he needed to come down from the high of a life-or-death fight. His heart pumped and his vision swam, but he stilled his nerves and checked on the security guard at his feet.

The guy wasn't moving for a long time.

Maybe ever.

Slater glanced at the digital interface built into the side of the elevator and noticed the cable car had automatically begun its descent back toward the ground floor. If it continued on that path, it would arrive back at the same corridor the concierge had guided Slater into a minute previously.

Slater ran through his memory, wondering if there would be any witnesses to greet him. It had seemed like a fairly secluded stretch of the lobby, reserved for whales and high-net-worth visitors only, which meant all would be well if the concierge had returned to his desk.

If not, Slater would have some explaining to do.

But as he stared at the panel of buttons symbolising nearly fifty floors he had the choice of visiting, he realised the lobby was by far the best bet. Any other option would effectively act as a random guess, except for level 22, which would see him burst out into a corridor filled with paying customers, carrying an unconscious guard on his shoulder.

So he left the control panel as it rested, allowing the cable car to descend straight back to the ground floor. He crouched on the soft carpet and touched a pair of fingers to the side of the security guard's neck, wading through a river of blood to do so.

He found nothing.

The guy was dead.

31

A s the elevator slowed, Slater's heart leapt into his throat when he realised he hadn't prepared for any kind of resistance. The control panel omitted a high-pitched *ding* to indicate it had arrived at the requisite floor, just as he dove for the dead guard's body and wrestled a Beretta M9 out of the holster at the guy's waist. In the chaos of the hand-to-hand fight, the man hadn't found a spare second to draw his weapon.

Slater disengaged the safety with a practiced flick of the index finger, swinging the barrel up to head-height as the doors whispered open.

Whoever lay in wait on the other side would either catch a bullet in the forehead, or a rapid outburst of commands to hit the floor and keep their head down.

In reality he required neither course of action.

The elevator doors slid open without a noise, revealing an empty hallway. In the distance, Slater heard the commotion of visitors moving in droves around the vast lobby, but this section of the ground floor was, just as he suspected, reserved for the high rollers and exclusive guests. There was no sign of the concierge — clearly the man had more important business to attend to than wait around to see if Slater would return.

Slater burst into action, re-engaging the safety and slotting the Beretta into his waist band. He would need both hands for the task ahead.

He hauled the badly-beaten corpse of the security guard out into the corridor, dragging the man unceremoniously by the collar. It proved messy work — Slater took the utmost caution not to get a speck of blood on his clothing. If he wanted to carry on like it was business as usual, he couldn't set off alarm bells with crimson stains on his wrists.

The corpse did nothing to help that, bleeding from everywhere at once. Slater's breath caught in his throat as he managed a glimpse at the damage he'd inflicted on the guard's face.

He had untamed power, and he was afraid what he might do with it if he confirmed his suspicions of a darker side to Mountain Lion.

So far, though, he had nothing.

He had a relentless stream of Forrest's men coming at him — something he had no choice but to defend himself from — but other than that, there was no proof of any kind of sinister intentions behind Forrest's actions. Slater didn't even know what the man looked like. He was rolling with gut feelings, positing the potential reasons for kidnapping a nine-year-old girl and holding onto her for such a significant portion of time.

Slater hurried the corpse across the corridor, exposing himself to potential arrest and life imprisonment if law enforcement decided to stroll in at that moment. He shouldered the door to a small storage room inward and left the dead man in a bloody heap next to an empty bucket and mop. Then he turned on his heel and closed the door quietly, checking in either direction for any surprise arrivals.

Still empty.

His heart pounding in his chest, he crossed to the same elevator — the doors were in the process of whispering closed — and sliced between them, re-entering the same cable car with a second to spare. If he'd missed that opening, it would have been a painful wait for the next elevator.

He rode the twenty-one floors to the same VIP room with his pulse pounding. There was nothing he could do physically to mute the sensation — the fight had been savage, and a split second of reaction speed either way could have turned the tide.

Despite dominating the encounter from start to finish, Slater knew he'd come dangerously close to death.

A sensation that never grew old.

And, more importantly, he didn't know whether he'd showed up on any cameras in the process.

He checked the roof of the cable car but found nothing visible. If cameras had captured the ordeal, there would be an army of security heading his way, and nothing he could do to change that. He'd left the Beretta on the dead man's body out of necessity — the first time he'd stepped into the VIP room, they'd waved a metal detector over his suit to make sure he hadn't come to cause any trouble.

That was the reason he'd entered Mountain Lion unarmed in the first place.

The elevator made a brisk return to level 22, and the doors sliced open before Slater even had a chance to compose himself. He stepped out to face a largely confused

Asian man in a tailored suit, no taller than five-foot-six, staring around the hallway as if he'd lost his wallet.

'Everything okay?' Slater said, like he hadn't a care in the world.

The man snapped to attention, delivering every ounce of customer service required for a role in such an exclusive location within the casino. He beamed, flashing a row of white teeth, and it was as if there had never been a problem at all. 'My sincerest apologies, sir. It seems one of my staff was meant to be here to greet you. I do apologise again — this is completely unprofessional of him.'

Slater stared left, then right. 'Huh. That sure is odd.'

'Certainly. I'll be sure to follow it up immediately.'

'Sounds like a plan.'

'Are you here for the VIP room?'

'Yes.'

'Right this way, please.'

The man turned and set off at a brisk pace down the hallway, no doubt determined to resolve the situation of his missing employee — which bode trouble for Slater. He was operating on a limited time frame. He'd hoped to eliminate the guard in such an effective fashion as to raise no concern about the guy's whereabouts. But he'd forgotten the golden rule of VIP rooms — no-one misses a minute of required work. These were the best of the best in terms of hospitality and attention to detail.

So he didn't have long to make his move.

The small man ushered Slater toward a vast opening built into the end of the corridor. Shaped like a giant church entrance, the pathway led through to a bustling hive of commotion — Slater heard the excited murmuring of high-rollers, and the distinct clicking of casino chips against felt tables. He made to stride directly past the man beside him, but something made him pause.

'Where do you think your man has disappeared to?' he said, posing the question with as much innocence as he could muster.

'I'm not sure, sir. It's quite unlike him. The cameras in the hallway will show where he went. I'll go check them now. Good luck on the tables tonight, sir.'

With a slight bow, the man turned on his heel and set off down the corridor at a brisk pace, hustling past the entrance to the VIP room and ducking into a side passage manned by two stern-faced security guards. The alcove rested around a bend, meaning the guards hadn't seen Slater's initial arrival.

It had saved his life.

Slater froze on the spot, halfway between the VIP room and the elevator, plagued by indecision. The head of security would see the footage of his employee being dragged into the elevator — Slater doubted the elevators would be blocked from view. Then the situation would become a ticking time bomb, counting down until all the security in the complex descended on him.

He had minutes, if not seconds.

It would have to be a brazen, all-out move to get himself downstairs. He would have to approach one of the most important-looking figureheads in the VIP room and insist on being ushered to the darker section of Mountain Lion immediately.

If one even existed.

He'd have to be off this floor before the head of security alerted his staff.

There was almost no chance it would work.

Or he could retreat.

He stared at the elevator doors, beckoning him, urging

him to make the smart decision. But when had he ever done that?

Forward, or backward?

Forward.

Always forward.

Slater strode straight through into the VIP room.

32

It only took a simple, four word request from one of the security team inside the entrance to the VIP room to flip the entire situation on its head.

Slater had started scanning each face in the room the moment he entered, eyeing dozens of baccarat and black-jack tables sprawling across a grand chamber-like space, with a high-domed roof reminiscent of a cathedral. He had a limited amount of time to accomplish what he wanted — he imagined the head of security navigating to the correct archive of footage, playing the tape, witnessing Slater wrench the guard into the elevator and return minutes later on his own.

He was so desperate to seize advantage of any opportunity he could get that he ignored the three-man team of suit-clad security by the entrance, barging straight past them, urgency in his gait.

One of the men reached out and seized Slater by the shoulder, his grip firm enough to indicate they knew something below surface-level.

Slater stopped in his tracks, ruffled by the sudden

change in momentum, fully aware of the ticking clock in his head.

'What's up?' he said, his tone biting. 'I've already been granted access to this room. I'm a regular.'

The member of security who had grabbed him — a powerfully-built Chinese man with a thick jawline, a buzzcut and an earpiece in one ear — creased his mouth into a hard line and narrowed his glare. He could see right through Slater's charade.

Slater wondered what the hell had changed.

'Sir, this way please,' the man said, and the atmosphere shifted.

They know.

Everything came together, a giant synapse firing inside Slater's head that connected the dots. On the way in, no-one had checked how many chips he was carrying — it had been an odd request on the concierge's part to ask in the first place. Slater had gone along with it, in sheer survival mode, not thinking of the ramifications.

They'd caught Samuel Barnes with a hundred thousand dollar Mountain Lion chip in his hands.

Fuck.

They knew Slater was hiding Shien — as soon as he'd pretended to lose the chip gambling at a rival casino, they'd seen straight through the facade and moved to intercept him. They couldn't do it in the lobby because he'd already been on his way up to the VIP room, but here it would be as simple as ushering him out of sight and falling on him in droves.

Slater shot rapid glances in every direction at once. There were dozens of men and women in formal attire dotted around the expanse — far too much collateral. He eyed holsters on the waists of the three men surrounding him. Each of their safeties on their sidearms had been disengaged. He could probably wrestle one weapon free, but three at once — unlikely. Besides, even if he dealt with these men there would be pandemonium in the VIP room. The crowd would surge for the elevators and the emergency stairwells, and it would be simple enough to catch a stray bullet in the chaos.

Too many variables.

Slater ran through every possibility in his head in the time it took the security guard to finish the sentence, 'Sir, this way please.'

Almost immediately, he nodded his understanding, feigning innocence. He raised an eyebrow, subtly questioning where to go.

The three person team settled into a practiced rhythm, one man on either side of Slater with a hand clamped down on each of his shoulders, the third taking up the rear to make sure he didn't make a wild break for it. An effective cordon, but Slater could sense the weakness in their grips. It was a subtle thing, something ordinarily not palpable, but underneath their suits he could sense the soft bodies of undisciplined men.

They might box recreationally at the local combat club on their off days, but they would all crumble against someone like Slater.

Confidence surged through him as they led him along one of the curving walls, keeping out of the way of the patrons. Some glanced in his direction, noting Slater's forceful departure from the premises, but most were focused on the hundreds of thousands of dollars in play on the tables before them.

They wouldn't bat an eyelid if Slater decked all three men right here.

But he didn't, because he knew he would get the opportunity in seconds. Sure enough the trio led him through a narrow door labelled "STAFF ONLY", hurrying him into a claustrophobic corridor with none of the luxuries afforded to the VIP rooms. The hallway provided direct access to the kitchen, where Slater could hear a dozen cooks slaving over hot plates in the distance, preparing gourmet delicacies to be funnelled out to the paying customers.

But there was no-one in sight, except for a fourth security guard striding fast toward them. The party would meet halfway along the corridor — Slater and his three buddies moving one way, the new arrival intercepting them for added support. The guy's face was twisted into a snarl. Dark purple bruising had swollen into place underneath one eyelid. Slater guessed he might have been responsible for Shien.

A second later the man confirmed it, unleashing a tirade.

'You really think you could just snatch someone like her out from underneath us and expect to—?'

His tone swelled to a crescendo, his rant almost complete.

Slater didn't afford him the opportunity.

He shot a dark look to his left, anticipating an instinctual reaction from the guard on that side. The Filipino man responded in predictable fashion. Filled with confidence, satisfied that he'd managed to hurry Slater out of the public eye, he returned the glare with equal verve, offended at Slater's attempt to appear threatening.

Slater hadn't intended to appear menacing.

He just wanted the man to look in his direction.

Without an inch of wind-up he headbutted the guy full in the face.

33

S later's forehead broke the guard's nose and he went down without resistance, letting go of his grip on the shoulder in the process. Slater leapt a full foot into the air and planted both feet on the collapsing guard's chest, pushing as hard as he could.

It achieved two things.

First, it sent the guard with the broken nose clattering into the wall — there was little space to move in such close quarters, which proved cumbersome — and second, it sent Slater careening back into the man on his right. He crushed the second guy against the opposite wall with enough force to squeeze the breath out of his lungs, and as he clattered back to his feet he stumbled once and narrowly avoided a swinging left hook from the guard taking up the rear.

The third man had been in place precisely to prevent Slater from breaking free, but he only had one attempt at a punch before Slater could capitalise. They were operating in the fine gaps that rested between milliseconds of hesitation, and Slater had spent what felt like half his life in those gaps. When he felt the displaced air of the man's overpowered hook swinging through the air beside his ear — the guy clearly had combat training if he could throw a punch that fast — he voluntarily bounced off the opposite wall and delivered a staggering uppercut against the underside of the third guy's chin.

Either a bone in Slater's hand shattered, or the guy's jaw cracked.

He couldn't be entirely sure in the heat of the moment.

He would find out once the adrenalin wore off.

The fourth guy — who had been approaching in a flustered hurry — didn't know how to react to the escalating situation, and chose to merely fall on Slater in a half-hearted attempt to tangle him up for long enough to gain the advantage.

Slater sensed the man bearing down on him and slipped a hand under each of the guy's armpits — known as underhooks in mixed martial arts. It gave him all the leverage, which he used to pivot on the spot and drop the guy on the back of his neck.

In the movies, taking a man to the ground never amounted to much.

In real life, where bodyweight was real and highly dangerous, Slater came down with the point of his elbow on the guy's throat, sandwiching him between the carpet and the weight on top of him.

He spluttered, horrified, his thorax damaged and all the fight sapped out of him.

Slater's mind raced, even as he demolished the four men around him. He noticed the Beretta M9 in the holster at the fourth man's waist while pivoting and thundering an elbow into the side of the second man's head. The guy dropped, shut off at the neurological power switch. Slater turned straight back to the guy with the injured throat and wrenched the Beretta free.

Slater sensed the first man — the one he'd head butted in the face — charging at him. Out of the corner of his eye he spotted hands darting for a holster at the waist. The guy was going for a gun. Violence and testosterone dripped in the air — this was the primal moment when one had to make a decision, regardless of the consequences. There would be no preventing the man from acting, and the distance was too great to subdue the man with his bare hands before the guy could reach for his weapon.

Slater hardened his nerves, twisted at the waist to line up his aim and fired two rounds. One in the chest, one in the head. The man's neck snapped back and he slumped to the carpet with a surprising lack of noise.

Stone dead.

Slater felt nothing. The violence still raged around him, shrouding him in a toxic haze, not allowing him to feel sorry for anyone until the fight had reached its conclusion.

He sensed the man with the damaged throat getting up from underneath him, sweeping his hands through the air in an attempt to throw Slater off-balance and send him falling to the ground.

Slater lined up his free hand and pumped it like a piston into the guy's forehead, bone against bone, rattling the human brain around inside its skull and sending the guy straight back where he lay, this time stripped of his senses.

Emptiness.

Stillness.

Quiet.

Slater knelt amidst his surroundings and focused on breathing deep, controlling himself, preventing any kind of murderous tendencies to follow him through to whatever came next. The life of a man who killed others yet tried to clutch onto some kind of moral compass was a hard life indeed. It took a certain type of compartmentalisation rarely seen in situations such as these. Slater had killed a man and knocked three others unconscious in the space of five seconds, and the all-out brawl had fired his brain into overdrive.

Attempting to bring his cortisol levels back down to normal took horrendous self-control.

The corridor lapsed into silence as he breathed, surrounded by a dead man and three men who might soon follow him if their injuries proved fatal — which they very well could. Nothing in Slater's conscious thoughts dwelled on the punishment he'd exacted — these men had tried to kill him, and wherever they'd been set on taking him would never have bode well for Slater.

He got to his feet, testing his injured leg as he levered himself upright.

Then one of the chefs from the kitchen at the end of the corridor materialised in the open doorway. He stared, mouth agape, at the carnage.

Reluctantly, Slater raised the Beretta to point square between the man's eyes.

34

S later stood uncomfortably still, tapping into a decade of maintaining calm in the most frenzied situations, to the extent where it took the chef a few moments to spot him amidst the sea of crippled bodies. Some were dead, some were injured, but everyone who had come into direct physical contact with Slater wouldn't be moving for quite some time.

Depending on how the chef reacted, he might face a similar predicament.

The man spotted Slater and froze in his tracks, staring down the barrel of the loaded Beretta M9.

Looking directly at his own demise.

Slater tightened his grip on the weapon and made no movement whatsoever — except, after a few seconds of stalemate, to raise one eyebrow. As if questioning what the chef was going to do next.

The man — a European guy in his late twenties — started to speak without moving his lips, effectively transforming into a ventriloquist out of fear. He must have figured that a single jerky, unwarranted move to either side would cause Slater to panic and put a bullet in his brain.

Smart kid, Slater thought.

'Can I walk away?' the guy said, four words that summed up the mortal terror no doubt coursing through his veins.

'Have you done anything wrong?' Slater said, barely raising his voice above a conversational volume.

'Uh...'

'Simple question. Don't overthink it.'

'No.'

'You're not involved?'

'No.'

'You're close with your employers?'

'Not really. I cook.'

'If anyone asks you what happened here... you got any particular allegiance?'

'I just cook.'

'Get out of here.'

The kid didn't move — Slater didn't blame him. His limbs would have locked up upon sight of the Beretta. If he truly did just cook — which Slater had no way of knowing for sure and no intention to hang around questioning him — then the sight of massive violence would freeze him like a deer in headlights.

Either that, or he was a phenomenal actor.

Slater doubted it.

In all likelihood the guy just cooked.

'You heard me?' Slater said.

'I heard you. I'm worried you might shoot me when I move.'

'You don't move in three seconds and I might shoot you.'

A weak threat, and something Slater had no intention of following through with.

But it gave the guy a choice, which he capitalised on by pivoting on his heel and disappearing from sight. He'd been attempting to act casual when he fled, but Slater could see the adrenalin spurring his movements, adding an extra burst of athleticism to his steps. Slater had seen it a thousand times before.

He breathed in deep through his nose, then out through his mouth, composing himself in the sudden silence. He tuned his ears to any suspicious noise from the VIP room outside, but it seemed like business as usual. Even though all-out physical warfare and unsuppressed gunshots caused a racket, Slater imagined the staff-only corridor had been soundproofed in some capacity, in case employees needed to make noise without disturbing the patrons gambling their life savings away.

As he stood motionless, surrounded by dead and unconscious men, he realised he was exactly right.

Act casual.

He tucked the Beretta M9 into the rear of his waistband, re-engaging the safety to ensure he didn't shoot himself and ruin everything he'd worked so hard for. Then he strode straight back out into the VIP room, adopting as relaxed a demeanour as he could manage given the fact he'd been fighting for his life seconds earlier.

Thankfully, Slater had been fighting for his life for countless years.

It had become as monotonous as breathing.

A couple of high-roller gamblers looked his way as he stepped into view, throwing him inquisitive glances as if to say, *What was all that about?*

They must have heard muffled punches — the gunshot reports tearing through the soundproofing.

They'd likely been dragged away by security many times

before, given the track record required to make it into a room as exclusive as this. Monstrous losses brought out the worst in people — Slater had lost count of the number of times he'd seen drunken fits of rage in casinos. Those who security deemed it necessary to remove seldom returned. So it came as a surprise to the whales that had seen him leave to watch him stride straight back into the room like nothing had happened, untouched and unperturbed.

Slater shrugged and gave a sheepish smile, as if to say, *Can't believe I got off so easily.*

No-one spared him a second glance. They returned their attention immediately back to the hundred-thousand dollar chips at play on the tables.

In the end, money trumped any kind of suspicion.

It simply wasn't worth the mental distraction.

Slater shoved his hands into his pockets to buy himself time on the stroll across the room, searching every corner for any sign of additional security looking his way. There were a couple of guards dotted around the outer perimeter of the room, but none had noticed his presence yet. He wasn't even sure if they knew of their co-workers' business — in all likelihood he was no more suspicious than any of the other patrons.

But, as he ducked his head to avoid detection and wandered in the rough direction of the entrance, he realised there was nothing he could feasibly achieve on this floor.

The head of security would have realised Slater's true intentions by now. He might already be storming toward the VIP room, surrounded by his men. There were countless variables — had Forrest been watching surveillance footage upstairs? Had the triad spotted him en route to Mountain Lion after identifying him as Shien's protector? How long could he leave Shien alone, bunkered down in the hotel room, before her father and his powerful friends tore Macau apart searching for her?

He was out of his depth, and he knew it. Trying to manoeuvre himself into the dark heart of Mountain Lion in a tactical way would almost definitely result in failure.

This far along the journey, he would have to brute-force his way through the final leg.

A thought flickered through his head.

You're barely getting started. You've achieved nothing.

That was reality. He realised he'd barely scratched the surface of what was happening in the underbelly of Mountain Lion — he had no proof of any kind of wrongdoing whatsoever, besides a small army of security intent on silencing him earlier. They wanted Shien back for a reason — if he discovered that reason had anything to do with his gut feeling, there would be hell to pay.

You won't be able to do anything if you don't make it off this floor.

He stormed straight out of the VIP room, speeding past an oblivious security guard in the process of picking his fingernails. The man either had no idea who Slater was or was so inept at his job that he couldn't see what lay right in front of him. Slater made it three feet past the guy before he raised his head — in Slater's peripheral vision, he watched the man recognise what stood in front of him.

'Hey... you're—'

The guy had been in the process of getting to his feet. For some reason, no matter how experienced the adversary, they were always surprised if Slater struck them in the middle of a sentence. Something about interrupting the theatrics felt unnatural — how could Slater ruin a moment by not allowing the guy to finish his words?

But that was exactly how it unfolded, and as usual it

paid off. The guy's jaw was slack halfway through the line delivery, clearly intent on causing a scene and pulling him up in front of the rest of the VIP room. Slater's fist scythed through the air with a practiced whip-like motion and caught the man directly on the chin, whipping his head to the side in unnatural fashion.

The lights went out, and he crumpled.

It had taken a half-second to complete the action — Slater found that all the suspicion of a violent confrontation came from the immediate aftermath, when adrenalin was pumping and cortisol was shooting through the roof. So he kept his pulse low and caught the man by the shoulders even as his knees were giving out.

He gently lowered the guy to the ground, loudly proclaiming, 'Whoa, whoa, whoa, you okay, buddy? What's wrong? Oh, no...'

Genuine concern laced his tone, and that was what drew the most attention. The facade wouldn't hold up for long — some of the patrons would have seen the punch out of the corner of their eye, but it had happened so fast they wouldn't have been sure quite what they'd witnessed. Slater's subsequent demeanour would confuse the hell out of them for just long enough to suppress a full-scale panic.

Slater finished lowering the guy to the ground and slipped straight out of the VIP room.

'Hey...' a voice cried.

He ignored it.

He bee-lined straight for the same door he'd seen the head of security slip through moments earlier and barged straight into a restricted area, reaching for the Beretta M9 simultaneously.

35

The two triad henchmen stepped into the marble lobby of one of Mountain Lion's rival casinos with purpose in their stride. They were headed for the front desk, adamant that their anonymous tip would pay off and that soon the situation would be back under control.

Right now, they weren't sure exactly who wanted them dead.

Seemingly everyone.

As they strode across the spotless floor, Tak spoke first. 'How the hell did Forrest find out?'

'You tell me,' Antoine said.

'We fucked up. There's no going back until we sort this out. Jerome told us as much.'

Antoine pressed two fingers to his eyeballs, riding out a wave of stress. 'What did he say exactly?'

'He asked us if the accusations were true. I told him they were — we don't know how much evidence he has. He could have been testing us — if we lied, he could have killed us. So I told him we did it, and he said he appreciated the honesty but he needed to distance himself from us until Forrest calmed down. Forrest is one of his highest paying customers, after all.'

'You think that's a lie?'

'No way to know. But you want to disobey him?'

'No. Are you sure this is the right move, though? You have more experience in this game.'

'Forrest knows we stole money from him,' Tak hissed. 'An obscene amount of money. Just think about that for a second. Think about what kind of a person Peter Forrest is. You think he'll ever let us off the hook?'

Antoine shook his head. 'That's a powerful enemy to have. He could pay the triad to kill us themselves.'

'He sure could. He could do a million things.'

'But going up against him isn't going to solve anything,' Antoine said.

Tak froze in the middle of the lobby and grabbed his naive colleague's shoulder. 'Think about what you just said. Where's it coming from?'

'What?'

'What part of you is saying that?'

'I ... I don't know.'

'You're scared of going up against him. Deep down you know it's the only way. We need to get rid of him and then melt into the background.'

'We can't do that alone.'

'No, we can't. That's why we're here. Are you following?'

Antoine looked around, and finally gazed up at the ceiling far above them. Almost staring straight through the solid surface. Searching the floors above with his mind. Something clicked. 'Oh.'

'Right.'

'This could go disastrously.'

'So could almost anything we do right now. This is the world, Antoine. This is what things look like outside your bubble.'

'I don't see a solution to this.'

Tak pointed to the ceiling. 'There's one up there. Now let's go get her.'

He approached the front desk, intent on using every shred of leverage he'd accumulated over his time as a career gangster to gain them the upper hand.

～

THIRTY MINUTES LATER, Tak and Antoine exited a lavish elevator, rejuvenated by fresh hope.

'They sure were accomodating to your demands.'

'I've done favours for their head office. Long ago.'

'Did I really have to wait outside?'

'I'm welcome in their inner circle. You're not. They don't trust you.'

'They should.'

'We got what we needed.'

'You sure you saw the footage correctly? I don't want to run into him up here.'

'He entered the building with the girl. He left alone. I triple-checked.'

'So this shouldn't be a problem.'

'It won't be.'

'Then why am I nervous?'

'Because you're used to things going your way. This is uncharted territory.'

'It sure is.'

'You'll get used to it. We might be on the back foot forever, if this doesn't pay off. And it probably won't.'

'Why are you saying that? For fuck's sake...'

'Better to accept reality for what it is than live in a pleasant illusion.'

'I'm not in an illusion. But you saw what this guy did to Forrest's men. And our own. You heard the reports coming out of the building on Beco da Perola? There's at least a dozen men dead. Most of them Forrest's. You think that's someone we can manipulate?'

'He has a weakness,' Tak muttered.

Without elaborating, he slid a keycard gifted to him by upper management into its slot underneath a polished door handle and pushed the broad wooden door at the end of the corridor wide open. It swung inward silently, revealing a luxurious presidential suite that a man who went by the name of Will Slater had booked hours previously.

If all went according to plan, they would find the girl still here.

'What if he told her to shoot anyone on sight?' Antoine muttered, his voice barely audible.

Tak grunted with hostility and slid a giant Desert Eagle handgun out of a custom-made holster at his side. 'It's a fucking kid, Antoine.'

Nevertheless, the sheer silence of the suite hung thick over them in a tense shroud. Tak stepped forward, tentatively moving through the open doorway, scolding himself for being so nervous to apprehend a nine-year-old girl.

He sensed movement to his left as he stepped into the main section of the suite, and wheeled on the spot, his senses firing, the barrel of the Desert Eagle coming up to lock onto its target.

With a sly smile, he realised he shouldn't have been so terrified.

Shien sat at one end of the giant dining room table,

unarmed, shaking with fear. She had known the sound of the front door opening could only spell disaster, but had effectively frozen in fright. She was, after all, just a child.

'Hey, honey,' Tak said, leering at their prize. 'You remember us?'

36

S later stormed into the security hub with devastation on his mind. The door was locked, but he simply hurled his weight at the centre mass, spurred on by adrenalin and immune to pain. The lock audibly snapped and he hustled straight into the room beyond.

The broad space was almost the same size as the VIP room he'd just exited from — Slater took one look at the bank of flatscreen televisions covering the closest wall and realised this place acted as the central security node for the entire floor. Its surveillance cameras displayed footage of five or six different rooms, each handling millions of dollars a minute as obscene quantities of casino chips flew across the tables. The rows of desks in front of the screens were surprisingly unpopulated — Slater figured he'd already dealt with the bulk of security on this level.

Left remaining was the head of security — the same short, rotund man who'd confronted him earlier — and a pair of heavyset guards complete with earpieces and sidearms fastened inside holsters at their waists.

A grave mistake, Slater thought.

Yet he understood the complexity of a structure like Mountain Lion Casino & Resorts, which meant these men might not be directly involved with the dark underbelly. In all likelihood they were, but Slater didn't want that playing on his conscience.

Thankfully, the pair had been in the process of responding to the commotion — the head of security must have seen Slater's brawl on the live feeds. The guards almost ran directly into Slater as he stormed into the room, taking them entirely by surprise.

Close range.

Slater smashed the blunt surface of the Beretta's magazine base into the bridge of the closest man's nose. He went down howling, unable to help himself, and Slater followed through with a thunderous front kick into the chest of the second guy, knocking him back into one of the desks. The guy sprawled over its surface in awkward fashion, destroying a bank of computers in the process.

Slater stomped down on the first guy's forehead as he hit the ground, a gruesome move to utilise but one that would ensure separation from consciousness. He held back enough to avoid permanent injury, instead knocking the guy out and throwing off his equilibrium for the foreseeable future.

Without hesitating, he used the first guy's temple as a springboard to launch himself onto the second guy, coming down on top of him with enough force to pummel his sternum, winding him. Slater followed up with a series of devastating elbows, restraining himself to ensure he didn't accidentally kill the man but dishing out a suitable amount of damage to prevent the guy from fighting back.

Out of breath, he crawled off the second motionless form, panting as he righted himself and aimed the Beretta across the room at the small, timid man — the only guy left awake in the entire space.

'None of that went the way you expected, did it?' Slater said.

The man didn't respond. He feigned some kind of vague hand gesture.

Slater narrowed his eyes.

'Are you trying to pretend you don't speak English?'

The man said nothing.

'We were talking earlier. I'll give you three seconds to answer me before I shoot you in the leg.'

The man visibly paled. He opened his mouth, searching for the correct choice of words but finding nothing.

'Just tell the truth,' Slater said.

'What do you want from me?'

'Information.'

'I cannot tell you anything. My employer will kill me. And it will be slow. Worse than anything you could do.'

'Your employer has enough problems as it is,' Slater said.

Still facing the man, he backtracked to the door and kicked it shut by ramming his heel into the edge of the wood. It slammed home, re-locking with a distinct *click*.

'You got any more men coming?' Slater said.

'You killed them all.'

'I killed one man. Because he tried to shoot me. Other than that, your men will be fine. They might have headaches for a few days. Nothing aspirin doesn't fix. Although, if you don't answer my questions with enough believability, I might get the wrong idea and go back to murder every single one of them. Understand?'

'What do you want from me?' the man repeated.

'I told you.'

'I told you also — there's nothing I can give you.'

'Yes, there is.'

'I'm sorry, sir. You will have to kill me.'

'It won't just be that. If I find out you're doing what I think you're doing, I'll make it slower and more painful than your employer ever could.'

'I doubt that. You don't have much time with me before others realise what's happening.'

'Do you keep young girls on this floor to please horny old men? Nine-year-olds — that kind of age?'

The man visibly froze, his features locking up at the sudden inquiry. 'What?! No, of course not.'

Slater believed him. It was hard to fake outrage of that kind — it seemed the man genuinely reviled being grouped in with that sort of crowd. Nevertheless, Slater kept his aim rigid, ensuring the barrel remained unwavering in the air, pointed directly at the centre mass of the man's forehead.

'Why should I believe you?'

The man squirmed, visibly uncomfortable, horrified at the thought of Slater thinking he was lying. Beneath everything, it seemed the guy had a shred of integrity. 'I swear.'

'Thought you weren't supposed to tell me anything.'

'I do not associate myself with those people.'

'Those people? Who are those people?'

The guy clammed up.

Slater surged across the room, sidestepping one of the unconscious bodyguards. He closed the space between them and clamped his meaty fingers over the guy's throat, squeezing hard enough to send veins protruding out of his forehead, turning his cheeks a deep shade of red.

When he released his grip, he waited a beat for the man to draw a staggering breath of air — then he jammed the barrel of the Beretta down the man's throat at the opportune moment, capitalising on the brief window of opportunity the guy afforded him.

The head of security coughed, spluttered, and his cheeks turned dark red. The shade of beetroot. He recoiled away from Slater, humiliated, in pain, horrifically uncomfortable and vulnerable.

Slater wrenched the gun out from between the man's lips, bringing a strand of saliva along with it. 'You're going to answer me.'

'They're not on this floor.'

'So something's happening in this casino. And you know about it.'

The guy threw both hands in the air, an exaggerated gesture to hammer his point home. 'What do you expect me to do? You know what happens if I talk about it?'

'You die?'

'Exactly.'

Slater jammed the Beretta against the man's temple — it was wet from the insides of his mouth. He squirmed, but didn't dare move. Slater moved the weapon back and forth against the wrinkles in his forehead, accompanied by a sickening squelching sound. 'You die right now unless you talk. You ready for that?'

'You are a good man, then?' the head of security said. 'If you are interested in these bad things happening? You must be some kind of vigilante?'

'Something like that.'

'Then you will not kill me. You are too noble.'

'One of the men underneath you is dead. Two, actually, if you count that elevator guard you were searching for earlier. I hit another one with so many elbows that his chances of recovery are less than slim. And none of them were as implicit in this scheme as you are. What do you think I'll do to you?'

'All talk,' the guy muttered with a wry smile.

Slater seized hold of his wrist, exposing the bare skin as the cuff of his dress shirt's sleeve rolled down. He pressed the Beretta against the tendons in the guy's hand and fired a shot, bracing for the recoil. The gun kicked back in his palm and gore showered across the bank of monitors opposite them. The guy's hand would prove useless for months, if not years, to come. In all likelihood, the limb would never be the same.

The guy howled and screamed and broke out in a cold sweat — Slater gave him no opportunity to recover. He clamped the same hand around his throat and began choking the life out of him, digging in hard enough for the man to think he was on death's door.

When Slater released his hold, the man spluttered and choked back tears, clutching his destroyed hand to his chest and staring up at Slater with venom in his eyes.

'There are certain levels of this casino reserved for human filth,' Slater snarled. 'Am I right?'

The guy couldn't resist any longer. Sweating and crying, he nodded. 'Yes.'

'You know what happens on those floors.'

'Yes.'

'You've done nothing to stop it.'

'I got no choice.'

'There's always a choice. You know which floors handle young girls?'

The man stared at him with visible disbelief. 'No... what did you say?'

'You heard me.'

'I don't know anything about that. I swear.'

'I'm sure you've heard rumours.'

'I always thought they were just rumours.'

'Bullshit.'

'What do you want me to do? I need this job to provide for my family. Just because people on other floors are doing—'

Slater backhanded him across the face, cutting him off. 'You could have anonymously gone to the police. Or anyone, really.'

'Look...' the man said, clearly frustrated. 'Who the fuck are you to tell me what to do?'

Slater smirked. 'I was wondering how long it'd take you to get angry. I'm not going to kill you, but I couldn't care less how much damage you take. I can see it in your eyes. You know about a single floor. Worse than all the others. Right?'

The man nodded. 'I won't lie to you anymore. Just don't kill me.'

'I think I've caused you enough distress.'

Relief plastered the guy's pale complexion. 'Thank you.'

That was intentional, you idiot, Slater thought. *Now you think we're best friends. Now you're going to tell me everything you know.*

37

'Y**ou know there's a floor for the scum of the earth but you don't spend much time thinking about it because you'd prefer not to know it exists. But your job involves sending people there occasionally — customers on this floor who show darker tendencies. Right?'

A pause. Then the guy realised Slater was onto him, and nodded.

'I don't know what they do there,' the man said. 'I never asked.'

'You must have been told what to look for.'

'If they seem ... I don't know the English word.'

'Seedy?'

'Something like that. If they look like they want something more than gambling. Something worse.'

Slater felt rage building, but he crushed it. He needed this man on his side.

'You sent them to take advantage of young girls,' Slater said. 'You got kids? You said something about a family.'

'Two.'

'How old?'

'Eight and eleven.'

'Girls?'

'Yes.'

'Imagine the men you sent away naked, on top of your children. You still happy about what you do?'

'I've never been happy about it. But I don't think about it.'

'You ever in contact with those secret floors?'

The guy shook his head. 'Each of the floors in this building is run by a different junket. We don't deal with each other. Only the boss.'

'Junket?'

'Illegal organisations, run by whoever. Triad. Private owners. They each operate their own economy. So, on our floor, we have full discretion over what we want to do with the gambling profits coming in. We can give wealthy customers lines of credit — that sort of thing. Each floor does its own thing, and we all report to Mr. Forrest. He gets a cut of everything.'

Slater listened to the spiel, formulating a plan in his head. 'I killed a couple of your men. I knocked almost all the rest unconscious. There'll be hell to pay when they come to and the bodies are found...'

The man said nothing, frozen in fright. He had no idea where the conversation was headed. As far as he was concerned, a psychopathic killer was in the process of determining whether he lived or died.

Slater reached into his jeans pocket and withdrew his smartphone — in all the commotion of the last twenty-four hours the screen had cracked in several places, turning the display into a spider-web of shattered glass. Nevertheless the phone still worked. He unlocked it, scrolled to the inbuilt voice recording application, and hovered a finger over the *record* button.

He tilted the phone toward the head of security, and raised the Beretta in his other hand.

'You're going to say these words,' he said, keeping his voice low. '*It took you long enough. You got the girl okay? Your payment's here.* If you say anything other than those thirteen words I'll put a bullet in your head, and I won't feel a shred of remorse about it.'

The guy flapped his lips, speechless. He hadn't quite worked out what Slater meant yet.

Slater gave him no time to think.

'Go,' he said.

He hit *record.*

'It took you long enough,' the man said, struggling to stop his tone from wavering. 'You got the girl okay? Your payment's here.'

Slater didn't take his finger off the *record* button.

'I ran into some issues,' he said. 'When Forrest realises you're going to the police with this, he'll tear you apart. I want to be out of the country before that happens. You're a brave man for standing up to someone like that. The cops will handle everything. They'll make things right. Good luck, my friend.'

The head of security stared at Slater with his mouth agape, the horror of what he'd implicated himself in dawning on him. When a man's reputation hung on the line — as Forrest's did with these secrets — he would go to unfathomable lengths to protect himself and save face.

The man no doubt understood how doomed he was if anyone in Forrest's employ heard those words.

Slater ended the recording. For good measure he dragged the file onto the front page of his home screen, ensuring it wouldn't take much of a search to find it. He tucked the phone back into his pocket and smiled.

'Please,' the man said. 'Don't show that to anyone. I will die. Have you stolen one of Forrest's girls?'

'I'm not showing a soul. But if I wind up dead in this casino, you can be damn sure that file will turn up on a rudimentary search of my body.'

Everything dawned on the man at once. He squirmed uneasily in his seat. 'You want the worst floor in the casino?'

Slater nodded. 'Yes, thanks.'

'Level 44.'

'Can I get there using the elevators?'

'Yes. You won't be allowed in, though. It takes an invite.'

'Or a recommendation from this floor. From you.'

The guy had broken out in an uncontrollable sweat. 'Fuck.'

Slater recognised the threat had dissipated — no-one in the immediate vicinity was looking to take his head off. He lowered the Beretta to his side.

'They search you when you get to level 44?' he said.

'Of course,' the head of security said. 'No weapons.'

'I'll drop it just before I get to the elevator. That way you can't kill me on this floor and destroy the recording.'

'I don't think I could kill you even if you dropped it now.'

'Your men might try.'

'Seems they already have.'

All the urgency had sapped out of the man — his lackadaisical demeanour stunned Slater. The audio recording had manipulated the guy into compliance so effortlessly that it felt unnatural. But all the resistance had left his body at once, his shoulders slumping forward and his expression one of dejection.

Slater spun on his heel, passing the two bodyguards

only just beginning to crawl out of unconsciousness, and wrenched the door to the security hub open.

'Remember,' he said. 'If I get to that floor and it turns out I'm not welcome, it'll be your head when that audio surfaces.'

The man said nothing. He simply gulped back fear.

'Make the call. And do it fast. It's in your best interests to make sure I get out of this casino alive.'

The guy nodded. 'I'll do my best. Please don't get yourself killed. You don't know what kind of man Mr. Forrest is.'

'I have an idea of what he's like. It won't turn out well for you.'

Little did the head of security know that Forrest was no doubt facing a relentless torrent of issues, given the mess Slater had become entangled in. But he had no intention of solving the man's problems — only worsening them. Every sign led to a dark secret on level 44, one that involved innocent children and disgusting predators.

And Slater was set to stride into the heart of it.

He shut the door behind him — confident that the head of security would do everything in his power to assist him — and made straight for the bank of elevators. He passed the entrance to the VIP room along the way, flashing a glance inside to check on the situation.

Two uninhibited security guards had wandered across the room to tend to the man Slater had knocked unconscious. Neither of them must have seen the strike take place, because they were treating him like someone who'd fainted. The guy had his head bowed and his rear end planted on one of the chairs running along the curving wall of the VIP room. He had his elbows on his knees and he was taking deep, rasping breaths, still disoriented by the blow. Soon his cheek would swell and his memory would return.

By then, Slater would be long gone.

The customers were entirely ignorant of the guards, treating them like they weren't there. They held money in higher regard than the wellbeing of the staff surrounding them. Bouts of fainting were none of their concern.

But soon the men Slater beat down in the corridor would wake up, and they would call for reinforcements, and shit would truly hit the fan.

By then Slater would be in the elevator, and it would be up to the head of security to ensure he didn't get bottle-necked into a trap.

He hoped the man would do his job well, and contain the panic to a single floor of the Mountain Lion complex.

He called for an elevator with a digital interface built into the far wall, and one arrived within seconds. As the doors slid open, he spotted a large opaque decorative vase propped up on an antique wooden table near the end of the corridor and dropped the Beretta M9 into its neck with as much practiced nonchalance as he could manage.

Nothing to see here.

Slater noticed there was someone inside the cable car, but he didn't think twice before stepping straight through the doors — any kind of hesitation would draw suspicion.

The doors sealed, trapping both occupants in silence.

Slater entered his intended destination into the digital display, and crossed his hands behind his back as the elevator lurched up the shaft.

He craned his neck to manage a sideways glance at the man alongside him. The guy was roughly the same height as Slater, in his late forties, with short salt-and-pepper hair. Slater noticed dried blood underneath the man's nose, and deemed it prudent to get a proper look.

He made eye contact with the guy, and stared straight into a mask of pain.

The man had stifled any audible exclamation of agony but his face told a different story, wracked by a combination of stewing anger and discontent. He clutched one of his hands awkwardly against his chest. Slater stared at the appendage and noticed it was wrapped in a blood-soaked cloth.

The guy shrugged, as nonchalant as one could be given the circumstances.

'Rough night?' Slater said.

'Something like that,' the guy muttered, returning his gaze to the ground.

They lapsed into silence — Slater didn't deem it necessary to prod. They were two men in a dangerous world, each carving their own path through it. Slater had no idea what the man did, and he didn't care. He was focused on his own trajectory.

Then the man's gaze wandered to the digital interface displaying the prominent number *44,* and his expression changed.

Recognition spread across his face.

In some capacity, Slater realised this man knew what was going on behind closed doors in Mountain Lion.

Was it worth pursuing?

He wrestled with his thoughts as the elevator powered toward its destination.

38

The matte black limousine with dark tinted windows screeched into the underground parking lot in a burst of energy. It braked hard in a soulless concrete space with white walls and grey floors, and its rear door flew open with the kind of urgency that signified the presence of a desperate man.

Peter Forrest stepped out into home territory, but there was no sigh of relief to be found. In fact his motions came with a certain twisting sensation in his gut, undermining everything he did. He couldn't shake the feeling that anything he attempted from this point onward would prove entirely useless. The world was falling apart around him — the two missing digits on his right hand barely crossed his mind.

He clutched the wet crimson cloth tighter over the ragged stumps and stumbled away from the limousine. He'd barely conversed with the driver throughout the journey, but the man knew what to do.

Shut his goddamn mouth.

Forrest couldn't expose any weakness, and if rumours

spread about his predicament the end would come faster. That was half the reason he hadn't received a moment of medical attention since the beating. Both public and private hospitals were out of the question — the triads had infiltrated society in Macau to an unimaginable extent. Anything Forrest wanted would need to be acquired from within these very walls.

He made a mental note to call the resident medical team up to his suite as soon as possible.

It sank into the pit of a thousand other churning thoughts and became lost in the madness.

He made for a bank of disused elevators — these shafts were cordoned away from public view, reserved for Forrest's high-roller clients with all manner of vices. They led to the VIP rooms and the private brothels and the ... darker places.

Another problem, a voice in the back of his head whispered. *If the authorities find the girl you're ruined, too.*

The girl.

The goddamn girl.

Everything came back to the girl.

As soon as she'd been whisked out from underneath him all hell had broken loose, and Forrest couldn't imagine order being restored anytime soon.

If at all.

He slammed the call button on the dusty panel alongside the elevators as the limousine peeled away and disappeared into the bowels of Mountain Lion's underground maze. Forrest had issued construction of ten levels underneath each tower. Some for parking. Some for maintenance and storage supplies. And some for...

Well, he didn't like to dwell on those choices.

He'd made them regardless, and now they would cost him his life and his reputation.

Unless he could pull off a miracle.

A lavish elevator arrived seconds later and he limped into its comforting interior, surrounded by luxury but overwhelmed with burdens. He thumbed the command to ascend to the highest floor the elevator could reach — which would deposit him at one end of the rooftop emporium — and hoped his journey would go uninterrupted.

When the cable car slowed to a halt to receive a patron on level 22, Forrest bit back fury and opted to seethe silently in the corner. The doors whisked open, and a powerfully built black man in a wool jumper and designer jeans sauntered into the elevator and tapped a command into the digital display alongside him.

In his hurry, Forrest had almost forgotten what he looked like.

It didn't take long for the man to notice. His eyes wandered over to Forrest and he stared at him for a beat, clearly shocked. Forrest shrugged.

'Rough night?'

'Something like that.'

Forrest was in no mood for conversation — especially not with a random stranger — and it was only when he caught a glimpse of the number 44 displayed on the digital interface that his eyes widened and realisation set in.

You dirty bastard, he thought.

Level 44 didn't accept guests without a rigorous pre-screening method. Junkets from various levels selected the vilest customers from their gaming rooms and sent them on their way if they expressed interest in paying a premium for a different kind of service.

Forrest had realised long ago that the fastest way to turn a profit was to satiate all needs, no matter how strange the requests.

The stranger, the more lucrative, he'd found.

The man seemed to recognise that Forrest was onto him. He froze up, rigid, thoughts no doubt churning through his head.

The elevator slowed, and the doors slid open to reveal a nondescript corridor, albeit a little darker and moodier than other floors. Of course none of the sensitive business took place up here — the level operated as a central node to figure out what the customer wanted, and to transact payment.

The real business took place far below Mountain Lion, in sections of the complex that no-one could accidentally stumble across.

The stranger didn't give Forrest a second look — clearly ashamed by his actions. He strode straight out into the lowly lit hallway, and the doors immediately closed on him.

Have fun, Forrest thought.

He continued to the penthouse level. The elevator beeped a confirmation and deposited him onto the same walkway where he'd handled the baccarat dealer the night before.

He took one glance at the vast emporium lying dormant, sweeping out in every direction all around him — the upper level of Mountain Lion hadn't been opened for business ever since shit had hit the fan. Forrest needed the space to breathe, to de-stress and mull over his options without worrying about civilians staring up at him. He paused on the walkway for a moment before crossing it and covering the three flights of stairs up to his penthouse.

The entire suite had been crammed into the uppermost portion of the glass-domed exterior, wedged into a private alcove like a giant chunk had been gouged out of the wall. Forrest had explicitly requested the design during Mountain Lion's construction — it afforded him a view over the entire emporium, as well as the elevated jungle he'd constructed to house the two Tsavo lions.

Sometimes he looked down on his empire, searching for a glimpse of the pair of beasts amidst the lush canopy of leaves. Every now and then he managed to spot them, and they charged him with confidence.

Now, every ounce of willpower had been sapped from him.

With heavy limbs, his footsteps echoing in the cavernous space, he ducked through to a winding stairwell twisting up through the foundations of the building. They culminated at the entrance to his suite. He stepped through into a world of luxury, a hollow and broken shell of a man.

He slumped to the floor just inside the entranceway, next to the chunk of plaster he'd kicked out of the wall. The weight of the world rested squarely on his shoulders.

He thought of level 44.

He thought of how fast he'd sunk into corruption.

He realised — if he had even a hope of surviving the coming chaos — he would need to take drastic measures.

He slid his phone out of his pocket and dialled a number saved simply as "Enforcers."

It was answered in moments.

'Yes?' the gruff voice on the other end of the line said.

'Are you ready to roll?'

'Always. That's what you pay us for.'

'I need you.'

'Where? Macau?'

'Definitely Macau. I need you in this very building.'

A pause. 'I don't follow.'

'How much do you know about level 44?'

'Enough.'

'You know where that floor leads?'

'Yeah.'

'You know how to follow every trail to its conclusion?'

'I'm sure we can work it out.'

'You're one of the only people who knows the extent of what I do. I need you on your A game.'

'When am I not?'

'Okay. I'm giving the go ahead. Shut it all down.'

'Loose ends?'

'None.'

'That'll be messy. That's dozens and dozens of people. Staff, customers. The lot.'

'All of it. Shut it down.'

'If we do... I'll have to bury my head in the sand for the rest of my life.'

'I can't let anyone trace those businesses back to me.'

'So end them quietly, boss. Don't do this.'

Forrest smashed his good hand against the wooden floor, hard enough to come close to breaking a bone. He winced in pain, but it stifled the rage. 'I didn't call you to talk me out of it. I called you to do what I ask.'

'You're telling me and my men to cause a massacre. I don't take it lightly.'

'I don't say it lightly. Know that there's no other option.'

The man on the other end of the line paused. 'You're fucked, aren't you, Peter?'

'Yes. Yes I am.'

'Shutting the floor down won't change a thing, then.'

'It might. It's the only choice I've got.'

'Is this a direct order?'

Forrest took a deep breath. 'Yes.'

'Then I won't say anymore. It's what I signed up for.'

'Good luck.'

'We won't need it.'

'I know. I think I'm talking to myself…'

The line went dead, and Forrest dropped the phone. He was left alone in his opulent penthouse, considering the gravity of what he'd ordered.

39

S later sensed the deprivation in the air the second he stepped out of the elevator.

He'd elected to leave the battered man beside him at peace — even if the guy knew what went on within level 44, there was no way to discern his level of involvement.

He would live to see another day.

Besides, Slater had issues of greater importance on his mind.

He stepped into a dark corridor with moody lighting, aware that he was unarmed, wondering what would transpire next. Underneath his steely demeanour he could sense inklings of rage trying to fight their way to the surface.

Memories from a different time.

A more vulnerable time.

He could mentally picture every acute sensation of helplessness — knowing where his mother had been taken, but powerless to stop it.

He wasn't powerless anymore.

He wondered how long it would take to snap.

The elevators doors sealed, and Slater found himself alone in an unknown corridor. He sensed the building all around him — boxing him in, pressing down on him, surrounding him. He had willingly headed straight into the madness, and he was relying on the actions of a man he'd blackmailed to ensure he made it out the other side alive.

What would the head of security do?

Help him — or take a risk and have him arrested?

The answer would come soon enough.

Slater stood there, his boots sinking into plush carpet, his breathing shallow, waiting for the slightest sound of movement. Ahead the corridor twisted ever so slightly to the left, so the end was concealed from view. He assumed it had been designed that way deliberately, to leave new arrivals in a state of confusion, stuck in limbo while they waited for someone to greet them.

Maybe that made them inclined to pay more.

Set them on edge, right off the bat.

It sure worked to throw Slater off his game.

He stood awkwardly, waiting, watching, wishing for the familiar bulge of a firearm on his hip but finding no reprieve.

Suddenly, footsteps sounded ahead. More than one person. Coming at him fast.

The blood drained from his face.

They would appear around the corner at any moment, armed to the teeth. There was nothing to hide behind, no doorways to duck through. Slater began to understand what a devastating predicament he'd got himself into when a man and a woman in formal corporate attire hurried into view, flustered and out of breath. Both were Asian, in their thirties, and both had no visible weapons on their person.

They weren't charging at him like enemies.

They were charging at him as if they'd dropped the ball themselves.

Slater understood. The head of security must have made the call to inform the staff on level 44 right as Slater got into the elevator. Obviously, customer satisfaction reigned supreme when dealing with such sensitive circumstances. He guessed there was always someone waiting to greet new arrivals, and the only reason for his lack of service was due to the late notice.

These members of staff had been inhospitable, which put them on the back foot straight away.

Slater capitalised on their unease.

'Took you long enough,' he said, his tone curt.

They pulled to a halt in front of him, still adjusting their behaviour, sliding into the polite and pleasant demeanour atypical of a resort's front-of-house. Juxtaposed against the sickening stench of despair in the atmosphere, it rubbed Slater the wrong way.

He wouldn't have to play the part for much longer.

'We do apologise, sir,' the man said, his English perfect. 'We were told you were on your way at the last second, unfortunately.'

'You usually get more notice?'

The woman nodded hard, her mannerisms exaggerated. 'Yes, sir. We need time to provide the best service we possibly can.'

'Well, you've got a lot of ground to make up then, don't you?' Slater said.

All the scorn and outrage of a pompous prick, he thought.

Just what he was going for.

'I believe we can do that,' the man said. 'If you would, please—'

He gestured down the corridor with an outstretched hand, ushering Slater along.

'Where are we going?' Slater said.

'Somewhere more private, where we can discuss what you're looking for today.'

'We can't discuss that here?'

'No, sir. We employ discretion here. It's for your own benefit.'

'Very well.'

The pair parted to allow Slater through, and they followed him at a brisk walk as he strode deeper into the floor. As he walked along the curvature of the hallway, the lighting seemed to fade, the shadows amplifying in the lowlight. Slater doubted the choice was for aesthetics — if anything, it seemed to hide the true intentions of the staff on this floor. He found the quietness unnerving, but what had he been expecting? Clearly it would be in upper management's best interests to keep the number of staff aware of these practices at a minimum.

Which made him wonder who the man in the elevator had been.

Peter Forrest? he thought.

Perhaps.

For now, he would focus on what he could control.

The pair of Mountain Lion staff led him into a sitting room packed with traditional Victorian decor. A polished oak statue of a snarling lion sat dormant in one corner of the room, awash in flickering shadows as a raging fire crackled in a broad fireplace. In front of the mantel rested two hard leather couches with wooden armrests on either side, facing one another directly to allow for conversation by the fireside.

Slater grew sick to his stomach as he sat on one of the

couches, allowing the pair following him to slide quietly into their respective places opposite. The silence that unfolded was not a pleasant one — it was laced with the uncertainty and illegality dripping in the air.

The fire crackled, and the pair studied him.

He stared straight back at them, considering the act of killing both of them, and finding no remorse anywhere in his mind. He imagined anyone in his shoes with sadistic tendencies would feel comfortable right now — they were isolated from the rest of the world, burrowed into a private refuge to cave into their most twisted desires.

'I hope your screening wasn't too intrusive,' the woman said. 'You must understand why we need a strict interview system.'

Slater connected the dots in a brief flash of thoughts, assuming the head of security wanted him to possess the upper hand and would therefore have made his arrival seem as unsuspicious as possible. If there were rigorous entry protocols to deem Slater applicable for the services on level 44, the head of security would have told them he'd passed with flying colours.

The man's own reputation was on the line also.

'It didn't bother me. I've done this type of thing before.'

They tried to conceal it, but both their shoulders slumped ever so slightly, some of the tension dissipating as they realised Slater had experience in these kinds of circumstances. He wondered if the difficulty of conversation increased with debuting psychopaths, men and women who gave into their vices for the first time in the comforting lure of Mountain Lion.

'What type of thing?' the man said. 'So we're clear…'

Slater feigned hesitation.

'You can tell us,' the woman said. 'Anything goes on this

floor, sir. We are here for your service. You shouldn't feel shame — it is perfectly normal.'

'Girls,' Slater said, acting as if he were embarrassed.

In truth, he was crushing down a rage so dark he didn't know how he might react three seconds from now. He didn't let it show, at all costs.

He needed visual proof.

Then he would turn destructive.

'What age?' the man said, with as much weight as if they were discussing what to select from the breakfast menu at the buffet.

'No older than ten,' Slater said.

'We happen to specialise in that field,' the woman said. 'But we charge quite a price. We have to preface all discussion with that disclaimer — I'm sure you understand.'

'How much?'

'What are you looking for?'

'To spend the night here.'

'A full twenty-four hours will cost you one million Hong Kong Dollars.'

'I can do that,' Slater said. He rummaged in his pocket and came out with a pale orange casino chip. 'These are the equivalent of—'

'Yes, sir,' the man said, taking the chip with a wry smile. 'USD chips. For the convenience of our American guests. A service we provide for peace of mind.'

Slater plucked a second chip out of his pocket and handed it over in succession. 'That comes to two hundred thousand USD, which is one-point-five million HKD if I'm not mistaken.'

'Will you be needing change?' the woman said.

'I was wondering if you could throw on a few bonuses for a hefty tip.'

'Such as?'

'Two girls. For twenty-four hours. And as long as they're still breathing after, it doesn't matter what physical condition they come back to you in. How's that sound?'

Slater's insides churned with every word, but maintaining a poker face had become something ingrained into his subconscious. He raised an eyebrow as the pair considered the offer, twirling the two casino chips in their thin fingers. They glanced at each other momentarily, then the man nodded to the woman to proceed.

'It depends what you want to do to them.'

'Whatever I want. I'm paying for privacy.'

'No permanent injuries.'

'Nothing they can't recover from. With time.'

The woman shrugged. 'How about this? Another pair of these chips and you can do anything besides kill them. Permanent injuries will be on the table. We want to appeal to anyone's kinks if the price demands it.'

Slater paused.

Did they know he only had four hundred thousand on his person? Had that information been passed up the chain, from the concierge to the head of security on level 22 to the staff on level 44?

Whatever the case, it confirmed the moral integrity of the people he was dealing with. He'd sunk to the darkest level he could think of, and they'd followed him down.

Now, there was nothing else to do but locate the product.

He would protect as many of these girls as he could.

And he would tear this floor apart to do so — the entire casino, if he had to.

Pure fury settled over him as he extracted the other two pale orange discs and passed them across. 'We've got ourselves a deal.'

The pair smiled, and rose from the leather couch, the transaction completed. Slater imagined a hefty commission would be headed their way for the sale.

In a few minutes, they wouldn't be around to receive it.

He got to his feet, barely able to control himself, and raised an eyebrow in question.

Where to?

The man smiled — a sickening gesture. 'Not on this level, sir. The product is kept below the complex. Underground. We have a whole sub-level dedicated to satisfying your needs. If you would please follow us.'

Slater sauntered after the pair, his hands balled into fists, his veins pulsating in his neck.

He thought of the raw strength powering his system, and how effortless it would be to beat both staff to death with his bare hands.

Not yet.

That would only be two.

He wanted every involved party lined up on the chopping block.

In that moment, he wanted nothing but vengeance.

So he followed them to a private elevator shaft cordoned off from the rest of the floor, and accompanied them into a smaller cable car devoid of the luxuries afforded to the usual Mountain Lion customers. It was a soulless metal box with harsh fluorescent lighting, and it whisked the three of them down into the depths of the skyscraper.

Far underground.

Far from public access.

40

S later couldn't understand how the staff weren't able to sense the raw anger pulsating out of his every pore.

Perhaps they were used to operating in tense atmospheres, where paying customers lapsed into silence given the nature of the deeds they were here to carry out. Perhaps they *could* sense his fury but had no way to excuse themselves from the situation, roped into doing their jobs even if they had to handle a volatile customer.

They thought they'd seen it all before.

Not like this.

Not like Slater.

There was no display on the interior of the industrial-style elevator to indicate what floors they were passing, or where they were headed. Slater imagined this cable car was reserved for a short express trip to a pre-determined holding facility.

Deep underground.

Burrowed away from detection.

'There's no need to be nervous,' the man finally said. His

voice barely rose above a whisper but in the pure silence of
the cable car it jolted Slater, along with the woman to
his left.

Ah, Slater thought. *You're misinterpreting this situation, my
friend.*

'Sorry,' he said. 'It's not my first time doing this kind of
thing but it still feels like I might get caught.'

'There's no need to worry about that,' the woman said.
'We've accompanied hundreds of men down here. None of
them have been caught. You have nothing to fear.'

Slater screamed at himself to delay the retribution —
every fibre of his being felt like driving the woman's head
into the far wall of the cable car hard enough to split her
skull open.

*You bitch, I'll show you what it feels like to feel
fear when—*

His thoughts ceased as the elevator reached its intended
destination and the doors powered open.

They stepped into a featureless corridor — this one
more workmanlike than the floors above ground, without
the expensive carpet or the ornate decorations or the attention to detail. Instead the floors were concrete, and the walls
were concrete, and everything resonated with the indescrib-
able stench of fear.

Slater's stomach groaned as his insides churned. He
battled down the sensation and stepped into hell.

A dozen doorways on either side of the long hallway led
into private rooms — certain doors were closed, and others
hung wide open. Slater didn't know how to interpret that,
but he caught a glimpse inside one of the empty rooms on
the way past and studied a collection of plush couches
arranged in semi-circular fashion.

'What's this for?'

'Waiting rooms,' the man said. 'While the girls are prepared.'

'Where is everyone?'

'We keep them in one of the larger rooms before calling them through. But, because you paid handsomely, we're happy to fast-track you.'

'Thank you.'

Slater surged forward with feigned enthusiasm, and at that moment his knee decided to buckle, landing with awkward weight on one of the ligaments. He grunted in discomfort and righted himself, straightening up as beads of sweat sprouted out of the pores at each corner of his forehead. He hadn't fully collapsed to the ground but it certainly threw the staff off their game. They stared at him, bewildered.

'Sorry,' he muttered. 'Bum knee.'

'Not a problem, sir.'

It didn't help to become aware of his injury. With each subsequent step he second-guessed himself, wondering if he could beat down everyone on this floor if he risked blowing out a tendon with each sharp movement. Some of the pent-up frustration leeched out of him, replaced with worry.

He fought for control of the anger in his veins as he followed the pair of staff past the final waiting room at the end of the hallway.

He had to hold onto the rage.

Slater glanced through the open doorway as he passed by, his ears picking up a low murmuring that could only mean one thing. He stared at a quiet procession of men in a consistent wardrobe of business attire — they were mostly older Asian men, with a few Europeans and a handful of Caucasians thrown into the mix. All civilians, dressed in suits with their ties unfastened and their collars open. There were eight or nine of them — Slater didn't have time to make a precise headcount given the brief look he was afforded — but they all sported the expression of deer caught in headlights.

The customers.

The high-paying visitors.

They clearly didn't want to be hanging around with similar-minded men, either due to shame or introversion. They had come down here to conduct private dealings, and they had all been set on edge by having to sit in the presence of others.

Maybe it was a tactic to whittle more money out of them once they were called through to the next leg of the journey.

Because Slater had — as the man put it — paid hand-somely, he carried straight on, striding after the staff, afforded his own privacy instead of being forced to hang around in the company of other sick and twisted minds. In the back of his mind, Slater made a mental note of the room's location.

He would come back for them.

The rage had started brimming again.

They led him through a maze of twisting corridors — he committed each turn to memory so he was able to find his way back on his own — and came to a halt in a narrow, claustrophobic concrete hallway that seemed more sinister than each of the previous ones. There were a handful of locked doors built into the wall at random intervals, each of the entrances flanked by a pair of heavyset bodyguards. Slater counted six members of additional security in total, each dressed in turtlenecks and suit jackets with leather holsters at their waists.

They were all armed.

And they were all bigger than Slater.

He noted the details, but barely paid attention to them. He'd expected resistance. None of it would faze him. All the guards stood frozen in place, still as statues, staring at the opposite wall without even a shred of interest in the arriving parties.

They'd clearly been told not to make eye contact with the guests.

'You can make your selections here,' the woman said, her voice hushed. 'Two girls. Take your time — there's no rush. We'll get them ready for you and have them delivered to one of our suites, where you can spend twenty-four hours with them. All the amenities will be provided — we provide a full service. Any questions so far?'

'None,' Slater said, barely managing a response.

His veins tingled in anticipation for what was to come.

The pair of staff produced a set of keys between them and each unlocked a separate bolt on the nearest door. They stepped straight through, gesturing for Slater to follow suit.

He hurried past the pair of guards flanking the doorway and stepped into a darker space.

He laid eyes on a sight he wouldn't forget for the rest of his life.

41

I t was a miniature cell block, constructed in a cramped, stifling fashion due to the size of the prisoners. Slater cast his eyes over two rows of emaciated young girls, most of them Asian but a handful sporting a wide range of ethnicities to accomodate any preferences customers might have. He counted eleven in total.

They stood motionless in their cages, watching him with dead expressions. Their gazes were placid — they were drugged to the eyeballs with the same cocktail administered to Shien.

Right there, right then, every ounce of common sense shrank away, replaced by something intense and animalistic and primal. Slater didn't care how many men he had to fight through to make it out of here. Whatever the price, he would pay it. The realisation that Shien had been heading for these cages hammered home, and it all culminated into a single boiling point.

He couldn't contain himself any longer.

After a brief pause, the woman said, 'Do you like what you see? Any of them can be yours.'

Slater didn't allow any sign of suspicion to leak, signifying what was coming. One moment he stood rigid with his hands by his side, frozen in between the pair of staff as the man to his right shut the giant steel door behind him, sealing them off from the corridor outside.

'Take your time,' the guy said. 'There's plenty of options, as you can see. All of them will fulfil your every request.'

And, just like that, Slater snapped.

He sucked up everything that had been building in his chest ever since he'd stepped out onto level 44 and transferred all that kinetic energy into his right leg, which he used to hammer home against the side of the woman's throat in a twisting roundhouse kick. Technique and the power of rage sent his shin bone into the delicate tissue around her neck with the force of a turbo-charged baseball bat, wiping the smug expression off her face in an instant. An audible *thwack* ripped through the space, and the woman collapsed against the bars of the nearest cage. The young child inside darted back, out of harm's way, withdrawing into the shadows.

Slater caught a glimpse of the suffering in the girl's eyes and used the anger to follow up with a scything front kick, dropping his lead leg to the floor, loading up, and then smashing the flat heel of his boot like a steel piston into the woman's face. Already permanently injured by the high kick to her neck, the front kick finished her off, punching her nose into the back of her skull and breaking all manner of bones in her face.

She died on impact — there was no doubt about it.

As her corpse slumped to the cold floor of the holding cell hallway Slater pivoted on the spot, searching for the man behind him with a laser-targeted jab. He simply flicked his balled fist in a straight line into the bridge of the guy's nose. He hadn't put any power behind him, but he utilised enough momentum to shatter the guy's septum with a half-hearted flick of the wrist. The guy froze in place for a half-second, prevented from calling out for help by the force of the punch.

Slater had never intended anything with the jab other than to keep the guy in place for the single moment in time it took to line up and launch another kick.

He thundered the same shin bone into the side of the guy's temple, putting his soul into the kick, throwing it with such ferocity that it landed with enough force to keel the guy over where he stood. He dropped like a stone, face first into the concrete, shut off at the power switch by the round-house kick.

Slater stumbled back into the steel bars, thrown off balance by the staggering effort he'd put into the single strike. It had landed with pinpoint accuracy, and might have even killed the guy on the spot. For good measure he stomped down on the man's throat, thinking of every time the guy had ushered rich sociopaths into this very room.

With a spluttering wheeze, the man suffocated as his vital organs caved in.

Slater felt nothing. He sensed the gazes of nearly a dozen children on him, but no-one said a word. Maybe they'd been trained not to speak.

He conducted a rudimentary search of each body, but no weapons turned up. Having crossed over into operational mode, tearing his gaze from corner to corner with a feverish pace, he turned and soaked in the sight of the closed metal door. There were no sounds of commotion outside — just silence. He imagined every room in this section of Mountain Lion was soundproof — they all sported the same dark, decrepit aesthetic with minimal lighting and deep shadows.

Slater didn't know what they were trying to achieve by making the concrete surroundings appear so sinister, but he vowed to use it to his advantage.

He paused, turning to the room — all the girls were staring at him with wide eyes and pursed lips. They were hungry, scared, and drowsy.

'Anyone speak English?' he said, keeping his voice quiet to prevent detection.

A couple of them nodded.

'I'll be back for you all. In a few minutes. I need to take care of something out there, then I'll be back. You'll all get home safe.'

None of them offered any kind of response. They continued to stare.

Much like Shien had.

Detached from reality. Co-operative. Unresisting.

Slater tasted cold fury on his tongue.

He turned, took a deep breath, and yanked the steel door open.

42

Six men, Slater remembered before he stepped back out into the corridor.

All armed.

But their jobs consisted of standing around and appearing menacing to the guests. An intimidation tactic, of sorts. They were down here to convince any newcomers not to try anything brash.

But had these hard, tough men ever needed to act in the heat of the moment?

And if they had, did it simply involve dragging a scrawny irate businessman back to the surface?

Slater would find out.

He carefully pulled the steel door shut behind him, concealing the pair of bodies laying inside the holding cell from view of any curious onlookers. He stepped directly into the presence of the two bodyguards, flanking him on either side, both in the realm of six-foot-three with powerful builds and tight clothing to accentuate their musculature.

Slater had a powerful frame underneath his jumper, too, but he didn't feel the need to show it off.

He bowed his head, a sheepish expression on his face as the bodyguards glared at him.

He turned to face one of them, still refusing to make eye contact. 'Uh, there was a bit of an accident in there, and, uh...'

'What?' the man spat, a single syllable that sliced through the air, demanding answers.

'The woman fainted — you got a doctor around? It's her birthday too.'

None of it made any sense, and it resulted in the bodyguard brushing past Slater in a flustered hurry, shouldering him aside to see what had happened for himself. As soon as he forced the door open Slater had a hand around the Beretta M9 at his waist.

He wrenched the gun free almost before the guy had recognised what was happening, thinking, *Fifteen rounds.*

The bodyguard to his left noticed the action first, so Slater twisted at the waist and fired two rounds at an upward angle through the top of his head. Before he'd even begun to collapse Slater pivoted back to face the man — now weaponless — wheeling around in the doorway, involuntarily flinching away from the sound of the gunshots while his mind attempted to process the dead bodies inside the holding room.

Slater put a bullet square between his eyes to save him the trouble of realising what was happening.

The pair of guards cascaded to the ground on either side of him, falling almost poetically. The other four dotted down the corridor were slow to respond, wrenched from the motionless states they'd been resting in for hours to meet the explosive appearance of all-out violence head on. A couple reached for their holsters.

Too little, too late.

Slater methodically unleashed a torrent of twelve successive rounds, emptying the magazine into the four men. They were lined up like bowling pins and Slater had nothing to be cautious about hitting — he simply had to drop four targets in a concrete tunnel.

Like playing a video game on easy mode.

Six men died in the space of two seconds, and before the last man had even slumped to rest Slater discarded the empty Beretta and yanked a fresh weapon out of the nearest man's holster. He barely stopped to check his progress. Everyone around him was dead, and he only needed the simple confirmation before he took off back the way he had come, making a beeline for the waiting room home to a group of ten paedophiles.

He gave no thought to what was about to transpire. He smashed open doors left half ajar, retracing his path through the sub-level, employing tunnel vision. Conscious thought had ceased to function — all the pain of his childhood and the suffering he'd witnessed within Mountain Lion had shut him down, turning him into a soulless weapon with a single aim.

Kill every single person in this complex that knew about the sex slavery.

He had become unstoppable.

Like a freight train barrelling towards its target, merciless and unforgiving.

He reached the corridor in question and spotted the open doorway leading to the waiting room, where nearly a dozen twisted souls waited to satiate their vices. His finger tightened around the trigger and he realised he was about to commit murder at an unfeasible scale.

He didn't care.

He surged forward.

Then he froze in his tracks. He sensed movement at the other end of the hallway, coming in the opposite direction. Heading straight for him. By rough calculations he estimated there were at least five or six men, judging by the quantity of footsteps.

More importantly, he heard the racking of slides and the clatter of automatic weaponry bumping against body armour.

Fuck, he thought.

There was a small army headed his way, armed to the teeth.

How?

He didn't have time to think, or consider. Any number of avenues could have collapsed — he'd infiltrated this casino by propping up a house of cards that could have crumbled at any moment. The head of security might have figured he could explain his way out of the recording, and sent in the cavalry to demolish Slater.

Whatever the case, he needed time to consider.

To plan.

Being caught in the open would achieve nothing.

So he darted to one side of the hallway and squashed his bulk into a jagged alcove set between two giant concrete slabs. There wasn't enough space to conceal himself entirely, but most of his torso managed to power into the gap, and the rest became draped in shadow.

Slater held his breath, clutched the Beretta at the ready, and waited for all hell to break loose.

Sweat ran off his face — the sub-level had become stifling, choked by stress and tension. The warmth seeped into everything, hanging thick over him. He narrowed his eyes and waited for the arriving party to materialise around the bend.

He would have maybe two seconds to determine how to proceed before they spotted him.

That'll be enough, he told himself.

A few feet ahead, he heard concerned voices emanating out from within the waiting room. Paying customers, disgruntled by the time they'd spent in limbo.

You won't have to wait much longer, Slater thought.

All of a sudden the approaching party roared into view in a tight cluster of motion — even from their strides Slater could sense they were elite, eons beyond the minimum-wage security down here. He spotted Kevlar vests and tactical gear and high-powered assault rifles with attached sights and thick suppressors.

A hit team, their faces hard and their movements practiced.

They knew combat. They knew it well.

Slater realised he didn't stand a chance.

Half-heartedly, he raised the Beretta slowly, lining it up with the mercenary at the front of the pack.

'Here goes nothing,' he whispered.

But no-one saw him. None of the unit — he counted five men total — even glanced his way. They weren't focused on anything past a certain doorway.

A waiting room.

Oh, Slater thought.

He shrank back into the shadows, and watched as the unit surged through the open doorway, entering the same space as the customers.

'What the hell is this?' one of the businessmen shouted, puffed up on outrage and confidence. His voice floated out into the corridor where Slater stood motionless, somewhat aware of what might follow.

If Forrest's at breaking point — how might he react?

Like this.

'Sorry, gents,' one of the mercenaries said. 'We've been instructed to shut this little outfit down. Don't take it personally.'

'What the fuck does that involve?' a European voice snarled.

Suppressed automatic gunfire bit the air, five weapons firing at once, an unrelenting stream of brutality that made Slater flinch where he stood, despite the years he'd spent on the battlefield.

No words followed, but he knew he was listening to the sound of ten men dying.

43

The gunfire ceased seconds later, but Slater found none of the obvious effects of hearing loss — the suppressors had taken care of that. Of course any gunshot is still biting, and the idea of any round being fully quieted was reserved for fairytales, but he found himself able to think without the horrendous high-pitched whining that often cropped up in the aftermath of unsuppressed automatic weapon discharges.

He shimmied out of the alcove, crouching low on one side of the hallway. These were Forrest's men, and Slater couldn't wait for them to go quietly. They would ensure everyone in the waiting room had been stripped of their existence before pressing further into the sub-level, eliminating any trace of the sex slavery operation. Slater had no choice but to confront them.

And — with the element of surprise still resting firmly in his hands — he felt like he had a chance.

'Clear?' one of the men said from inside the waiting room.

'We're good. The sick fucks deserved it.'

'Taking the high road, Pierce?'

'Get fucked. They're a level below us.'

'You sure? We've got to kill the product, too. What have the girls ever done to deserve that?'

'I don't see you protesting.'

'Pays the bills. We good to go?'

'Everyone reloaded?'

'Yeah.'

'Yep.'

'Uh-huh.'

A pause. 'Alright. From what I know there's two guards outside each—'

He didn't get to finish the sentence, because the man chose that moment to walk through the open doorway, materialising in front of Slater in a glaring side profile.

Slater had no choice but to act.

A single pivot to the left, and he'd be spotted.

Outnumbered five to one, the only way to get through this would be relentless motion.

He nailed a round through the side of the man's temple, the bullet vicious in its intensity, exploding out the other side of the mercenary's head in a shower of gore. The corpse crumpled where it stood, but by then Slater was already on the move, shouldering the dead guy aside and unloading all fourteen additional rounds into the waiting room, dropping mercenaries left and right, sending lead into limbs and foreheads. His trigger finger pumped at a lightning fast pace, and before the surviving hostiles had the chance to return fire Slater recognised the sound of an empty magazine and ducked back out of harm's way.

There was only one guy left alive, and he came screaming out into the open at a flat-out sprint, intent on capitalising on Slater's empty magazine.

Slater had poised himself directly alongside the doorway and he caught the man's charging momentum full in the chest, knocking both of them back across the carpet in a tangle of limbs. In the carnage Slater kicked out, still off-balance, his heel catching the barrel of the man's carbine rifle. The gun twisted away, breaking the mercenary's trigger finger in the process. It clashed against the opposite wall, out of harm's way.

Even though the haze of adrenalin and testosterone and the pure savagery of combat, Slater sensed something give in his bad knee. As he landed on the concrete with the mercenary's weight slamming down on top of him, his leg buckled at an awkward angle and something snapped — either a ligament or a bone, he wasn't sure which. He couldn't even feel the sensation but he understood the extent to which it would impede his movement.

He had to deal with the six-foot, two-hundred pound, furious elite combatant on top of him in the next few seconds, or he would be beaten to death when the guy realised Slater was unable to walk.

Scrambling on the ground, rolling for position, both men fought with everything they had. It didn't take Slater long to realise the guy was a trained jiu-jitsu practitioner — an untrained hostile could be isolated and shut down in the space of seconds. But as Slater locked his legs around the guy's waist, pinning him in position, the mercenary dropped an elbow into Slater's stomach and wrenched his lower body free from the hold.

He transitioned into side control, covering Slater's chest horizontally with his entire bodyweight. Slater bucked and writhed, but the power of leverage trumped any kind of adrenalin boost. The guy flattened himself out across

Slater's upper chest and used his right elbow to smash scything blows into Slater's forehead.

The first elbow caught Slater hard enough on the temple to stun him momentarily, allowing the mercenary time to drop a second, similarly powerful strike into the bridge of his nose. Hot pain flooded his senses and blood burst from both nostrils.

Slater coughed, spat, and recognised that another couple of those would strip him of any ability to retaliate. He would be brain dead in moments.

The mercenary loaded up a third elbow, but he became greedy. He lifted his entire torso a few inches off Slater to transfer all his bodyweight into another strike. He must have thought Slater was on the verge of unconsciousness — perhaps Slater appeared more hurt than he actually was.

The brief half-second of opportunity opened up, and Slater seized it.

He bucked hard at just the right moment, levering himself out from underneath the man. The guy tumbled onto his rear, left with nowhere to transfer the energy he'd built up in his right arm. It took him a second to compose himself — certain victory had been *right there* in his grasp — and by that point Slater had hurled himself across the guy's seated bulk, acquiring top position in the blink of an eye.

And he had jiu-jitsu ability in spades.

From there it became fairly straightforward. Hurting everywhere but still functioning, he used the small window of space between their frames to drop a quick succession of hammer fists into the guy's cheeks and chin, sacrificing power for output. The shots were short and sharp and no doubt frustrating as all hell for those on the receiving end.

The guy squirmed, his airways restricted by Slater's fist smacking him repeatedly across the face.

After a couple of seconds he gasped for breath, and Slater used the moment of distraction to slice his legs into place across the man's stomach, seizing full mount position.

Now you give up your back.

The guy lay facing straight up in the air, exposed to all manner of punches and elbows as Slater saw fit. To avoid taking the brunt of the damage to his unprotected face, he instinctively rolled onto his front.

If Slater wanted to, he could have choked the guy unconscious right there.

Like clockwork.

But he didn't feel inclined to do that. He recalled what the unit had said.

We've got to kill the product, too.

If Slater hadn't been here, the five-man hit team would have murdered each and every one of the young girls in the cells, chalking it up to an operational necessity. They were no more noble than the men they'd just killed in the waiting room. They didn't deserve a quick and painless demise.

So Slater waited for the guy to roll onto his front, exposing the back of his neck, and then he dropped devastating elbows without hesitation or remorse, targeting the top of the guy's spine. One after another hammered home, facing no resistance, and after five or six of the massive blows Slater felt the mercenary stiffen underneath him, his limbs locking up.

He was either unconscious or close to death.

Not good enough.

Slater clambered off the man — who made no effort to move from his pronated position — and fetched the assault rifle he'd knocked out of the guy's hands seconds earlier.

An M4A1 carbine, complete with an array of optional attachments, almost brand new.

He didn't think twice.

He simply advanced toward the paralysed mercenary and lined up his aim.

44

W hen it was over, and all the members of the hit team Slater had injured over the course of the firefight had caught a bullet squarely through the top of their heads, he stood in disbelief amidst a sea of devastation.

There were bodies everywhere. The dead customers, resting in pools of their own blood and sprawled across various pieces of furniture where they'd died before understanding what hit them. The hit team, five men kitted out in tactical gear, tasked with shutting down a sensitive portion of Forrest's empire. The bodyguards further down the hall, who had been inefficient and slow to respond and had paid the price with their lives.

Slater caught his breath, alone with an entire floor of corpses, and gazed around at the men who had met their demise with such brutality. Blood drenched the walls. It pooled in puddles on the dusty concrete floor, coagulating into muck.

All in all, Slater figured the world wouldn't miss any of these people.

In fact, it would be better off without them.

What now?

He didn't know. Ever since he'd followed Shien into the limousine he'd been moving based on what felt correct — a gut reaction to circumstances that had changed as rapidly as he could feasibly comprehend. Without Shien by his side, his stomach churned. She was safer bunkered down in the hotel room rather than following him through this hell hole, but he didn't want to leave her unattended any longer than necessary.

Besides, he was in bad shape.

The two elbows from the mercenary had delivered damage that would take days — if not weeks — to heal. He couldn't be sure if his nose was broken or not, but blood flowed freely from his nostrils all the same. A pounding headache had sprouted into life deep in the recesses of his skull, thumping and pulsating behind his eyeballs. He took a step forward to navigate around one of the mercenaries' bodies but his leg caved in, folding in on itself as his knee landed at an awkward angle.

Pain flared. He grunted, beginning to sweat in the claustrophobic surroundings, and adopted a strange limping approach to movement — he leant most of the pressure on his heel, stepping forward with his right foot twisted at an awkward angle to alleviate the weight on his damaged ligaments.

Besides that, everything else hurt equally. His body weighed heavy, all his limbs drooping toward the floor as they searched for energy. No amount of physical fitness could sustain the output required for all-out combat. Brawls to the death used one hundred percent of one's capacity, pouring every ounce of strength into fighting to stay alive.

That simply couldn't be repeated over and over again — it was more draining than running a marathon.

So Slater found himself hobbling with a pathetic gait for the private elevator, retracing his steps to the shaft that would whisk him back up into Mountain Lion's public spaces. From there he could work his way out of the casino — he couldn't imagine he would face much resistance that he hadn't already dealt with.

In the dark underworld of the complex, he would be resting on top of the most wanted list.

But he imagined ninety-nine percent of the casino staff had no knowledge of this world.

For good reason, too.

On his way to the elevator, he considered his next move. Part of him wanted to retreat to the rival casino's hotel room and heal up while contemplating his next move — both for Shien's protection and his own recovery. Another part of him recognised that urge as weakness — there wouldn't be a more prudent time than the present to take advantage of the gap he'd carved in Forrest's defences.

He thought of the man with the bloody hand in the private elevator.

Was it him?

Was he Peter Forrest?

It had to be. His gut told him Forrest had been placed firmly on the defensive, throwing his enforcers at the situation in an attempt to restore order through sheer force.

Slater glanced back at the dead hit team and realised he had to finish this now.

Forrest wouldn't allow him a second chance.

If he took time to heal, the man would use his resources to vanish into nothingness.

But why hasn't he already done that?

The thought plagued him as he chambered a fresh magazine into the M4A1 carbine, striding fast for the elevators. He glanced at the walls on either side of him, flashing by, sparse and concrete and bare, and realised his surroundings had skewed his perception. If he'd been standing on the highest floor of the complex, looking out over an emporium and set of towers that he'd built with his own resources and determination, he would understand why a billionaire businessman wouldn't be inclined to start fresh.

Forrest had too much pride.

He would do anything to save his empire, because without it he was lost.

Slater channelled the darkness still churning inside him, tapping into it. Forrest had been so determined to keep his casino operation afloat that he'd sunk into moral depravity to get his profit margins up. Slater had met a hundred — no, a thousand — men and women like him before, and the urge to wipe them out never faded away.

Besides, these were special circumstances.

Slater had seen first-hand the raw suffering on the young kids' faces.

He would make an express trip to the top floor, settle the racing emotions in his head with a bullet through Forrest's brain, and then come back for them. He'd do his best to ease them back into the world, but he wasn't a counsellor or a psychologist. He couldn't help them at any subtle, deeper level. But he could drag them out of this hell hole.

He was an enforcer.

Sensing a narrow window opening up in Forrest's defences, he called for the elevator using an archaic two-button system. These private facilities were barebones, nothing like the contemporary digital wonderland of Mountain Lion's public face. This was a workspace, through and through. It turned Slater's stomach end over end as he tasted the sterile air.

What horrors hadn't he been able to prevent?

What had unfolded down here before he'd chanced upon this madness?

Then all his thoughts tore away from hypotheticals as he realised the elevator was due for arrival in a couple of seconds, maximum. He heard the cable car rumbling on the other side of the steel doors, descending fast.

It had already been on the way down when he'd called for it.

Veins pumping, adrenalin suddenly skyrocketing, he lurched the M4A1 carbine up in a tight arc and had it locked onto the narrow slit between the steel doors in a heartbeat.

They wouldn't be expecting him this close.

It would be a battle of reflexes.

When it came down to that level of subconscious combat, Slater never failed.

So with supreme confidence he exhaled as the elevator touched down on the other side of the doors. A brief second of utter silence unfolded, then the doors whispered open — so quiet that Slater could hear nothing but the sound of his own heartbeat in his ears and the distant hum of some kind of generator.

There were three people in the elevator. The more archaic, primitive side of Slater's brain recognised the shape of their forms and formulated a plan of attack in milliseconds. His barrel already lined up with the middle silhouette, so it would simply be a matter of pulling the trigger, then working his aim from left to right and dropping all three targets before they even realised he was there.

But then he realised he'd aimed high.

What? That never happens?

Because the middle figure was somewhere in the vicinity of four feet tall.

And young.

And female.

The two men accompanying her on the ride into hell had seemingly been prepared for this exact predicament. They each had the cold barrel of a semi-automatic pistol pressed into the sides of Shien's temple, sandwiching her between the guns. Her eyes watered from the pressure, a sight that set Slater's temperament spiralling wildly out of control.

Before he could capitalise on the brief sliver of opportunity he had to react instinctively and drop the two men, the moment slipped by.

The four of them found themselves in a stalemate of the highest stakes.

'Will Slater, isn't it?' one of the men said in perfect English. 'I'd put that rifle down if I were you.'

45

S later understood the gravity of the situation. He had experience in this kind of predicament — where the very lives of everyone around him, including himself, rested on how he chose to react.

But it didn't make the conversation any easier.

'I'm sorry,' he said to Shien, all he could think of, encapsulating every furious thought running through his head. 'I shouldn't have left you up there.'

'No, you shouldn't have,' the first guy said. 'What were you thinking? Here we were, thinking we were up against some kind of superhuman, but then you go and do something like that. Can't see a way out of this, can you?'

'You want me dead?'

'No.'

Slater simply raised an eyebrow. The M4A1 remained locked in place, unwavering. The trajectory narrowed between the first man's eyes — if either of them fired a bullet into Shien's head, Slater would have them both dead in a split second, tearing his aim from one man to the other.

He had no doubts about that.

At the end of this stand-off, he would be the only one left alive.

But then none of it would mean anything, and the girl he'd spent what felt like a lifetime trying to protect would die. After that any kind of vengeance would be hollow.

Shien had to survive.

His mind hardened as he searched for a way to ensure that.

Any way.

'Then what's this about?' he said. 'If we're not enemies?'

'My name is Tak,' the taller man said. He looked Filipino, well-built with short hair and a pronounced jawline.

A powerhouse of a man.

The suit draped over his frame looked like it cost several thousand dollars. He hovered his weapon in place beside Shien's head with a practiced calmness. The man had experience in tense situations.

'You know my name,' Slater said.

All of their sentences came out distorted, changed by the gravity of the stand-off. The tension ran thick in the air. Slater didn't move his gaze an inch from Tak's forehead.

'This is my colleague, Antoine,' Tak said.

Slater didn't dare look across. 'He knows my name too.'

'We want to talk to you,' Tak said.

'Does your friend Antoine speak?'

'I'm a little more accustomed to these situations than he is.'

'I see.'

'I'll do the talking.'

'Fine by me.'

Shien whimpered, unable to help herself, barely managing to contain her emotions. By now Slater imagined the drugs had entirely worn off, leaving her in a state of unrest, fully perceptible to what was going on around her.

And there was no situation quite like having two loaded pistols shoved into each side of your head.

The whimper — only a slight squeak from below Slater's peripheral vision — triggered the rage. Unable to control his own actions, he started to tighten his finger around the trigger.

You can make it, he told himself. *You don't need to bargain with these men.*

But he stopped himself at the last moment. He would never be able to forgive himself if he misjudged the timing by the finest millisecond and Shien wound up getting caught in the crossfire.

It seemed Tak recognised the hesitation on Slater's end, for he chose that moment to continue. 'We were the ones who released her last night.'

Slater paused. 'You guys are the ones who tried to rob Forrest?'

Tak hadn't been anticipating that. He was slow to respond — it would have gone unnoticeable to the general population, but in these circumstances Slater picked up every detail. His eyes and ears and nostrils were attuned to the environment in a manner exclusive to a life-or-death situation. He noticed everything.

'Yes,' the man said, rolling with it. 'That's us.'

'Why should I care what the two of you have to say?'

'Because otherwise we'll blow this kid's brains all over the wall. You might kill us after that but what good will that do? You've already sacrificed so much for her. Don't stop now.'

As if the man could read Slater's mind.

Shien whimpered again, recognising each word for the

consequences they spelt. The sound grated on Slater's eardrums, threatening to yank the anger out of the internal compartment he'd stuffed it in.

'It's just the two of you?' Slater said.

'There was a third.'

'What happened to him?'

'You tell us.'

Slater paused, thinking back to the apartment complex, to the hallways drenched in wet rot and the testosterone-fuelled carnage of close quarters combat between two men who wanted nothing more than to emerge the victor. An intoxicating memory, all things considered. One leeching with primal sensations — after all, when stripped down to its raw reality, that was the only reason anyone did anything.

To survive.

So he shoved aside his natural instincts and elected to please the two men in front of him for as long as it took to find an opening. But not before returning a dose of their own medicine — they'd toyed with him by threatening Shien, so he'd make sure they wrestled with their own emotions in turn.

'Your man had a jewelled earring?' Slater said, thinking back to the lone wolf he'd shot dead in the hallway.

'Yes. That's him. Jin. Our partner.'

'How long have you three been working together?' Slater said, keeping his tone casual, as if nothing at all were out of the ordinary.

'As long as I can remember.'

'Oh. That's nice. He didn't die well.'

'What?'

'I shot him dead. Round straight through his forehead. Like what I'll do to you if you decide to kill her.'

'Could you live with yourself if that happened?' Tak said,

his voice ice cold, the barrel of his firearm twisting slowly against the side of Shien's head.

Slater hadn't even got the chance to glance down and check what make the weapon was.

He couldn't move. Couldn't blink.

'Probably not. But I'd be alive. You'd both be dead. You ready for that?'

'As ready as I'll ever be.'

'I don't think you are.'

Tak said nothing.

'I think you came into this full of confidence and bravado but you didn't think of the possibility that I might just kill you where you stand.'

'You're too attached to this girl to do that.'

'Am I?'

He sensed Shien's gaze locked onto the underside of his chin, her eyes boring into him. He ignored it.

'You don't want to do this,' Tak said.

'You have no idea what I want.'

'Actually, I might have some clue. You want Peter Forrest dead.'

Slater said nothing.

'Am I correct?' Tak said after a few seconds of silence.

'Possibly.'

'Is that where you were headed right now?'

'Possibly.'

'Then I suggest we work together.'

'Why the hell would I do that?'

'Think about it. You have your issues with me — I kidnapped this little girl after all. Someone you clearly care about, despite what you say. I have my issues with you — you killed someone I considered a brother...'

'You sent him after me,' Slater said. 'Don't pin that on me.'

'And you got yourself wrapped up in this situation of your own accord. Don't pin that on us.'

'I was helping.'

'Were you?'

'What would you have done with her if everything had gone according to plan? If I never interfered and you got away with hundreds of millions of dollars?'

'We would have released—'

'You would have let a baccarat dealer and a young girl kidnapped for sex slavery purposes walk free after they'd both seen your faces? The only two loose ends. You wouldn't have tied them up, when they both mean nothing in the grand scheme of things? You think I'm stupid enough to believe that?'

Tak said nothing for a long stretch. 'But you interfered, didn't you? So we don't have to worry about what might have been.'

'You need me for this, don't you?' Slater said.

'Sorry?'

'I can tell you're desperate. It's okay. You don't need to hide it. But you're on Forrest's shit list, aren't you? He knows you're the one behind the transfer.'

'But we're not,' Tak said. 'We didn't do it. At least, our man didn't. Forrest caught up to him first but we got there afterwards.'

'Is he alive?'

'Who?'

'Samuel Barnes.'

A pause. 'You know him.'

'Who do you think went through with the transfer?'

The man froze. 'Why'd you do it? You ended up paying us nine figures. What was the point?'

'To stir things up. To create chaos. I'd say I did a pretty good job.'

'You ruined our lives.'

'They were already ruined — let's face it. I was the straw that broke the camel's back.'

'So what now?' Tak said.

'I'll help you,' Slater said.

'How am I supposed to believe you won't just—?'

Slater let go of the M4A1 carbine in one smooth motion, letting the rifle clatter to the floor between the elevator doors, a gesture laced with enough stress to make a lesser man lose consciousness. If his buttering hadn't worked and Tak decided to shoot Slater between the eyes right there, he wouldn't be able to do a thing to stop it.

Unarmed, completely vulnerable, he stood still as a statue with his hands by his sides.

'You believe me now?' he said. 'I'll help you. I know what Forrest was running down here, and I want him dead. You want him dead for different reasons. Doesn't bother me — let's do this before he calls for more backup.'

Tak paused, mulling things over. Then, tentatively, he lowered the gun off Shien's temple. A red welt protruded from the side of her head, visible through her matted hair.

Antoine followed suit.

The four of them stood there, shell-shocked by the ordeal, by the closeness to death. Silence enveloped the corridor.

'He has a hit team,' Tak said, his voice quiet. 'Forrest does. They're enforcers. Ex-Special Forces. They'll be protecting him. It'll be tough. I don't even know why we're trying this.'

Slater jerked a thumb over his shoulder. 'They're all in a room back there.'

Tak raised an eyebrow.

'Dead,' Slater said.

'You're kidding.'

'I'm ex-Special Forces too. They met their match.'

'Five against one?'

'There's ... levels to the Special Forces.'

'What were you?'

'Something else. We going to do this or what?'

46

In one fluid motion, Tak and Antoine released Shien from their grasp.

Slater watched her run from them, crossing the slight gap between the two parties with all the energy her tiny limbs could muster. She threw her arms around him, unable to stop herself from the instinctive reaction. He relented for a moment, reaching down and holding her tight, silently reassuring her that everything would be okay.

Silently hoping she would understand.

'You need to stay here, Shien,' he said. 'You need to wait for us to come back.'

She parted from him and stood there, her frail hands clasped together, looking up at him with anguish plastered across her face.

'Will...' she said.

'I need to go, right now.'

'Will, don't go with those men,' she whispered. 'They'll kill you.'

Waiting patiently in the elevator, both Tak and Antoine

managed slight smirks. Slater turned to them and offered a sheepish shrug — *Kids, right?*

They nodded back.

Deep down, he believed every word.

And he knew it to be true.

'You can't come with us,' he said. 'We need to take care of this right now — there won't be any other opportunity.'

'What do I do? Are there dead people down here?'

'Yes. Don't look at them.'

'What if you don't come back?'

'I will.'

'I mean — what if you die?'

'Shien, trust me.'

'I can't stay down here,' she muttered. 'This is where they were keeping me. I think I know what they were going to do with me. I heard what you said before. This scares me so much, Will. I can't...'

'I don't have a choice.'

'Where do I go?'

'Follow the corridor. You'll find a room with a dozen girls inside — all around your age. Tell them it's going to be okay. And wait for me.'

The conversation dragged on — Shien pleading with Slater to stay with her, Slater insisting he had no other choice. By the end of the back and forth debate, both Tak and Antoine had dropped their guards considerably, evidently frustrated by the time it was taking Slater to persuade Shien.

'Clock's ticking,' Tak finally muttered.

Slater gave it no additional thought. He brushed straight past Shien, ignoring her fingers snatching at his wrist.

'*Will,*' she hissed as he stepped into the elevator, a single syllable laced with all the doubt and unease she felt as she watched her protector willingly follow the two men who had kidnapped her.

'I'll be back soon, Shien,' he said. 'I promise.'

She said nothing. Her options had been exhausted. Slater strode into position between Tak and Antoine and nodded his approval. Tak reached out and tapped the *close doors* button, and the cable car responded instantly.

The doors whisked closed, and the last glance Slater had of Shien was not a pleasant one. A look of abject horror had settled over her — she was now isolated in a strange corridor that reeked of fear. The man who had risked his life over and over again to keep her alive had just abandoned her where she stood.

Slater felt awful.

But not as awful as Tak and Antoine were about to feel.

As soon as the doors touched closed, Slater assessed the rough measurements between each man. He'd deliberately positioned himself half a foot behind Tak and Antoine, so it would take them a vital half-second of pivoting to get a wild shot off. Both their sidearms — which he recognised as identical Beretta M9s, much like every pistol in Macau, it seemed — were fixed on the ground.

They'd become complacent.

His gesture of dropping the carbine rifle and leaving it in the corridor had settled their nerves.

He wondered how long it would take them to realise he was still unarmed, and what a foolish gesture that would be if he truly intended to take the elevator up to Forrest's level with them.

He'd dropped the gun to make them relax.

Nothing more, nothing less.

Slater eyed the three-pronged neck tattoos snaking their way over each man's collar. He'd spotted the symbols within seconds of laying eyes on the pair. He'd registered it in the back of his head and made a mental note to not let it slip.

'Your triad,' he said, breaking the silence. 'They run level 44, don't they?'

Slater had spotted identical tattoos on the pair of staff who had interviewed him before bringing him down to the den of debauchery.

'Yes,' Tak admitted, realising there was no way out of an explanation. 'But—'

He didn't get to finish his sentence.

Slater backed up a half-step, raised one leg and smashed it into the small of Antoine's back. The less experienced man staggered wildly forward, crumpling against the front of the cable car as he failed to find his balance. By that point Slater had changed levels, crouching down as best he could given his wonky leg.

He wrapped both hands around Tak's Beretta and used the strength afforded to him by icy fury to wrench the gun free, tearing it from the man's grasp before the triad thug had even realised what was happening. From there it was a simple act of lining the weapon up with the underneath of Tak's chin — the safety had already been disengaged — and pumping the trigger once.

The bullet entered the soft skin around the man's jaw, hurling him back across the elevator. Slater stood and fired three successive shots into Antoine's chest — the man had only now managed to turn around from his awkward ricochet off the wall.

Blood sprayed from Antoine's chest.

Slater wheeled, put a bullet in Tak's forehead for good measure, then turned straight back to Antoine and blasted his temple apart in quick succession.

He reached out, slapped the *down* button at the bottom

of the elevator's panel, and waited for the cable car to change course and complete its three-second journey back to where it had started.

The doors opened, revealing Shien frozen in shock, gobsmacked at the turn of events. She turned her eyes away from the blood coating the walls of the cable car.

'Told you I'd be back soon,' Slater muttered, stepping over the bodies on his way out of the elevator.

47

F orrest realised, in an epiphany, how little money and power truly meant in the end.

He sat numb on the floor of his grand dining room, knees tucked to his chest, his forehead pressed against the cool glass of the sweeping panoramic windows. They provided an unparalleled view of Macau's skyline, just as he found himself surrounded by unparalleled luxury, sitting atop an unparalleled empire that no-one from his humble background had ever dared to attempt.

But he'd lost himself along the way.

Or had he ever found himself in the first place?

Fuck it, he thought. *Doesn't matter.*

He took a fifth giant mouthful of vodka from a tall frosted glass bottle, which proved the breaking point for his poor gag reflex. All the alcohol he'd hammered down his throat over the past hour came up in a projectile of burning liquid. He spewed the gunk across the floor alongside him, then rocked back into position, pale and sweating. He didn't have the energy to move. He stared out at the city and wondered when the next dose of bad news would strike.

The phone rang.

He grimaced — over the last few days he'd likened the sound of his shrilling mobile device to a virtual death sentence. He snatched up the smartphone and dragged a finger across the screen, answering the call.

'Please tell me you got the job done.'

'Uh, Peter, it's Jim.'

Forrest sat bolt upright, nervous energy coursing through him. 'Why the fuck are you talking to me? Where are the others?'

'They didn't want me to tag along, sir. I'm a newcomer, after all. They wanted me to sit back and check in with them every thirty seconds as a sort of accountability process. So I knew not to panic.'

'And?' Forrest said, although he knew exactly where the conversation was headed.

'I'm panicking.'

'How long's it been?'

'Six minutes since last contact. There's no explanation for it. They're all professionals — you know that. I think they're dead, boss.'

'*Fuck!*' Forrest roared at the top of his lungs.

'Are there cameras down there?' Jim said. 'Can we check?'

'Of course there aren't cameras. Can you imagine if someone accidentally got their hands on that kind of footage?'

Jim had been briefed on Mountain Lion's darkest secrets after being accepted into Forrest's team of enforcers. The kid only had a five-year stint in the Australian Special Air Service Regiment on his record, but a dishonourable discharge and a recommendation from one of Forrest's hometown contacts had led him to the doors of Mountain Lion with a mean streak and an insatiable addiction to money. Same as all the other enforcers Forrest employed — albeit, they had a little more experience.

'They're dead,' Forrest said with finality. 'Where are you?'

'HQ.'

'Get yourself up to my penthouse.'

'I don't think I have clearance to—'

'You're not following, Jim.'

Silence crept down the line. Jim didn't respond.

'This is it,' Forrest said. 'Everything's gone to hell. There's no way I'm going to make it out of here, mate. I need you to do something for me before you get on your way.'

'On my way?'

'Get as far away from me as possible.'

'Nah, Peter. Can't do that. You've been so good to me.'

'Then do one thing for me.'

'What's that?'

'I'm ninety percent certain there's a man on his way up to my penthouse to kill me. He's the guy who's been fucking with me this entire time, along with the triad and everyone else in goddamn Macau. But I stood next to this motherfucker in the elevator. I stood right next to him.'

'You sure it was him?'

'He was on his way to level 44. Then my entire team wind up dead on the live floor in the basement. It's him. He's the same guy who killed half my men when I sent them after the girl.'

'I can get myself in position.'

'No. He'll kill you, just like he killed everyone else.'

'Then what?'

Forrest paused, breathing hard before he made his next

move. He could recognise he was slipping dangerously close to lunacy, but he didn't care anymore.

'The zookeepers are on call twenty-four-seven, yes?'

'Uh, I think so.'

'Round them up. Whoever's in the complex. Tell them to put the pair of Tsavo lions on the walkway above the enclosure.'

'Is this some kind of sick initiation, you fuckwit?' Jim snarled, suddenly furious. 'Am I on a hidden camera show? Is the team gonna burst in here laughing their balls off because I got roped into believing something like this?'

Forrest let the laughter break from his lips, cackling and giggling and rolling around on the floor of his empty penthouse, succumbing to the madness. 'Oh, mate. I wish. I wish, buddy.'

'Peter. You don't sound okay.'

'I'm not okay. Get the fucking lions on the walkway or I'll have you killed myself. Understand?'

'You can't be serious.'

'Put. The. Lions. On. The. Walkway.'

'Why? What are you hoping to achieve?'

Forrest gazed out at his empire. 'I've achieved everything, Jimmy boy. I've got nothing left to achieve. But I can sure have some fun before I wind up six feet under. Go out with a bang, as they say.'

He picked himself up — a sorry sight indeed — and hobbled across the dining room to the other side of the penthouse. From here he could stare out over Mountain Lion's emporium, and the network of private walkways hovering above the luscious artificial jungle a couple of dozen feet below.

'I want to watch,' he whispered into the phone, not caring what Jim thought of him. 'I want to see the expression on this guy's face when he realises what he's walking into. The lions — oh my God. I knew I bought them for a reason. Let's have some fun with this, Jimmy boy.'

'Will you let me go if I do this for you?'

'Yeah, mate,' Forrest said. 'Humour me this one favour. Then go bury your head in the sand.'

'Alright, Peter. I'll get going. Good luck with all your problems.'

'Thank you, Jimmy boy. Thank you.'

48

'Now, I actually need to leave you,' Slater said. 'I'm not bluffing this time.'

They stood a couple of dozen feet inside the corridor, hovering in a stretch of the sub-level without bodies splayed across the floor. A rare sight, given recent events.

'I don't understand...' Shien said, tears in her eyes. 'You just said you wouldn't have really gone up there.'

'I wouldn't have gone up there with *them*. They were part of the reason you got kidnapped in the first place, Shien. Their organisation runs this floor. They didn't set you free out of any moral responsibility. They set you free because it would work best for them to pin their dirty dealings on you. Do you understand what I mean?'

'I understand they were bad men,' she sniffled. 'But I was being serious when I said you'd die up there.'

'The most dangerous men came down here, Shien. I killed them. No-one's left. Now it's just the guy who started all of this.'

'But *why?!*' Shien yelled.

It was the first time Slater had ever heard her raised voice. Previously she'd drifted through the chaos alongside him, drowsy to what was really going on. Then she'd regained full motor function and the detached mentality had given way to raw fear.

Now, she was angry.

'Will,' she said, after he'd had time to process the outburst. 'I don't get it. I don't get why you need to kill more people. We can leave. We can leave right now and no-one will follow us. Look at all the trouble you've caused around here. You think they're going to focus on getting me back? They'll be focusing on keeping themselves alive. We need to go, Will. We need to get out of here. I can't stay here any longer — I don't like the memories of this place. You don't need to do this.'

He paused, reeling from the tirade, recognising that she was absolutely right. He'd been surging forward with relentless momentum for such an extended period of time that it hadn't clicked yet.

The damage was done.

Forrest's organisation was in ruins. Slater now knew for a fact that the man had other enemies in the triad and God knows where else, all out hunting for his head. In truth, Slater could walk out the door with Shien and never return — and, at some point, Peter Forrest would meet his demise.

But that didn't sit right with Slater.

He'd never been one to walk away.

And seeing this conflict through to its bloody conclusion had become something greater than himself, something linked to a darker part of his past that he wanted to destroy forever.

'It's personal,' was all he could manage to say, suddenly overwhelmed by raw emotion.

Shien sensed it.

He wasn't sure how, or what level of genius she truly had, but all of a sudden he noticed the expression in her face shift into one of sympathy, of understanding and trust and approval.

'Go do what you need to do, Will,' she muttered.

Slater nodded. He found himself at a loss for words, unable to console Shien in any way.

He realised she didn't need consoling.

If anything, she was the one supporting him.

'I'll go get this done,' he said. 'Then we can work out where to go. But I need this. For me.'

'I know.'

He touched a hand to her shoulder and gave it a quick squeeze, trying his best to reassure her. 'Stay safe.'

'I'll be fine. There's no-one left down here, anyway. Hurry back.'

'That room I mentioned,' he said. 'With the girls. I was telling the truth. Tell them to stay as calm as possible.'

'Do they have the same stuff in their system that I had?'

'I think so.'

'Then I won't need to tell them to calm down, will I?'

Slater nodded. 'Right.'

'Good luck, Will. Even though I know you don't need it.'

Slater turned on his heel and snatched up the M4A1 carbine he'd dropped moments earlier. He thumbed the magazine release button on the side of the weapon and confirmed there were ample bullets. His rudimentary search revealed a full magazine. He hammered it back home.

'This won't take long,' he said.

He hauled Tak and Antoine's lifeless bodies out of the cable car, used the control panel to close the doors, and shot straight back up to level 44 with resolution on his mind.

49

T he process took at least a couple of minutes to complete, but Slater went through the motions underneath a foggy haze. Like he'd been placed under a spell, he lurched from movement to movement with a practiced urgency. The private elevator arrived at level 44 with a resounding thump and he hurried straight out into the plush hallways.

He knew that if he encountered anyone — anyone at all — on this level, he would gun them down in cold blood. Their sheer presence would spell all the guilt Slater was looking for — one didn't end up here by mistake. Somehow he hated the false veneer of luxury on this floor more than the stale industrial look of the sub-levels. At least the darker levels were honest. Everything on this floor reeked of toxic perfume, a musk that permeated the walls and floors and ceilings. Slater hurried straight to the bank of elevators accessible to the public, wondering why exactly Forrest had allowed them to reach his private penthouse.

After all, the man had been on the way to the top of the complex when Slater had encountered him.

He reached the bank of public elevators without incident. The corridors were silent — as if everyone who ordinarily populated this section of Mountain Lion had recognised the collapse of the operation underneath them and bailed from a sinking ship. The thought infuriated Slater — he pictured the staff delivering the girls to their customers sinking back into day-to-day life without repercussion, free from any guilt or wrongdoing.

They would commit the same crimes again.

People like that were destined to repeat the process.

Finding work wherever they could.

Of any nature.

He took solace in the knowledge that he had a lot of living left to do, and hoped he would run into them one day.

All of them.

Charged with rage, he stepped into a vacant elevator and entered the highest possible floor number available to him — 102. The cable car grumbled underneath him and shot toward the stratosphere, moving fast, leaving Slater no time to turn back.

Not that he ever would.

The thought was as foreign a concept as he could possibly fathom.

He snatched hold of the M4A1's tactical grip with one hand, slicing a finger inside the trigger guard with the other. He recognised his disadvantages — he was effectively operating on one leg, with no understanding of the layout of the top floor.

He had no idea where exactly Forrest would be hiding.

He didn't know whether there were reinforcements protecting the man.

All in all, a disaster. But Slater figured if he'd come this far, he could manage the final stretch. No matter how dire the circumstances.

Then the elevator arrived at its destination, slotting into place at the top of the shaft with a satisfying *click,* and the doors whispered open.

And the whole world went horrifyingly mad.

Slater had never sensed animalistic power like this. The hairs on the back of his neck bristled before he even had a proper glance at what lay in front of him. He simply sensed raw strength and sinewy muscle, nothing human. He realised if the elevator hadn't operated with such pleasant silence, he would have already been dead.

No fucking way, he thought, flabbergasted.

On the steel walkway leading away from the bank of elevators rested a gigantic predator, as tall as Slater and three times as heavy, facing the opposite direction. The beast sat on its haunches, its great back aimed toward him, rising and falling with each panting breath. It was watching, waiting, stalking. Slater stood still as a statue inside the cable car, not daring to raise the carbine rifle in his hands, not daring to do anything but stare in awe at the massive creature.

As his brain started operating again, recovering from the sheer shock of standing in the presence of such a terrifying predator, he connected the dots of what he could see.

It was a lion.

But it was unlike any lion he'd ever seen before.

For starters, the beast sat only a few feet from Slater's position, so close he could smell its skin. Being in such close proximity to a natural murder machine locked up his limbs, stifling him with terror. On top of that he soaked in the sight of the lion's hairless body, missing any kind of regal mane or lush golden coat typical of wildlife photos of the predators.

This was a different breed. A less aesthetically pleasing breed.

A savage breed.

Slater realised he had to act only a couple of seconds after the elevator doors swung open. If he remained motionless, frozen in fright, the doors would omit a harsh electronic beeping noise to signal they were about to close. That would put the beast on him in a heartbeat.

He couldn't fathom the proximity. If he wanted to, he could take a single step forward, reach out, and touch it. But if he moved in the slightest, it would twist on its haunches and launch itself into the cable car, goring him to a bloody pulp in seconds.

You have to do something.

Anything.

Seized by analysis paralysis — something Slater ordinarily didn't have much experience with — he opted to simply act. He'd made it this far in life operating off instinct, and he feared hesitating would ruin his luck.

Even if every bone in his body screamed to stay completely still.

He knew hell would break loose.

He moved regardless.

In one action he wrenched the carbine rifle up to shoulder height and depressed the trigger, clenching his teeth hard enough to break molars in an attempt to ride out the terror coursing through his body.

Pandemonium struck.

Unsuppressed gunfire erupted, deafeningly loud. At the same time the lion twisted on the walkway at a speed Slater couldn't fathom, bullets already embedded in its meaty back. He caught a glimpse of wide, gaping fangs and sinewy muscle exploding off the mark before the beast leapt into the elevator, reacting with instinct to the cacophony of noise.

Slater kept firing.

He let the entire magazine unload, round upon round hammering into the hairless lion as it shifted through open space at a dizzying rate. It passed between the doors with a single pounce, lurching off its own momentum. Bullets flew, blood spilt...

...and five hundred pounds of pure unbridled muscle mass hit Slater like a freight train, sending him crumbling off his feet and ricocheting off the rear wall of the cable car.

He lost his footing — and his hold on the M4A1 rifle — which proved useless considering he'd worked the gun dry on the lion. Thirty bullets were embedded in its hide, and the results showed. Instead of leading with its jaws and tearing Slater apart with a single shake of the head, the beast had splayed horizontally across him, treating itself as a battering ram as it succumbed to the laundry list of injuries.

It came down on top of Slater, all five hundred pounds crushing him against the back of the elevator.

His damaged leg screamed in protest, sending a cold bolt of agony up his thigh and through his core. He grimaced as the lion slumped across his legs, pinning him in place. It writhed and bucked in its death throes, bleeding from multiple wounds but hanging on for dear life.

It wouldn't die quickly.

Slater realised the mortal danger he was in as the lion turned to face him, its bloodshot eyes staring daggers into his soul. Instantly the pain of his leg fell away, replaced by an overwhelming survival instinct.

Still resting on its side, kicking and bucking as it died, it lurched at him. Slater saw a great maw slicing through the air toward him — if he did nothing, the massive jaws would clamp down on either side of his head.

Charged with terror, he shot both hands out and seized each of the lion's jaws in a powerful grip.

Both parties froze in place.

Slater had never felt strength like this. In a life or death situation he was able to overpower almost any adversary — a lifetime of powerlifting had gifted him with the strength of a bull. But as his veins pumped and the lactic acid burned in his arms and he squeezed with everything he had left in his system, he realised he was fighting a losing battle.

He couldn't overpower a lion.

Even a dying one, operating at less than ten percent of its usual capacity.

He stared down the beast's throat, its neck straining as it grunted with exertion. A milky haze had settled over its eyes — death was approaching fast — but it wouldn't get there in time.

Slater reached the point of failure. His arms buckled slightly at the elbows, relenting as the lion powered its teeth toward him. He sensed a gruesome death bearing down on him and let out a roar of his own, pressing with any reserve he could find within him.

The lion's jaws slipped back an inch.

It sensed Slater gaining the upper hand and surged forward, unloading all its primal energy into the struggle. Finally, Slater's arms could do no more. He buckled and collapsed, slumping over as he lost all feeling in his upper limbs.

And the lion took its final breath.

It drooped its head onto his chest, exhaling with the kind of finality Slater had seen hundreds of times before in the men he'd killed.

He'd never quite found himself in a situation like this, though.

The beast faded on top of him, its massive paws going limp, its jaws hanging slack. Slater eyed the sharpened, yellowing teeth inside its gums — only half a foot from his now-unprotected face — and let out a sigh of relief.

He still couldn't feel his arms.

They'd worked harder than he thought humanly possible to keep the creature at bay.

Working his way free would prove cumbersome. All the crushing pressure of a five-hundred pound monster bore down on him, and as soon as he chose to focus on the situation at hand the pain came screaming back into reality.

His leg was fucked.

To put it mildly.

Ligaments and bones and all manner of juicy tendons in the side of his leg groaned for relief, already injured and pinned in awkward fashion underneath the dead lion.

Slater inhaled sharply to prepare for the agony involved in moving the beast, inch by inch, off his legs. His vision swam — a quick assessment of the situation revealed the M4A1 carbine lying on the other side of the lion's hulking mass, its magazine empty, a fresh one necessary. Slater had a spare magazine tucked into the belt of his jeans, but without a gun to hammer it into, it proved useless.

He started shifting the lion as best he could, pushing with as much exertion as he could manage against the beast's stomach...

...and then he froze.

No.

He'd glimpsed it out of the corner of his eye, barely noticeable amidst the shadows draping the other end of the walkway. The path cutting across the vast open space was mostly illuminated by the natural light spearing in through the giant glass-domed roof of the emporium. But a stretch of the steel mesh at the other end hung underneath the lee of a complex constructed in the side of the glass dome, mostly shrouded from the general public's line of sight but providing a gorgeous sweeping view over both Macau and the emporium itself.

Forrest's penthouse had to rest within.

There was no other explanation for the strange architectural layout.

But that wasn't what had seized his attention so abruptly.

Slater stopped moving. He lost all willpower instantly, what little strength he'd been clutching onto sapping out of him in a single moment. He stared straight into the new pair of predatory eyes, wide and menacing and attached to a body just as muscle-clad and destructive as its dead twin's.

Another lion.

It had noticed him — and it spotted the corpse of its mate, slumped in a bloody heap over Slater's legs, trapping him in the cable car. It bowed its head and began to stalk, pawing without a peep of sound across the walkway.

Advancing.

Eyes wide.

Gazed locked.

Slater realised immediately he was a dead man.

He could do nothing. The advancing lion was just as vicious as its mate — in fact, even more so. Its muscles swelled with the intensity of an apex predator preparing to strike. Somewhere in the back of his mind, he recalled some nature documentary that said when prey can see the advancing beast, a lion would seldom charge from more than seventy feet away.

Slater figured he had a couple of seconds before the lion broke into an all-out sprint and tore him cleanly in two in his compromised position.

He gave one final heave, wrenching his legs with everything he had left. They barely budged an inch. Pain from his torn ligaments screamed up into his stomach, threatening to bring up the food he'd digested earlier that morning. He slumped back against the wall, panting, sweating, shaking.

The lion crept closer.

He closed his eyes and waited to die.

50

Forrest managed a smirk as he brought up a surveillance feed of Mountain Lion's lobby on his phone and spotted Jim hustling for the exit as fast as his legs would allow. The man wore simple jeans and a leather jacket, with a faded duffel bag draped over one shoulder.

All his possessions in the world, hanging by a strap.

In some way Forrest envied the man. Jim could disappear and start fresh, worming his way around until the heat died down. Forrest had created something titanic, and he was linked with it. He would go down with Mountain Lion — nothing else was feasible.

Briefly he considered the fact that he could have slipped away. Earlier that morning would have been the ideal time — use his offshore accounts to tuck himself into a third world hole for a few months until he worked up the courage to form a new identity.

But that wasn't Peter Forrest.

It never had been, and it never would be.

His empire was his life. When it ended, he would too.

He would go out on his shield.

Jim had done his job. It hadn't taken long to navigate the Tsavo lions onto the walkway — the zookeepers had hurried them along with the use of electric cattle prods, a strangely effective method given they didn't find themselves in a predicament where they could get attacked. From there they'd left the predators alone, thoroughly confused by Forrest's demands.

Now, they were nowhere to be seen.

Forrest was alone atop an empire of riches that would soon come crashing down.

He hurried to the viewpoint, in a trance-like state, uncaring about anything except watching the mysterious African-American man get mauled to death at the final hurdle. He gazed out across the walkway — and the vast emporium below — and spotted one of the Tsavo lions resting on its haunches, almost placid, with its back to the bank of elevators. It had chosen the perfect position to rest — any unsuspecting arrivals would be mauled.

What if someone else comes up? One of the staff?

They had no reason to. Forrest hadn't requested anyone. If they found themselves being gored by a lion it was no-one's fault but their own. Besides, Forrest had long ago abandoned the idea of remaining morally pure. Killing anyone and everyone had become his bread and butter.

Or, rather, getting his men to do it for him.

Much more effective.

There was no sign of the other Tsavo lion. Forrest imagined it was buried somewhere in the supports underneath him, prowling the darkness, investigating this strange new area.

One of the elevators arrived and the doors opened — Forrest noticed the action out of the corner of his eye. He whipped his gaze around and froze, anticipating madness, drawing every ounce of pleasure and satisfaction out of the situation until the chaos caught up to him.

Gunfire erupted, silhouetting the gigantic beast behind muzzle flashes. Forrest watched in fascination. It was like a horror movie unfolding before his eyes. The lion twisted and pounced, firing like a rocket off the mark as it launched into the elevator.

Then, nothing.

Forrest squinted, but from his elevated position he couldn't see directly inside the cable car. Nothing happened for a full minute. Cold sweat broke out across his brow.

What the hell's going on?

He couldn't fathom the man achieving the impossible. He imagined the Tsavo lion could take a swathe of bullets to the body before it succumbed to pain — and it would have torn the man's head off by then. The one-way windows running along this stretch of Forrest's penthouse covered a significant stretch of space. He wondered if he could get a better view in another room.

Moving fast, ignoring the pain coursing through his mangled hand, he hurried through to the next room across. By this point his hand was beyond recovery — he hadn't received proper medical attention in due time and he'd elected to simply wrap the finger stumps in a bloody cloth. It wouldn't be long before infection set in.

He didn't intend to be alive by that point, anyway.

Unless he could pull off a miracle.

He hurried to the far corner of the empty room and crouched down, peering at a new angle along the walkway.

The lion had come to rest on its side, slumped across the same man he'd shared an elevator with earlier.

Just as he suspected.

The guy who had played a major role in bringing his empire to its knees.

Or, in reality, exposing major flaws in the system that Forrest had created himself.

He'd sabotaged himself.

But, as he realised the African-American man was pinned in place, going nowhere, he sensed movement underneath him.

The second Tsavo lion materialised, stalking along the walkway, headed straight for the elevator.

The guy was now unarmed, having exhausted his ammunition.

Forrest grinned maniacally. He forced all thoughts of salvaging the situation aside and focused entirely on enjoying what came next.

You've got time, he thought. *Get a front seat experience.*

His mind racing to the point of delusion, he hurried away from the floor-to-ceiling windows, heading straight for the front door of his penthouse. From there he could navigate to the walkways and hear the sound of the man's death with his own ears. That would bring him inner peace.

That would be the silver lining for the subsequent collapse of his empire.

He hurled the front door open and set off on a mad dash for the grimy concrete stairwell that led to the walkways. He preferred the elevators, but he'd reach the walkways faster taking the manual route, and time was of the essence.

He made it two flights down before he sensed movement directly in front of him. He looked up and jolted in surprise as a tight-knit party of bodies hurrying in the other direction crashed into him. The sharp twists of the stairwell made it easy to tangle up, and Forrest tumbled, dropping hard onto one of the dull concrete steps. He grimaced and reached out a hand to steady himself, barely giving it a second thought.

Wrong hand.

The two stumps where his fingers used to be slapped against the concrete, devolving him into a wreck. He curled into a ball, surrounded by hostile bodies, some of which rained down blows on his exposed liver. He cried out, the confidence sapped from him in a single moment.

Someone had come for him.

This was it.

But who?

The powerfully-built Asian man who reached down and hurled Forrest to his feet with a steady hand sported a familiar face. He thought he would never see the man again. He thought he'd moved on from that part of his life.

He'd thought wrong.

'What are you doing here?' Forrest snarled, his pain turning to anger. 'We settled things. You have my money.'

Jerome leaned in and pinned Forrest against the wall, flecks of spit forming in the corners of his mouth. Surrounding him were five furious triad gangsters, armed with pistols and sub-machine guns and shooting daggers at Forrest from their positions on the stairwell.

'You thought it would be that simple?' Jerome hissed back. 'Fucking me over?'

'What?'

'You know exactly what I'm talking about.'

Forrest couldn't form a response before Jerome hammered his fist into his gut. He doubled over, coughing, and Jerome backhanded him across the face, knocking a tooth loose. Forrest spat blood onto the stairwell.

'What do you want?' Forrest moaned. 'If you're here to kill me, just get it over with.'

'I want to know why you did what you did.'

'I have no idea what you're talking about.'

'I want you to lead me to Tak and Antoine. I know they're in this building somewhere.'

'What?!'

'You heard me.'

'How am I supposed to know where they are? I haven't been in touch with them since—'

Jerome threw a vertical elbow, jamming his forearm into the bridge of Forrest's already damaged nose. Forrest howled and slumped to his knees, a pitiful sight on the cold stairwell.

'Why lie?' Jerome said.

'I'm telling you...'

'Then why do we have footage of them strolling straight back into Mountain Lion an hour ago? And, even better — they had the girl. I see what you were doing to me.'

'What?!'

'It was all bullshit. You were hoping I'd come after Tak and Antoine and Jin. You wanted to cause internal disruption in my ranks. Make everyone doubt each other. Then you could swoop in and take over.'

'No...'

'You've been paying us handsomely for long enough. That became too much, didn't it? You wanted all of Macau for yourself?'

'Jerome, I'm telling you,' Forrest repeated.

'What will your words do? We have the visual proof.'

'I don't know what they're doing in my casino.'

'Have you found them, then? Have you killed them?'

'No.'

'Why not?'

'I've been a little preoccupied.'

'Where are they?' Jerome hissed. 'I know you're hiding them. They double-crossed me and then they shit their pants when I told them I was onto them. So they slunk back here with their tail between their legs.'

Forrest couldn't speak. At a loss for words, he snivelled and bowed his head.

'Don't feel like talking?'

'What's the point? You won't believe me.'

'I want the truth. That's all, Peter.'

'I don't know anything. That's the truth.'

'You're right — I don't believe you,' Jerome said. He pressed his fingers into Forrest's throat like pincers, holding him upright. 'Except I think I know what might make you talk. Tak and Antoine spread all kinds of rumours while they were around. They said you have a walkway hovering over a lion enclosure? And you use it to kill people?'

Forrest went pale. 'They're lying.'

'I don't think so. Why don't we go pay it a visit? Maybe that might loosen your tongue. You can tell me where my old employees are, or I'll feed you to them.'

'No,' Forrest mouthed, paling, at a loss for words. 'No, no, we can't do that. The lions are—'

Jerome thundered a fist into Forrest's mouth, shutting him up. The pain amplified, sending him into a groggy stupor.

'Quiet, now,' Jerome muttered. 'Let's go.'

Forrest opened his mouth to protest, now white as a ghost, but Jerome struck him in the face again. Forrest's head slumped. Two of the triad thugs snatched him underneath each armpit and began dragging him down the stairs.

'No,' he muttered through bloody lips. 'The lions ... are out.'

But no-one heard him.

51

S later stared death in the face, and braced himself for the most painful few seconds of his life.

Conveniently, they would also be the last few seconds of his life.

The hairless lion advanced toward him, with pale skin and bloodshot eyes and a menacing gait. Slater imagined it sprinting the last stretch, its mighty jaws clamping down on his unprotected upper body. No amount of strength in his arms would hold off a fully healthy lion — especially considering he could barely feel his limbs. It had taken all the power in his system to keep a lion on the verge of death at bay for a few seconds.

Any kind of resistance against this new arrival would result in catastrophic failure.

He would only be prolonging his death.

In his final moments, he thought of Shien. He prayed she would take initiative and find her way home. Maybe she could even usher the other kidnapped children to safety. As long as she made it out of Mountain Lion before the entire complex went into lockdown to deal with the chaos, Slater could rest easy.

He hoped he'd done enough to save her.

The lion continued to stalk, prolonging the inevitable, closing the space between them.

It was eighty feet from the cable car.

Seventy.

Sixty.

Fifty.

Its giant limbs tensed up. The lion bared its teeth, its eyes widening, the rush of an imminent charge crackling in the air. Slater's insides went weak as he rode out the stress. He tasted raw fear, unlike anything he'd ever felt before. Human hostility — no matter how terrifying — had its limitations. This kind of natural fear knew no bounds.

Then, from the other end of the emporium, the sound of footsteps. Multiple bodies moving through space, bursting out into the open, clattering against railings in haste. The lion obscured Slater from view, but he heard low voices ringing through the space.

The lion didn't care.

It burst off the mark.

Slater tensed up, expecting the inevitable, watching it close the gap, spelling his death.

Then, from across the walkway, '*What the fuck is that?!*'

'I told you!' another voice roared, sounding congested, as if its owner had both nostrils clogged. 'Nobody listened to—'

The voice was drowned out by automatic gunfire — Slater realised far too late the party was firing down the walkway, directly at the lion. Bullets slashed past the sprinting predator and thudded into the rear wall of the elevator, some sinking home only a few inches above Slater's head.

He recoiled away from the impacts, flattening him into the gap between the dead lion and the wall as best he could.

Then there was nothing to do but wait in terror. Chaos reigned across the emporium — bullets flew, men shouted and barked commands, a low roar emanated from somewhere between the two parties, steel rattled, muzzles flared, and after a few seconds of Slater's hearing being drowned by madness he heard the distinct shriek of a man being mauled to death.

Slater kept his head down as the wall behind him thudded with the impacts of stray bullets. Directly on top of him, the first lion's corpse twitched involuntarily, spasming in the elevator with enough force to rock the cable car in place. His heart leapt at the sensation. As he burrowed further into the carpet — now soaked with blood — he realised he could wriggle one leg free from underneath the crushing weight of the dead lion.

He grimaced and worked his good knee back and forth, yanking it inch by inch out from underneath the slab of meat, all the while ducking as wild shots ricocheted off the cable car. Pandemonium struck — more horrific screeches echoed through the vast space beyond.

Goddamn, Slater thought.

When the gunfire ceased after a brutal stint of madness, Slater wrenched his bad leg free with a gasp and leapfrogged over the dead lion, tumbling in a heap onto the other side. He splashed down in a puddle of the predator's blood — barely noticing the disgusting surroundings — and snatched up the M4A1 carbine, ejecting its magazine with a practiced motion. The magazine shot free and Slater slammed the fresh one home.

He powered to his feet — a difficult task indeed — and hobbled out of the elevator, leaving the foul stench of the dying lion behind.

He observed the carnage.

With a wheeze and a groan of desperation, the second lion hobbled from one side of the walkway to the other, limping away from a fresh kill. Blood drenched the sides of its mouth — it had done well. Another bullet from one of the new arrivals slammed into its torso, spurring it on. The lion omitted a final yelp of anguish and dove for any kind of safety it could find.

In this case, returning home.

Slater watched with mouth agape as the mortally wounded beast lurched over the railing, tumbling like a rag doll toward the jungle canopy below. He realised it was instinctively returning to its enclosure, fleeing from the steel bite of the bullets dotting its hide.

The lion smashed through the canopy, five hundred pounds of bodyweight destroying a portion of the broad jungle leaves. It disappeared from sight, crashing to the forest floor below. Slater estimated the drop at a couple of dozen feet. He wasn't sure if it had died on impact, but the beast would succumb to its wounds before long.

He sized up the trail of devastation the lion had left in its wake.

Three of the men on the walkway had been brutally mauled, leaving no doubt as to their fate. Their wounds weren't survivable — Slater merely glanced at the bloody corpses before turning away. His stomach churned at the sight. A couple of others had been dumped on their rears further down the steel path, shocked into immobilisation by the sight of the predator bearing down on them. They clutched sub-machine guns in their sweaty palms, the barrels smoking.

They couldn't believe their luck.

They'd survived.

That's a shame, Slater thought.

He hobbled a few steps away from the bank of elevators, stepping out onto the walkway — the structure dizzyingly high amidst the emporium — and raised the carbine rifle to his shoulder. He let twin bursts of fully automatic gunfire fly, dropping each man where they sat. The pair crumpled, their weapons clattering to the floor.

Slater locked his gaze on the only two men remaining on the walkway, both unarmed, both flabbergasted at the horrific turn of events.

Peter Forrest, beaten half to death, and a muscular Asian man with the identical neck tattoo of the triad snaking its way past his collar.

Even though neither were armed, Slater didn't want any trouble. He lined up his aim and put a bullet through the triad gangster's thigh, dropping the man where he stood. Forrest yelped in fright and cowered away from Slater, leaning over one of the railings in an attempt to minimise his target area.

He was no threat.

Slater deployed his best poker face and placed as much weight as he feasibly could manage on his bad leg without passing out. The pain proved staggering, ripping through him with all the force of a gut punch, but he kept his balance. Sweat broke out across his brow, but it meant nothing.

He could function.

For now.

'Look, mate,' Forrest said, clutching the railing for dear

life, his knuckles turning white. 'You're the guy from the elevator, yeah? I'm sorry, mate. I don't know what I've done to you.'

Slater pulled to a halt in front of the pathetic man. The triad had dished out unbelievable punishment, to the point where his face had swollen beyond recognition. It looked like he'd been stung by a thousand bees at once. He could barely keep his eyes open through the swelling.

'You haven't done anything to me,' Slater said.

'Then what do you want? For fuck's sake, just leave me alone.'

Slater said nothing. He stared down at the man who had caused such suffering, who had stripped innocent children of their freedom and forced them into a line of work barely imaginable. He wondered how many girls he had used up and murdered, their bodies dumped when their ability to serve the paying customers proved suddenly useless.

He wondered if Forrest had ever given it a second thought.

But, in his desperate, snivelling state, Forrest took the silence as a form of hesitation. His mouth opened in a half-gasp as he sensed an opportunity, displaying his emotions without a second thought.

Getting your face smashed into a pulp often stripped you of the ability to employ subtlety.

'Do you want a job, mate?' he coughed. 'Y-you seem like the type of guy who can dish out a fair bit of damage. What do you say? Help me get my feet back under me and I'll make you rich, brother. Richer than you can imagine. There's work to be done, but—'

'The girl. Shien.'

Forrest paused. 'Yeah? What about her?'

'Where are her parents?'

'Her dad's dead. He got caught up in all this shit. Not his fault. Not mine either.'

'And the mother?'

'Probably halfway to Texas by now, mate.'

'How do you know she's from Texas?'

'I thought about kidnapping her instead of their daughter. But … she's not in the picture. She won't want anything to do with this.'

Slater lapsed back into silence, twisting the M4A1's barrel in imperceptible semi-circles, mulling over what to do next.

'Look,' Forrest said, 'did you hear what I said about a job? I've got some openings. Clean this mess up and I'll give you millions of dollars. Millions. I just need time to—'

Slater offered a half-smile, barely putting any effort into the acting job.

Humouring the man for a single second.

Forrest was clutching at anything he could. His face lit up at the sign of the smile. He grinned through a bloody set of teeth. 'Millions of dollars, mate. All yours.'

Slater reached down and hauled Forrest to his feet, dragging him up by the collar. The roughhousing didn't seem to deter Forrest in the slightest. He desperately held onto the false reality that Slater was his ally. Like a teenager believing their crush was head-over-heels in love with them because of momentary eye contact.

Slater peered over the edge of the railing, staring down into the artificially lit jungle enclosure. From somewhere on the dark forest floor, he thought he heard a noise similar to a weak growl.

'You think that lion's still alive?' he said, passing it off as simple banter.

Forrest smirked. 'Dunno. Fifty-fifty, mate.'

'That's better odds than you gave those girls.'

Forrest started to open his mouth to speak but Slater swung an uppercut that crashed against the underside of the man's chin and knocked a fat wad of teeth loose in a spray of blood. Then he hauled the pathetic billionaire over the railing, barely putting any effort into the act. Forrest tumbled headfirst over the side of the walkway and fell silently into the jungle canopy.

Too terrified to scream.

52

S later didn't bother to watch the ordeal. He wanted to wrap this destruction up in the next minute or so. He turned to face the last hostile left alive in the emporium — the triad figure with a useless right leg and a bad neck tattoo.

'You someone important?' he said, his voice cold, his bones drained of energy.

The madness had taken its toll on him. He could barely see straight as he used the railing to lend assistance to his mangled leg.

The triad member had gone horrifically pale — Slater realised he must have severed an artery with the thigh shot. The guy was bleeding out, already sprawled in a puddle of the crimson stuff.

'You could say that,' the guy muttered, his English good. 'You have no idea.'

'Let me guess. Head of the triad?'

The man nodded.

'Thought as much,' Slater said. 'What's your name?'

'Jerome.'

'That's not your name.'

'It's what everyone calls me.'

'You're the one who ran that basement operation, huh?'

Jerome paused, but Slater had spent enough time around liars to understand exactly what that pause meant.

Whatever words came out afterwards would mean nothing.

They would be false.

Without question.

'We had no choice,' Jerome said. 'Forrest paid our organisation to offer him protection and enforcement throughout Mountain Lion. He couldn't keep the complex running without dipping into the horrible stuff. It started out as bread crumbs, but ... I'm guessing you saw what it became.'

'I sure did.'

'That's why I'm here,' Jerome said, his tone confident but his eyes pleading for a break in the interrogation — to compose his thoughts, to arrange his defence. 'That's why we came. To make things right. You saw how we beat him half to death. We were here to put a stop to all the sex slavery. We're gangsters, but we have morals.'

'That's why you came?'

'Yes.'

'It wouldn't have anything to do with your two friends I killed in the basement, would it? You didn't show up to get them back?'

Jerome took a moment to respond — the hesitation revealed all. Both of them sensed it. Acceptance spread over the man's face. He wasn't talking his way out of this one.

His entire demeanour shifted in the blink of an eye.

'Alright — we weren't here to make things right,' the man snarled. 'Don't know why I bothered trying to hide it.

But it doesn't make a fucking difference. You're going to help me.'

'Am I?'

'I'm bleeding out. Get me to a hospital or you won't make it out of Macau. I'm God here. You understand? I run this fucking region.'

Slater had heard it a thousand times before. The same old spiel, laced with outrage and scorn and supreme confidence.

The only way bad men knew how to gain leverage.

Through intimidation and threats.

'What do you think you'll do if I die here?' Jerome spat. 'Where do you think you'll hide? You don't know what's coming.'

Slater gazed around. 'Seems like all your men are dead.'

'There's more. There's hundreds more.'

'That's odd. I don't see them.'

'You take one step out of this casino without me by your side and you'll be a dead man walking.'

'Somehow I doubt that.'

'Macau is mine. If you think—'

Slater unloaded three bullets into Jerome's face. He'd listened to the gangster go on for long enough. Nothing he said would have ever affected Slater's mindset — he wanted to cleanse the earth of anyone involved in this kind of operation. Excuses proved useless.

Excuses wouldn't bring his mother back.

The final gunshot faded away, blisteringly loud initially before fading into a soft echo rolling along the emporium walls. Then that too dissipated, leaving Slater entirely alone at the top of Mountain Lion Casino & Resorts. He let the carbine rifle fall to his side and gazed around in a state of shock.

A dead lion in the elevator. Dead men scattered about the walkway. Dead men underneath the complex, their corpses left to be discovered in the most incriminating of settings. Their legacies would be ruined, their lives lost, because they felt the need to satiate their twisted vices.

He'd done enough.

Not just for his time in Macau — but for a lifetime.

You crossed that bridge long ago, he thought.

He should have stopped halfway into his career. But he'd carried on pressing forward, throwing himself into combat time after time, adding scar after scar to his mental state until he'd devolved into a broken man by the time he'd finally left the service to his country behind.

From there he'd plunged into hell in Yemen, and followed it up with a war for the ages in Macau.

To this day, he couldn't ascertain whether he found trouble, or trouble found him.

But his work here was done.

He honed in on the total silence draped over the emporium and stared up through the glass-domed ceiling at the cloudy sky. It was late afternoon, and he hadn't slept in what felt like days. He dropped the carbine, recognising the finality with which it hit the steel mesh of the walkway.

Signalling an end to the chaos.

For now.

For a brief stint of his life where he could recover from the craziness. Put his feet up for as long as it took to heal back to full health. Maybe he'd revisit the stem cell clinic in Zurich. There were a thousand options, all of which he had the opportunity to capitalise on.

But first, he needed to sort out the future of a young girl waiting in the basement of the complex for him to return.

He limped for the elevators in tentative fashion, ignoring

the cable car containing the dead hairless lion. For superstition's sake, he strayed as far away from the beast as he could manage, calling for the elevator at the very end of the line.

It arrived in seconds — clearly it was a slow day for VIP customers — and he hobbled into the centre of the thickly carpeted box, thumbing a button on the panel.

He wiped blood from his face, winced as fresh pain coursed through seemingly everywhere at once, and leant back against the metal banister to take the pressure off his mangled leg.

All in a day's work.

Before the doors closed, he thought he heard a low growl resonate up from below the walkway, piercing the air. Slater tuned his ears to the sound, just as a follow-up scream of pain tore through the emporium.

Then silence.

Peter Forrest, murdered by his own pet.

A wry smile spread across Slater's face as the doors sliced closed.

53

I t took less than ten minutes to devise an exit plan.

Shien had acted years ahead of her age, finding the keys to each cell on one of the dead guards and freeing each of the young girls one by one. By the time Slater arrived in a bloody heap at the correct sub-level, a broken mess of his former self, Shien had arranged the drugged-up children in an orderly line by the bank of elevators.

She saw Slater hunched over, dripping blood onto the thick carpet.

'Oh my God,' she whispered. 'Will...'

'Told you I'd be alright,' he said with a bloody smile.

By now Shien had grown accustomed to the violence, and none of the other kids were in a suitable state to react to it. They stared at him, glassy-eyed, probably seeing him as some kind of apparition. He stumbled through the elevator doors and sucked in deep breaths as he thought about their next move.

'There needs to be a discreet way to leave,' Slater said. 'From this floor. Forrest would have made sure of that.'

'I don't understand,' Shien said.

'Don't worry. Talking to myself. But there'll be a way out from here without walking through the front door.'

'Isn't everyone dead?' Shien said. 'Why can't we just walk out?'

'Even if there's no-one behind the cameras, I don't want to attract attention. I'm not in the right state to defend all twelve of you.'

'So where do we go?'

'Like I said. There's got to be a back way.'

'I can look if you want,' Shien said. 'There's no-one else down here — I already checked the whole floor. You killed a lot of people, Will...'

'Wasn't all me.'

'Well, you're in no state to go running around looking for a way out. Let me do it.'

Slater's fatherly instincts took over but he cut himself short. He could barely see straight, let alone run up and down the corridors searching for an exit. He nodded, his mannerisms weak, leaning on one of the concrete walls, relishing the cool touch of the stone against his cheek.

'Stay here,' Shien said.

'You sure?'

'I'm fine. The drugs aren't in my system anymore. I can think properly.'

'Yeah, but ... you're nine years old.'

'And you're half dead.'

'True.'

Slater blinked hard, composing himself, racing through a list of hypotheticals once they found themselves out of Mountain Lion. Shien seemed to read his mind.

'What are you going to do with them?' she muttered, lowering her voice. 'There's so many of them.'

'I'll take them to the police. There's not much else I can do.'

'And what about me?'

Slater stared at her, recalling what Forrest had told him about her parents — about the lack of a home she had to return to. 'We'll figure that out later, Shien. For now let's get out of here.'

'You know something,' Shien said, narrowing her eyes. 'About me. What is it? What did you find out?'

Slater grimaced — horrific injuries removed the ability to conceal emotions. 'Now's not the time.'

She shrugged. 'Suit yourself. But you'd better tell me eventually.'

'Search for a way out,' he said. 'And keep these girls close by. There's something I need to do — to buy us some time once we get out of here.'

'What?'

'Hold on.'

He staggered past the posse of children, following the curvature of the corridor in slow-motion, effectively operating with one leg. Shien made to follow him but he held out an open palm.

'No,' he said. 'I've got this. Start looking for a way out.'

It took him three painful minutes to reach the cell block. With his vision swimming in murky waters, he found the corpse of the man from level 44 and slipped a pair of bloodstained fingers into his jacket pocket, retrieving the four bright orange casino chips he'd handed over earlier that day.

He tucked them into his own jeans pocket and limped for the elevators.

On the way back, he passed Shien exiting one of the rooms, shaking her head in frustration. 'Nothing so far.'

'I'll be back in five minutes,' Slater said.

'What are you doing?'

'Getting us a bankroll.'

~

THROUGH SHEER DUMB LUCK, Slater managed to exchange the chips without interruption. He rested his forehead against the glass security screen separating him from the cashier, barely able to keep himself upright. When he straightened up, he noticed a bloody imprint left behind on the sheet — a clear mark where his temple had rested. He gulped back unease and waited while the cashier counted out four hundred thousand US Dollars, all hundreds.

The woman behind the screen barely gave him a second glance — a true professional. Anyone else would have gawked at the sight.

Slater recalled a time not so long ago when he'd found himself in the depths of Yemen's mountain ranges, clutching onto his life by a thread. That had felt different, though. Survival out in that wasteland had been something primal — he'd formed a connection to the land while stumbling out of hell, shot and beaten and barely conscious. There had been nothing around for dozens of miles in any direction. Here, surrounded by easygoing tourists and wealthy patrons, overshadowed on all sides by luxury, his injuries became more noticeable.

He stood out like a sore thumb.

The cashier bound the bills into four tight bands and tucked them discreetly into an expensive-looking carry bag emblazoned with the Mountain Lion emblem. Slater slid a hand under the thin partition and took the bag, nodding gratefully to the woman.

She nodded back.

With that he pivoted — albeit slowly, taking care not to aggravate his leg any further — and limped his way back across the vast lobby. This giant dome of a room was situated adjacent to the main casino complex. Slater passed elderly men in suits and women in regal gowns and tourists with their shirts tucked into their shorts twirling fifty-dollar casino chips eagerly through their fingertips as they hustled for the closest tables.

The facade of importance.

None of this mattered. Slater saw the complex in a new light — all the activities important to the bottom line took place far out of sight, either in VIP rooms with obscene table limits or below, in sterile concrete rooms that reeked of fear and suffering.

The areas open to the general public facilitated an illusion.

There was also an inevitable delay. Slater gazed around and noted it appeared like there was nothing wrong at all — customers seemed happy, staff seemed pleasant. No hint could be found that Mountain Lion's owner lay dead on the top floor, torn apart by his own exotic pet, accompanied into the great beyond by dozens of gangsters and killers from all walks of life.

Astonished by the ridiculousness of it all, Slater pressed forward, staggering past groups of civilians with all the time in the world.

Slater had little time.

Then he almost ran directly into a man, both of them headed in opposite directions and unfocused on their exact trajectories. Slater bumped shoulders with the guy and a twinge of abhorrent pain tore up his leg. He suppressed it with a wince and turned to make eye contact.

He froze in place, recognition spreading across his face.
Samuel Barnes mimicked his actions.

54

'You're alive,' was all Slater could think to say.

Samuel wore a plain black long-sleeved shirt and baggy jeans, both of which were draped unnaturally over his frame. Slater realised the clothes weren't his — they had been given to him by his captors. The man looked as if he'd aged ten years since Slater had seen him last. Heavy black bags hung underneath his eyes and his cheekbones protruded from his face. His features were hollow and gaunt. He stood hunched over, his shoulders slumped, the baggy clothing no doubt covering an array of bruises and injuries.

'Yeah, man,' Samuel said, his voice hoarse. 'I'm alive.'

'You okay?'

'Been better.'

They both remained frozen in place, two statues in a sea of moving bodies. Passersby ignored them — they had their own destinations in mind.

Will Slater and Samuel Barnes assessed each others' injuries.

'What happened?' Slater said.

'I came back here. After you left me in that apartment complex. I tried to cash in the chip you gave me.'

'And?'

'They grabbed me straight away.'

'Who?'

'I don't know. All of them. First a guy called Forrest wanted to know what I'd been doing — but obviously I couldn't tell him because it was his own men who black-mailed me. Then those guys came in afterwards. The triad guys. They wanted to know what happened to the money. I didn't know shit, man. You took the laptop.'

'I'm sorry,' Slater said. 'I could have done more.'

'You seem pretty banged up yourself.'

'I don't want to think about it. That'll make it worse.'

'That some kind of battlefield mentality?'

'Something like that. Where are you headed?'

'Me?' Samuel said, staring vacantly over Slater's shoulder. 'Don't know, mate. I just got out.'

'From where?'

'Holding cell. They told me they were going to kill me tonight. Don't think they had much use for me when they realised I didn't know shit.'

'What changed?'

'Everyone disappeared. The men guarding me got called somewhere. To deal with some ... problem.' He stared at Slater as he finished the sentence, connecting the dots silently. 'What'd you do?'

'Stirred up some trouble.'

'Is it bad?'

'Only a matter of time before this place falls to pieces,' Slater said.

Samuel went pale and cast his eyes skyward. 'Like ... structurally?'

'No,' Slater said with a smirk. 'Behind-the-scenes stuff. They won't be in business much longer.'

'Triad?'

'You heard of someone called Jerome?'

Samuel's eyes widened. 'Everyone has. Did you piss him off?'

'I killed him.'

Despite the commotion all around them, silence laced the space between the two parties. They both stood there, Samuel's mouth agape, comprehending what had unfolded inside Mountain Lion.

'You need to get out of here,' Samuel said.

'I'm working on that.'

'No — I mean, right now. You don't know what you've just done.'

'I've pissed off some pretty important people in the past. I'm still here.'

'Not like this.'

'Good thing I'll be out of the country soon, then. I take it you're thinking the same thing.'

Samuel nodded. 'Just ... lucky to be alive, man.'

'How'd you actually get out?'

'The door was wonky. I could work on levering it open when there was no-one around — but there were always people around. Until you showed up. Then everyone disappeared.'

'So I inadvertently put you in this place and got you out. Consider it even?'

'I'd have been dead if you never showed up in the first place. The triad would have killed me, and then the girl. Is she still alive?'

'She's still alive.'

'Job well done, then,' Samuel said.

Slater found himself astonished by the transformation he was witnessing. Gone were the nerves and the stuttering — instead Samuel stood before him with a placid expression on his face, dejected and reserved. Accepting of his circumstances. Slater looked into his eyes and wondered what kinds of physical punishment they'd dished out on him.

They'd certainly changed him.

'Where are you going now?' Slater said.

'Don't know, man. Out of here.'

'You got money?'

'No.'

'You got a passport? Any personal belongings?'

'No. Can't go back to my place. They'll be watching it. When they find out I'm gone.'

'I think you're the least of their problems right now, Samuel. Go get your stuff, and get out of Macau. And while you're at it—'

Slater reached into the carry bag and snatched up one of the four bundles of bills the cashier had provided him with. He handed it across, making sure to be discreet.

'There we go,' he said. 'Now you've cashed your chip in.'

Samuel stared down at the money, tears brimming in his eyes. It seemed his emotions were finally forcing their way to the surface. 'Thanks, man. Don't even know who you are.'

'Don't thank me,' Slater said. 'We can skirt around it as much as we want, but I left you for dead in that apartment complex. That's the truth. Don't rely on me for anything. Go start your own life with that money and do something with yourself. Forget I exist.'

'Don't think that'll happen anytime soon.'

'Good luck, brother.'

Samuel stared at him. 'You too, man. With ... whatever it is you do.'

'I piss people off, it seems. It's a full time gig if you do it well enough.'

'Don't run into any of Jerome's friends.'

'Why not?'

'They'll kill—' Then he paused, likely remembering what Slater had done in the apartment complex, the sheer ferocity with which he'd barrelled through a small army of hitmen. 'Don't worry. Do your thing.'

'Get yourself out of Macau.'

'On it.'

Samuel turned and disappeared into the crowd, a pale shell of his former self. Another victim of greed and corruption and the lust for power. Slater couldn't remember a time where he hadn't operated in this murky world. It surrounded him, overwhelmed him, consumed him.

But he kept his head afloat.

Even with such riches and the unrelenting demonstrations of what kind of life one could live when they turned a blind eye to morals, Slater had never faltered. Never wavered. He prided himself on that.

With dark memories of his time in Macau on his mind, and an intricate web of pain receptors screaming for attention throughout his body, he ghosted through the masses covering Mountain Lion's lobby.

Heading back into its dark heart.

55

'Will,' Shien said, her voice as stern as always. 'Let me drive.'

'Not a chance,' Slater mumbled.

The damage to his leg had caused him the most distress. Cuts and bruises and knocks to the head were uncomfortable, but nothing Slater hadn't handled a million times over. On the other hand the agony coursing through his knee carried with it a sensation he hadn't experienced for quite some time.

Yemen, a voice in the back of his head whispered.

He allowed himself a smirk — how could he have forgotten so quickly? He realised his entire life had been made up of a series of grievous battlefield wounds, interspersed with short periods of respite. Frankly he found it hard to believe he'd made it this far without turning into a cripple or a brain-damaged zombie. Since he'd first stepped foot in the United States military and been whisked from division to division until he ended up in a career too unbelievable to fathom, Slater had been operating as a war machine.

Sometimes he wondered when he would reach his expiry date.

If he kept this pace up, it wouldn't be long.

Then he looked across the centre console of the stolen limousine at Shien resting peacefully in the passenger seat, her knees tucked up to her chest as the vehicle bounced and jolted over potholes...

...and he realised it didn't matter how much damage he accumulated over the long term.

As long as he could succeed — whatever the cost — the satisfaction would outweigh the permanent consequences.

He'd lived his life that way for as long as he could remember.

He wasn't about to change it anytime soon.

The escape from Mountain Lion had unfolded in anticlimactic fashion. Upon returning to the basement sub-level, Shien had ushered Slater and the dozen drugged children up a narrow concrete passageway. The path opened out into a private garage, lined with supercars and luxury SUVs that Slater imagined belonged to the line-up of dead customers in the waiting room.

A discreet entrance and exit, far away from the public eye.

As he suspected.

One of the vehicles in the fleet of company limousines had to suffice, since Slater had to transport a dozen passengers, even if only temporarily.

So he found himself behind the wheel of a dark, slim vehicle with tinted windows and more than enough room inside. Shien had opted to slide in the passenger seat alongside him, but not before ferrying the girls into the centre compartment and securing their seatbelts. All of them complied without protest, walking zombies until the effects of the drugs faded away.

Slater had watched patiently in the rear view mirror as Shien operated, something in the back of his mind telling him he should be the one in charge. But, slumped over the steering wheel with his vision swimming back and forth, his leg sticking straight out in front of him in the footwell in an attempt to minimise the horrendous pain, he realised he was now relying on the courage and tenacity of a nine-year-old.

And he wouldn't have had it any other way.

Now they twisted through the congested streets, headed away from the main gambling strip, plunging into the bowels of ordinary civilisation. Slater could see Shien staring at him out of the corner of his eye, clearly concerned for his wellbeing.

'I'm fine,' he said, breaking the silence.

There was no word from behind them. Slater had the glass partition open so he could hear anything the drugged girls felt the need to utter, but so far nothing had come. They sat in absolute silence, still as statues. The effect was almost eerie.

'I can't drive,' Shien said. 'But neither can you right now.'

'I'm doing okay. I haven't crashed yet.'

'You will soon.'

'Not far to go.'

'Are you sure this is the right idea?'

Slater took his eyes off the road for a moment, a risk he was willing to take. He locked eyes with Shien, silently pleading with her to understand. 'Think about it. There's nothing else I can do.'

'I thought you killed everyone back there,' Shien said. 'So can't we take our time?'

'That world is a hydra,' Slater muttered.

'What?'

'Cut one head off and two more take its place. I've seen it many times before. But Forrest is done. That's all that matters. That's all I was trying to accomplish.'

'Why? If you know you won't stop bad things from happening...'

'Bad things will always happen, Shien. I'm one guy. I can't do everything — it took me a significant portion of my life to learn that. But I can focus on one thing at a time, and I can get the job done. That's just how it works. If I think I can take down all organised crime in Macau, then I'm an idiot.'

'You did a lot, though. You put a stop to some bad people.'

'That I did. So you can understand why I need to pass these girls off.'

'What if there's bad people in the police?' Shien said. 'I've heard of that happening before.'

'I can't save everyone, Shien. All I can do is my best. It's why I had to leave Samuel in the apartment complex, and it's why I need to hand these girls over. If I try and protect all of you, it'll do more harm than good.'

'We're here,' Shien said.

Slater twisted the wheel and pulled sharply into the near-deserted parking lot — the end destination set into the limousine's inbuilt GPS. He pulled to a halt in front of a long, low building with blocky letters arranged above the entrance. They spelled the name of the complex in several different languages.

Public Security Police Force of Macau.

Shien stared up at the unimpressive building with concern — Slater noticed the lump in her throat. By now the sun had started to set, plunging their surroundings into lowlight.

'How do you know there's no bad men in there?' she said.

'Not everyone's bad, Shien. If they were, everything would be chaos.'

'Are you sure?'

Slater stared at the young child and realised the experiences of the past two weeks had changed her. For better or worse, he wasn't yet sure. She might have previously been hopeful and optimistic, searching for light even in places it didn't exist. Now he could sense her judging everything, assessing everyone for threats.

He couldn't imagine her trusting anyone for quite some time.

Slater flashed a glance behind the driver's seat and spotted all eleven girls sitting rigid in their seats, their backs pressed against the leather and their gazes unwavering.

'I can't send them in on their own,' he muttered.

'You can barely walk,' Shien said.

'Don't need to walk.'

He slumped in his seat and leant one shoulder on the horn — the noise cut through the quiet of the parking lot like a jackknife, hammering across the open space and piercing through the open windows of the police station. Slater gulped back a ball of nausea, struggling to prevent himself from vomiting, and waited a full five seconds for the discordant sound to fade away.

Within seconds a pair of officers materialised at the front entrance, hands by their holsters in an instinctual response to the interruption. Slater forced his door open and hobbled out of the driver's seat, leaning on the chassis for support. His face still bloody, he waved the man and woman over.

Shien clambered out of the passenger seat, recognising that Slater could barely move. She hurled open the rear door and began ushering the children out of their seats one by one, guiding them toward the pair of officers.

Slater immediately noticed the concern on the officers' faces. They took their hands away from their weapons and bent down, folding at the knees to welcome the kids into reassuring arms. The woman turned and barked a command in Chinese through the open doorway. Another pair of officers appeared at once, hurrying out to meet the strange procession of new arrivals.

Once all eleven of the children had been transferred across, Slater sensed eyes on him — the only adult amidst the strange scene. The officers were looking to him for answers — one of them rose from her knees and touched a hand to the sidearm at her waist. She took a step toward him.

Slater subconsciously understood that he couldn't stay.

The carnage would be traced back to him.

And he had never stayed in one place for too long.

He locked eyes with Shien across the roof of the limousine. 'Tell them these children were found in the basement of Mountain Lion Casino & Resorts. Tell them to be prepared for what they'll find there. Tell them to leave no stone unturned when they investigate.'

Shien wrestled with the translation for a moment, then fired off a string of rapid-fire Chinese to the approaching officer. The middle-aged woman paused in her tracks, digesting the words, then turned to look at the group of young girls.

She could seemingly sense that Slater meant no harm.

'Get in the car,' Slater said to Shien.

Shien turned back to him. 'What?'

'Get in.'

'You don't want me to stay with them?'

'No.'

'Will, maybe it's best... you know. To return to my family.'

'Shien,' Slater said, fighting to mask the emotion in his voice. Despite his best attempts, his tone wavered. 'Just get in.'

She understood all at once. Her upper lip began to quiver, and anguish flared in her eyes. The sight wracked Slater's own mindset — he'd been putting the revelation off as long as he feasibly could. But sooner or later she had to know.

He didn't know where they would go.

He didn't know what they would do.

But they couldn't stay here.

Wrestling with the knowledge that her parents were gone, Shien ducked back into the passenger seat, fighting back tears. She slumped over, hyperventilating, a sea of emotions washing over her.

The female officer watched Shien slip back into the car. She widened her eyes, reaching for her weapon.

Fuck, Slater thought.

He crammed himself back into the driver's seat and stamped on the accelerator — he'd left the engine running for a reason. Tyres squealed and the stretch limousine shot away from the police precinct before the officers had the chance to detain any and all witnesses. Slater kept tense in case he heard the deafening blast of a gunshot headed in their direction — he doubted the limousine was bulletproof — but no shots came.

The officers mustn't have deemed it prudent.

There was no threat.

Just a fleeing witness.

Slater lurched the vehicle back onto the uneven surface of the road and rocketed away from the station, leaving the children in the safest hands he could find, internally unsure about his decision but understanding that he needed to focus on his own survival. He had pulled those kids out of hell, and that was all he could do.

He couldn't individually return them to their families while dealing with half of Macau wanting him dead.

So as Shien broke down alongside him he accelerated into the darkness, unsure what his next move would be but determined not to stop.

He never stopped.

56

Miles away from the bright lights of the luxury casinos, Slater pulled the limousine to a final stop on the side of a dingy, unlit street strewn with rubbish and filth.

It had been an uncomfortable journey. He'd initially intended to provide words of reassurance to Shien but over the course of their trip, it had become obvious that he was in no state to offer the girl guidance. He could barely string a sentence together, let alone find the necessary words to soothe her and take her mind off the revelation.

So he simply concentrated on the road ahead and let Shien process the news as best she could.

When they finally pulled to a halt, after nearly half an hour of pitiful, body-wracking sobs drifting across from the passenger seat, Shien turned to him with bloodshot eyes and a running nose.

'How did you find out?' she whispered.

'Someone upstairs told me.'

'They killed them?'

'They killed your father. Your mother ... is fleeing the country.'

Shien paused, digesting Slater's words. He wondered if there were still traces of the drugs in her veins — despite the initial breakdown she seemed to be processing the information in a coherent manner. She nodded, staring over Slater's shoulder, deep in thought.

'I didn't think she would hang around.'

The words took Slater by surprise. 'You didn't?'

'We weren't that close. I loved my Daddy more than anything.'

Her bravado threatened to shatter under the weight of the sentence. Her upper lip began to tremble again.

Slater reached out a hand and touched it to her shoulder. 'We'll figure this out. I've got you this far, haven't I?'

'Where will we go? How will you look after me? You'll get arrested if I'm a missing person — you realise that?'

'I haven't thought that far ahead,' Slater muttered. 'Too much is happening at once.'

'This won't last long.'

'I'm not the person to take care of you, Shien.'

She froze. 'You have to. I can't survive on my own. I'm too young. I don't know how the world works.'

'I get that. But I can't hang around forever. We both know that. I'm not that guy. I ... wander. And I kill people. Neither of those things are suitable for someone like you. That's why I don't have kids.'

'So where do we go from here?'

Slater paused, riding out a massive headache sprouting to life behind his eyes. He closed them momentarily, leaning back in the seat, then opened them a second later to scrutinise his surroundings.

They were in the middle of nowhere.

Out this far on the outskirts of Macau, the streetlights barely functioned as the darkness settled over the rundown buildings all around them. The resulting shadows could conceal all kinds of undesirables. Even with the driver's window open just a crack, Slater sensed the stench of poverty and desperation in the air.

They were in the slums.

'We lay low,' he said. 'For as long as it takes for the attention to die down. I have contacts ... from my past. Maybe we can sort out false identities. Start fresh somewhere. I don't know... I'll work it out when—'

Involuntarily, his eyes drooped shut. He slumped over the wheel, hitting his forehead on the top of the leather. Shien leapt across the centre console out of concern and tiny hands grabbed his shoulders, heaving him back upright.

'Will,' she said. 'You're hurt bad. You need a doctor.'

'Triads ... might be in the hospitals.'

'They might be everywhere. You need help.'

'Let's ... get to safety. Come on. Let's find a place.'

He reached out and fumbled with the door handle, prodding and yanking until the release mechanism kicked in and the door swung outward into the filthy alleyway. He stepped out, searching for flat ground with his good leg. He pitched and levered himself upright, breathing hard, swimming in a sea of darkness and suffering.

'Come on, Shien,' he muttered. 'Let's—'

A shape materialised out of the darkness, surging into range before Slater even had time to recognise it as a man. The newcomer pushed Slater into the side of the limousine with one hand, heaving him off-balance without any effort at all. A gun appeared in the murky night and the barrel slammed against Slater's temple, pinning him upright against the side of the vehicle.

On the other side of the car, Shien screamed.

'Who's the girl?' a deep voice said.

Slater squinted, wading through the haze of semi-consciousness, desperately trying to make out who stood directly in front of him. He saw redness and shadows and the sharp glint of steel. He felt the cool touch of the gun barrel on his skin. Sweat leeched from his pores, running onto the metal. He winced and slumped further down the side of the limousine, giving in.

He couldn't fight any longer.

'Who's the girl?' the voice repeated.

He thought he recognised it.

'Just kill me, for God's sake,' he muttered.

'If I were here to do that you'd have been long dead.'

'Who are you?'

'You really can't see me?'

'I'm beat half to death, in case you couldn't tell.'

'Oh, I can see that. But up to this point I was under the illusion that William Slater was a superhuman. Since when did injury stop you, brother?'

Brother.

The word triggered something in his memory. For a moment, head bowed, pulse racing, he thought the impossible. 'Jason King?'

The man laughed. 'Close enough. In fact, it'd be awfully convenient if you could tell me where he was. But that's not what I'm here for.'

'Who are you?'

'I'm the guy you called in Yemen when you needed to save the world.'

Slater paled. He had spent the last few months running from his old division, the clandestine black-operations unit that had single-handedly forged him into a destructive killer. They hadn't parted on good terms, and Slater had spent his time since the forced retirement lying low — for the most part.

An unintended barrage of all-out warfare in Yemen had culminated in a chemical weapon on the streets of inner-city London. Slater couldn't have made it to England in time. He'd been forced to call on the resources of his old employers, men and women who no doubt wanted him dead for deserting his position at such a crucial time.

Frankly, he was surprised the man standing across from him hadn't found him sooner.

'You took your time, Williams,' he muttered through bloodstained teeth.

Russell Williams let the barrel of his sidearm drift down from Slater's forehead.

'You look like death,' the man said. 'Par for the course, though.'

'When do I not?' Slater said, spitting a ball of crimson onto the dirty concrete between them. 'You sure you're not here to kill me?'

'Like I said, that would have happened days ago if it was my intention.'

'You been following me?'

'Intermittently. You're a hard man to keep track of.'

'You found me, though.'

'That I did.'

'So what are you here for?'

'To apologise.'

57

They made an odd trio — Shien, Slater, and government handler Russell Williams.

Three people from vastly different backgrounds, sitting on their rears in the muck of an unlit alleyway, their backs resting against the chassis of a dark limousine. Slater welcomed the respite — no-one would think to come looking for them out here. He had crucial time to talk, and recover, and formulate a next step.

First, he had to work out what the hell Williams was doing in Macau.

'You couldn't have called?' he said.

'Given the extent of your contribution to our country, I thought it'd be best to deliver this message personally.'

'What message?'

'You're off the hook.'

'I'm going to need more information than that.'

'I've been busy,' Williams said. 'Ever since you and Jason King absconded. The two best operatives our government has ever seen — gone, just like that.'

'We had our reasons.'

'I now know that. The internal investigation took a little longer than necessary, but ultimately it all comes back to Ramsay, doesn't it?'

That piece of shit, Slater thought.

When King had taken certain liberties concerning an operation in Russia, the mysterious handler known only as Ramsay had detained the pair in an effort to rein them in. It had resulted in catastrophe, with both King and Slater vowing never to return to active service after a whirlwind of chaos in Dubai.

Now, King was gone. Vanished into the depths of the free world. Enjoying retirement.

Slater knew the man would never return.

He knew he would never see Jason King again.

And he was perfectly fine with it.

'Where's King?' Williams said, as if reading Slater's mind.

'Your guess is as good as mine.'

'Come on, Slater. You know something.'

'We went our separate ways.'

'Somehow I find that hard to believe.'

'If you really want proof, find the hospital in Sohar — a port town in Oman. They'll confirm everything I'm telling you. We were together there, and then we weren't. King was done with this life. I wasn't. We parted ways there — there wasn't much else to discuss.'

Williams stared at Slater's bloody clothing, and the mass of cuts across his face. 'You sure aren't done with this life.'

'And Uncle Sam's okay with that?' Slater said incredulously. 'With knowing I'm out here in the wild, putting my skills to use?'

'They're not okay with it. But they're willing to forget you exist. As a compromise for what Ramsay put you through.

Just as you and King went down your own paths, we can too.'

'A clean slate?'

'A clean slate.'

'So I go off,' Slater said. 'Do my own thing. You promise me you won't track me down and silence me.'

'We promise.'

'Who's to say you won't break that promise in future? No-one will ever know.'

'If that was our intention, you'd be dead. I don't know how many times I need to repeat that.'

'Enough to convince me.'

For added effect, Williams raised the gun in his right hand and pressed it to the side of Slater's temple without resistance. He mimed firing a shot, accompanied by his own personal sound effects.

'As easy as that,' he said.

'Maybe you're not going through with it because the girl's here.'

Shien perked up at the mention. She'd tuned out of the conversation, most of it flying straight over her head. Now she craned her neck to get a better earshot of what the men were discussing.

'Who is she?' Williams repeated.

'Someone who's been through a lot.'

'Wouldn't have anything to do with the state you're in, would it?'

'It sure does.'

'Someone got what was coming to them?'

'You could say that.'

Williams shrugged. 'Not much I can do about it.'

'You could kill me right here, right now. Would make things easier for you and your people, if we're being honest.

You wouldn't have the threat of my existence hanging over your heads.'

Williams glanced sideways at him. 'We're not too worried about that.'

'Oh?'

'Your psychological profile's been compiled pretty extensively over the years — as you can imagine, given the amount of leeway you had. We have reason to believe you're sane enough to cut ties with.'

'You sure about that?'

'You've got your head screwed on straight. And if you don't want to work for us, we can't force you. Despite what you might think.'

'You could try.'

'Wouldn't work out well, would it?' Williams said. 'For either of us.'

'You, mostly.'

'Let's agree to disagree, then.'

'So what is this?' Slater said. 'Just you giving me a friendly heads-up not to hide?'

'Pretty much. And to let you know that when we say "clean slate", we mean "clean slate."'

Slater didn't like where this was headed. 'What have you done?'

'All those juicy government funds you hoarded over the years. We took them back.'

Slater paused. 'I doubt it. I took precautionary measures.'

'We know. Zurich. That's cute.'

'Shit.'

'Didn't take long to trace your movements, and find your accounts. Even though the Swiss banking laws are strictly in favour of privacy, we convinced them otherwise. Just this one time.'

'How'd you manage to do that?'

'We can be ... persuasive. I think you forget what you used to do for a living.'

Slater nodded. 'Understood.'

'Think of it as a fresh start. You can work normal jobs. Make an honest wage. Earn an honest living. You and I both know you're too pure to steal your way into another fortune.'

'You think I have a problem with robbing bad people?'

Williams paused. 'You got cash on you right now?'

'A bit.'

'How much?'

'Three hundred thousand. Give or take.'

'Hand it over.'

'What makes you think I'll do that?'

'Because I'll kill you if you don't — and if I fail, you'll have the United States government hunting you down until the end of your days. You don't want that hanging over your head for the rest of your life. Hand it over. Clean slate. If we're doing this, we're doing it properly.'

Slater paused for the briefest of moments — in truth, there was nothing to consider. He reached into his jeans and withdrew the three bundles of cash he'd stuffed in his waistband. He handed them over to Williams, then lifted his cotton jumper to reveal his waistline was bare.

Drained of every last drop.

'You satisfied now?' he muttered.

'Not about satisfaction. This is a reset button, Slater. You're free to go and do whatever the hell you want with the rest of your life — whatever trouble you get in, it's on you. But you don't get any advantages due to your skillset. Start over. Be a good person. Don't get wrapped up in shit like,' he looked Slater up and down, 'whatever the hell you've got yourself wrapped up in.'

'Don't worry,' Slater said. 'Job's done here.'

'Is there going to be headlines plastered all over the news tomorrow morning?'

Slater spat another glob of blood across the sidewalk. 'What do you think?'

'Should be obvious what I think.'

'Trust your gut. I did the right thing.'

'I don't doubt that, or I wouldn't be sitting here.'

Slater turned his gaze to Williams and studied the man now that he'd managed to compose himself. Williams wore a black suit with a white shirt underneath, open at the neck. He kept himself in impressive shape for a desk jockey, complete with thick salt-and-pepper hair that showed no sign of balding, even though he'd have to be close to fifty by now. Overall, he looked good.

Then Slater's gaze wandered over to Shien, sitting quietly alongside them with her arms wrapped around her knees and her face pointed toward the ground. He noticed her eyes drooping — the past twenty-four hours had been a whirlwind, and now in the silence the girl was tired. She tucked her chin to her chest and began to doze.

Slater beckoned for Williams to lean in and lowered his voice. 'You need to take her.'

Williams froze, darting his gaze across to Shien and back to Slater.

'What?' the man hissed under his breath.

'You heard me.'

'Slater—'

'Take all my money, strip me of everything — I don't give a shit. But she needs a home.'

'She's your responsibility. I don't even know who she is.'

'Her parents were killed. Well, one of them, at least. The other bailed. She's had a rough time these past few weeks. Take her back stateside. Find her a foster home.'

'Not a chance. You know the kind of trouble we could get in for that?'

'Not really. And it can't be any more trouble than you'll be in with me.'

'Slater.'

Williams spoke with finality, with the kind of grave weight that words could only carry if they were backed by obscene power. The man had the control of the United States Armed Forces at his fingertips — Slater knew the kind of unofficial rank Williams possessed.

Making an enemy of him would be a death sentence.

But not before Slater could cause a storm.

'You know what I know,' Slater said. 'About how it all works. About the intricacies of the system. You know the kind of damage I can do in a short amount of time if I really set my mind to it.'

'We'll kill you. I could kill you right now.'

'Could you?'

They faced each other across a gap of less than a foot, both seated, their voices still low, tension running thick in the air. Beside Williams, Shien dozed where she sat, head still drooped.

'Let's not do this,' Williams said.

'Smart man. I'm half dead but I could still mop the floor with you.'

'Slater, I didn't come here to fight.'

'Then be reasonable. You've taken everything from me without much of a reason. I've sat back and accepted it, even though I didn't do anything to you and your people. Ramsay's actions are on you. But fuck it. Who cares? At least humour me by doing this one thing for me. I know you're a good man. I know you don't want to see her die.'

Williams paused, offering Shien another glance. 'And if she stays with you...'

'She dies. You know better than anyone what my life is like.'

'You can change it, you know.'

'Somehow I don't think I can.'

'You think you're destined to do this kind of thing forever?'

'Maybe. In the heat of the moment, impulse tells me to act. I've never ignored it and I don't plan to in the future.'

'You sure this is the only option?'

'If the people I was up against recover, they'll be looking for her. Get her away from here. Use your resources. Find her a home. A good home. She deserves it.'

'And what do I get in return?'

'How about the fifty-two million dollars I earned over the course of my career? How's that for a compromise? Not like I have much of a choice anyway.'

'Was it that much?' Williams said with a low whistle. 'I never got told specifics.'

'Uncle Sam. He pays well.'

'Not anymore. You and King were paid the equivalent of your worth. There's no-one like you two anymore.'

Slater shrugged. 'I'll survive. You'll do this for me?'

Williams paused, mulling over the offer. 'It's going to be a problem for us if I refuse, isn't it?'

'Yes.'

'You know you'll get yourself killed if you go up against us.'

'You think it's worth the trouble?'

The silence dragged out — ten, fifteen, twenty seconds.

'No,' Williams conceded. 'Probably not. But that's not why I'm doing it. I'm doing it because you did good goddamn work for us.'

'Thank you, Russell.'

'Don't worry about it.'

'You'll make sure she gets the best treatment?'

'The very best. You know as well as anyone what we can do if we apply our resources.'

'She deserves it. She's been through hell.'

'Because she met you.'

'She was going through hell before she met me.'

'You seem to consistently amplify problems.'

'I think I solve them. Different perspectives.'

'Keep going the way you're going and you won't be solving them for much longer.'

'That's my concern now, though, isn't it?'

'It sure is. This is goodbye, Slater. Forever. As of this second, the United States government doesn't recognise your existence. Go and do what you want with the rest of your life.'

'I was going to anyway.'

'Well, now you don't have to look over your shoulder for us.'

'I've got more enemies than you lot.'

'I can't imagine why. You seem to attract destruction.'

'Quite the life it's been...'

'You enjoy it?'

'I don't know if anyone can enjoy it. But I've never known anything else.'

'You think you'll keep getting into trouble?'

'Seems to be something I don't do too well avoiding.'

'Well, good luck. Maybe it'll be harder to wreak havoc on a limited budget.'

'You're still okay with leaving me with nothing? After everything I've done for you?'

'Clean slate,' Williams repeated.

Slater sighed.

The stillness of Macau's outer suburbs washed over them — for a moment the commotion and the tension died away, replaced by something close to a soothing calm. Slater struggled to his feet and stared down at the unlikely pair — Russell Williams and a nine-year-old named Shien.

Her eyes remained shut.

She was dozing in the silence.

Slater made eye contact with Williams, and they both realised what needed to be done.

Slater had put the girl through enough. He had never been one to mince words, and any time he spent unnecessarily lingering around would make it all the more harder to say goodbye. And that wasn't Slater's world — finding the correct thing to say, helping Shien understand why he needed to leave and find solitude.

At least for this portion of his life.

He was bred for the road, for chaos and confusion, for dealing with problems as he stumbled across them. This was not the life for a child, and sooner or later he and Shien would have had to part ways. He'd done his job — he'd spared her from a fate worse than death — and that was enough.

She would understand.

The sooner he faded from her mind, the better.

Memories had to die, so that she could live a full life.

So he nodded once to her tiny sleeping form and turned on his heel and walked directly away from her and Russell Williams, leaving her in the hands of a man he'd trusted with his own life for over a decade. He would do her no harm — Williams was a good man. Slater had no qualms over leaving her with him.

But he had qualms about leaving like this.

Stripped of everything he'd worked for, torn away from the concept of a secure retirement, he limped into the darkness, dragging his mangled leg behind him like a wounded dog.

Into the unknown.

And, deep down, laced with discomfort and unrest, Slater realised he wouldn't have it any other way.

No money, no future, no prospects.

Just a lifetime of experience as a warrior and a raging desire for trouble.

He ducked into the lip of a neighbouring alleyway and left both Shien and the U.S. government behind forever.

58

W illiams sat patiently on the sidewalk, watching Slater's silhouette mould into the night. He stared down at the three stacks of bills in his hand and shook his head in disbelief, tucking the bands into his jacket pocket. He hadn't been comfortable with the idea of stripping the man of everything he'd slaved away for, but it had been an explicit demand from the very top.

If Will Slater wanted to walk away from his old life, he had to leave his riches behind with it.

Strangely, Slater hadn't seemed perturbed in the slightest. Williams knew if he had fifty-two million dollars sitting in an account, he wouldn't part with it amicably. Besides, it represented a lifetime of Slater putting his life on the line for his country. It represented relentless hard work and commitment to a life that had been in no way pleasant. It paved the way for a portion of Slater's life where he could rest, and recover from over a decade of hell. Now that had all been thrown into disarray, for reasons that Williams considered entirely petty. He didn't agree with his superiors' judgment, but he was forced to carry out their orders regardless.

Frankly he'd been expecting more of a fight.

Then, suddenly, it all made sense.

Fifty-two million dollars provided comfort. It meant Slater could hole up in a luxurious retreat and live out the rest of his days in undisturbed peace.

Williams had seen the manic look in the man's eyes.

Slater was a man of movement, and struggle.

He wouldn't sit around enjoying life. He couldn't.

When the government stripped him of his fortune, it would force him into a nomadic lifestyle.

Something he embraced.

Beside him, the young girl who Slater had referred to as Shien stirred. She opened her eyes just in time to catch a final glance of Slater disappearing into the darkness — off to cause more carnage, no doubt.

'He's ... leaving,' she muttered, still slightly groggy.

'He is,' Williams said.

'Are you okay with letting him go?'

'Who's going to tell him otherwise? Slater does what he wants. Always has, always will.'

'What happens to me?'

'I'll make sure you're taken care of. How are you feeling?'

Shien watched the empty space Slater had occupied moments earlier. 'Like ... everything's going to be okay. I haven't felt that way in a while.'

'That's good.'

'You're not going to hurt me, are you?'

Williams followed her gaze into the darkness. 'I promised Slater I'd take care of you.'

'People go back on their promises.'

'Not when you're promising that man.'

'He's different.'

'He sure is.'

'Where's he going?'

'I don't know.'

'Will he be okay? He seemed hurt.'

Despite everything, Williams smirked. 'You haven't know Will Slater long enough. That's nothing to him. He'll be up and about in no time. You don't want to be around him when that happens. Now, come on. Let's get you out of here. We have a flight to catch.'

59

Two weeks later...
Zürich
Switzerland

O n a freezing morning in the Greater Zürich Area, a man in an expensive black overcoat stepped out from underneath a broad concrete archway, his boots making fine imprints on the light dusting of snow coating the sidewalks. Despite a slight limp in his right leg, any onlooker would consider him in phenomenal shape, with a powerful musculature clearly visible underneath his designer clothing.

He paused for a moment in the middle of the sidewalk, inhaling a massive gulp of the crisp morning air. He checked in either direction for any nosy civilians before sliding a gloved hand into the pocket of his overcoat and withdrawing a slim grey smartphone. He navigated to a banking application, refreshed the page, and couldn't resist flashing a grin complete with two rows of gleaming white teeth.

For Will Slater, it was a good day.

The opportunity had presented itself, and he'd seized it. It hadn't taken much critical thinking to recognise that everyone involved in Peter Forrest's dirty profits had swiftly departed from the land of the living a couple of weeks earlier. The triad had been thrust into tatters, and the culprits of the brazen theft attempt had been left with bullets in their heads in the sub-level of a casino complex. Forrest himself had died a gruesome death — a fact that had been confirmed to Slater on the evening news some time ago.

Mountain Lion had burst at the seams as a horrific list of illegal operations had been uncovered by a Macau task force. Hundreds of arrests had been made. Affirmative action had been taken without hesitation, and the Macau casino industry had gone into panic mode.

But none of that really mattered to Slater. He'd pulled a certain child out of the depths of hell, and that gave him all the satisfaction he was looking for.

He glanced one final time at his accounts, now crammed with money that had been resting in limbo for weeks.

No-one would miss it.

And Slater would put it to better use than the authorities. He still had a lot of living to do, and a lot of justice to dish out.

Sometimes it paid to habitually memorise crucial information.

Like account numbers, and confirmation codes, and triad bank details.

Four-hundred and thirty-five million dollars richer, he strode off down the street, wondering where the next chaotic sequence of events would occur.

He couldn't wait.

WILL SLATER WILL RETURN.

MORE BOOKS BY MATT ROGERS

THE JASON KING SERIES
Isolated (Book 1)
Imprisoned (Book 2)
Reloaded (Book 3)
Betrayed (Book 4)
Corrupted (Book 5)
Hunted (Book 6)

THE JASON KING FILES
Cartel (Book 1)
Warrior (Book 2)

THE WILL SLATER SERIES
Wolf (Book 1)
Lion (Book 2)

Join the Reader's Group and get a free 200-page book by Matt Rogers!

Sign up for a free copy of '**HARD IMPACT**'.
Meet Jason King — another member of Black Force, the shadowy organisation that Slater dedicated his career to.

Experience King's most dangerous mission — action-packed insanity in the heart of the Amazon Rainforest.

No spam guaranteed.

Just click here.

ABOUT THE AUTHOR

Matt Rogers grew up in Melbourne, Australia as a voracious reader, relentlessly devouring thrillers and mysteries in his spare time. Now, he writes full-time. His novels are action-packed and fast-paced. Dive into the Jason King Series to get started with his collection.

Visit his website:

www.mattrogersbooks.com

Visit his Amazon page:

amazon.com/author/mattrogers23

Made in the USA
San Bernardino, CA
09 January 2018